W9-BBA-222

A Cat in the Stacks Mystery

WHAT THE CAT DRAGGED IN

Miranda James

BERKLEY PRIME CRIME
New York

BERKLEY PRIME CRIME
Published by Berkley
An imprint of Penguin Random House LLC
penguinrandomhouse.com

ISBN: 9780593199480

Berkley Prime Crime hardcover edition / August 2021
Berkley Prime Crime mass-market edition / May 2023

Printed in the United States of America
1   3   5   7   9   10   8   6   4   2

Book design by Tiffany Estreicher

For John and Matt, with much love

Amor vincit omnia

ONE

I hadn't been down this road in over four decades, not since shortly before my paternal grandfather died. New houses adorned the landscape, taking the place of the fields of cotton and soybeans I remembered, among other crops, and I saw fewer cows and horses. To my surprise, I did espy several goats in one pasture.

My goal lay only three miles ahead, I thought, not completely trusting my rusty memory. "We'll be there soon," I said as I glanced over my shoulder at my passenger in the backseat.

Diesel, my Maine Coon cat, chirped in response. He enjoyed riding in the car, even if we were headed to the veterinarian's clinic. They made such a fuss over him there, he never seemed to mind when I took him. He would find today's destination fascinating, I was sure. There would be much to explore.

I spotted fewer houses along the road now and more

land dedicated to farming. Slowing, I could see my turn coming up. As I drove up the graveled drive, I realized that the old cattle gap right off the road was no longer there. I missed the sound of the car bumping over the spaces in the boards that I had always loved as a small boy.

Framed and shaded by five towering oaks, each well over a century old, the white frame house stood a couple of hundred feet back from the road on a gently rising slope. The front yard with its randomly placed small flower beds had recently been mowed, and the structure appeared to be in good repair. I pulled the car up close to the old, detached garage to park. I left the engine running for a moment.

Why am I hesitating? I asked myself. *What memories of this place do I have to fear?*

Nothing terrible had happened to me in my grandparents' house that I could recall. I thought perhaps I was feeling a bit overwhelmed by the past suddenly rushing over me. My childhood felt so far away, and yet here I was, at a place indelibly linked in my mind with those years of my life. A happy time for me, for the most part.

I didn't fear the memories themselves, I realized. I feared the feelings of loss the memories triggered, a longing to see my parents and my grandparents again. I blinked back a few tears and resolved to get on with inspecting the house. As an only child with no first cousins, I had felt the lack of family keenly when my parents died. My mother's parents had died some years before, and she had been an only child as well.

From the backseat I heard an inquisitive warble and a loud meow. Abruptly, I switched the engine off and got out of the car. I opened the back door for Diesel, and he hopped onto the graveled drive. We stood there for a few moments longer as I gazed at the building. This early-August day promised heat, and I could already feel the perspiration starting. I walked the several yards to the house and mounted the five steps up to the front porch. Diesel trotted along beside me, emitting an occasional chirp.

A faint breeze wafted along the open porch, and I sank into one of the elderly rocking chairs to stare out at the lawn and the road beyond. Diesel stretched out at my feet. I closed my eyes, and I could see my father and my grandfather sitting on the porch. My mother would have been in the house helping my grandmother prepare the Sunday meal. We visited my grandparents on Sundays twice a month. I was about four on the last Sunday we saw my grandmother. She died of a heart attack at home shortly afterward.

I had only vague memories of my grandmother, a short, plump woman with a loving smile. As her only grandchild, I knew that I was special. She spoiled me as much as my parents would allow, and now, all these years later, I felt a sudden pang for her. I wished I'd had many more years to get to know her, but that wasn't to be.

Forcing my mind away from my grandmother, I focused instead on the conversation I'd had earlier this morning with my lawyer, who also happened to be my son, Sean. When he told me that I had inherited my grandfather's house, I honestly thought he was kidding me.

"There must be some mistake. My grandfather sold that house right before he died."

"Weren't you listening, Dad?" Sean scowled as he leaned back in his chair and crossed one leg over the other. The light hit the polished sheen of his now exposed cowboy boot. I stared at it for a moment as I struggled to take in the import of Sean's news.

Another house—I had inherited another house. My paternal grandfather's farmhouse. That was what Sean was telling me, but I found it hard to understand how this had come about.

"Start over, and go slowly," I said, "with less legal jargon."

Diesel warbled in support, or so I imagined, and Sean grinned. "If Diesel is confused, then I guess I threw too many legal terms at you. All right, Dad, I'll go over it again."

Sean opened the folder of papers that he had closed only moments before and scanned the document on top, evidently my grandfather's will.

"Your grandfather, Robert Charles Harris, leased his house to one Martin Horace Hale until said Martin Horace Hale's death. The original date of the lease was almost forty-five years ago. Your grandfather died about three months later. At the time of his death, he was a widower residing in a nursing home in Athena."

I nodded. I vaguely remembered going to the nursing home a couple of times to visit my grandfather, but I was only about six at the time.

"There is correspondence with the will," Sean continued, "to indicate that, as your parents did not wish to occupy the house, it being out in the country, your grandfather decided to make other arrangements."

I nodded. "Dad had no interest in being a farmer. I know that disappointed my grandfather, and I think it caused some hard feelings between them. I thought that was why my grandfather sold the house and the farm."

"He never sold any of it. He leased the house and the

farmland to Mr. Hale for fifty dollars a year." Sean glanced up from the papers to look at me. "It's what they call a peppercorn rent, because according to the taxes paid, the property was worth quite a lot more."

"I've heard the term before," I said. "Was this peppercorn rent paid every year?"

"Yes, it was, without fail. The most recent payment was made in January of this year," Sean said. "It's in an interest-bearing account at the Athena bank."

"Who paid the taxes on the property?" I asked.

"Martin Hale," Sean said. "Part of the lease he signed. In return for paying the taxes, he kept all the profits from farming."

I thought about that for a moment. "An odd arrangement."

Sean shrugged. "I guess since Granddad didn't want to be a farmer, your grandfather did what he thought was best at the time. He obviously didn't want to sell outright. Maybe he hoped Granddad and Granny would retire there."

"They might have, I suppose," I said, saddened by the deaths of my parents at far too young an age. I felt a paw on my leg, and Diesel chirped at me. I knew he felt my sadness. I rubbed his head.

"I take it that Martin Hale died," I said, trying to focus on the present.

"Yes, about nine weeks ago," Sean said. "He was in California at the time, visiting family, and they didn't think to inform anyone in Athena until about a week ago, when the grandson came to clear Mr. Hale's effects from the house."

"Why haven't you told me about this before now?" I asked.

"Because I didn't find out any of it until a couple of days ago," Sean said patiently. "Mr. Hale's grandson didn't have any information about his grandfather's will or even the identity of his lawyer. He went through the house looking for his grandfather's papers, and he finally found them in an old dresser, or so I was told. He didn't do anything with them, however, until late last Friday. He reported his grandfather's death to the sheriff's department, asked about finding my father-in-law, and was referred to me."

"What did he tell you?"

"The basic facts of his grandfather's death," Sean replied. "He handed me an envelope marked *the lawyer*, and inside I found a brief explanation about the property. I was shocked, of course, but I decided there was no point in going into it with you until I'd had a chance to study the documents. Plus, I had to track down a copy of your grandfather's will."

Sean reached into a drawer and pulled out a set of keys, four in all. He handed them over to me. "I thought you might want to go out there this morning," he said.

I nodded. "Will you come with me?"

"I can't right now," Sean said, his tone regretful. "I have a couple of matters that I need to address this morning, but once I'm done, I can head out there if you'll give me directions."

That done, Sean assured me he would be along no more than thirty minutes behind me.

Diesel meowed loudly and brought me back to the here and now. "Yes, I know we should go inside. Even with the breeze it's humid out here." I felt the sweat rolling down my back. I couldn't remember whether the house had any kind of air-conditioning system, but I hoped it did. Sean had mentioned that the electricity was on, thankfully.

The key turned easily in the lock. The front door opened into a center hallway that stretched to the back of the house. I stepped inside and paused for a moment to look around. There were several rooms on either side of the hallway, four to a side. The parlor stood to my left and a bedroom to my right. The doors to each room stood open, and I meandered down the hall, Diesel beside me, stopping to look into each room.

The interior of the house was cool, and I felt the sweat beginning to dry. Diesel rambled in and out of the rooms, sniffing and chirping. My memories of the furnishings in my grandparents' day were hazy, but most of the furniture I saw looked old and frankly shabby enough to have been here in their time. The air in the house wasn't stale, but it did have that scent peculiar to houses that have been empty for a while, a mingled aroma of dust and must from lack of cleaning.

The original house had burned near the end of the Civil War, all its contents destroyed except for a few pieces.

The present house had been built not long after the end of the war. I remembered that much at least of the family history my father had shared with me.

Near the end of the hall to my right a door opened into the kitchen. The appliances at least were contemporary, I saw, and the house overall looked tidy, though more than a bit dusty. I kept memories at bay as I wandered, trying not to let myself be swept away by nostalgia. I opened the refrigerator and found it empty. Glad that I didn't have to clear away moldy items, I shut it.

Near the refrigerator I saw a door. Was it to the backyard? I couldn't remember. I opened it and found a set of stairs leading upward. That was odd, I thought. Then the realization struck me. *The attic.*

I suddenly felt an urge to shut the door and turn my back on it.

Don't be silly. You're not four years old anymore.

My grandmother had wanted to take me up to the attic, I now recalled. There were things up there that I could play with, she had told me. I had taken one look at those stairs and the darkness above and had run away. She didn't try to get me to go up there after that.

I laughed, a bit shakily, and Diesel rubbed hard against my leg. "I'm okay, boy, really I am. Just an old, foolish memory. We'll go up there."

Diesel evidently took that as permission because he scurried up the stairs. I had no idea about lighting, but as I stepped into the stairwell, I saw a switch and flipped it. The shadows above me disappeared, and I ascended slowly.

The musty scent I had detected earlier grew stronger here. Once I reached the top of the stairs, I spotted footprints on the dusty floor that looked recent. Mr. Hale's grandson had no doubt explored up here. Then I saw that the footprints went only a few feet into the attic. Evidently the grandson had seen enough and decided to leave the space alone.

I couldn't blame him. The jumble of boxes, old chairs, a large wardrobe in the far corner, and piles of junk would have daunted anyone. I didn't relish sorting through all this myself in search of family treasures, at least not until the area had been thoroughly cleaned.

The attic had some ventilation because it wasn't as oppressively hot as I had expected. I couldn't ascertain what ventilation there was, however, because of the accumulated stuff everywhere.

I heard a loud warble and looked around for my cat. I saw his footprints leading away from me toward the other side of the attic, but otherwise I saw no sign of Diesel.

"Where are you?" I asked, feeling slightly alarmed. "You'd better not be stuck in anything. I'll bet you're filthy by now."

The cat meowed loudly, the sound more muffled this time. I glanced around, trying to figure out where he could be. I caught a sudden movement out of the corner of my eye and focused on the old wardrobe. One of the doors was moving.

"Diesel, come away from there." I began to pick my way through the piles to retrieve my cat. He could be stubborn if he found anything to interest him.

I heard a loud thump, and Diesel chirped. I dodged around a stack of boxes and came to a sudden halt.

Diesel sat about three feet in front of me, his right paw on a human skull.

TWO

My first thought, after a moment of sheer horror had passed, was that Diesel had found a fake skull, probably plastic or resin. While I stood transfixed to the spot, the cat batted the skull with his right paw, and the thing wobbled sideways.

"Stop that." My tone came out harsher than I'd intended, but Diesel immediately quit touching the skull. I drew a deep breath and walked over to the cat's plaything. I squatted beside it, and Diesel moved close to me and trilled, perhaps an apology, more likely a question.

I stuck out a reluctant finger and rubbed the tip along the top of the skull. I drew in a sharp breath.

This was no toy. This was real.

I drew my hand back and bent closer to the thing. I could see bits of dirt clinging to it. From the attic? Or had it once been buried somewhere?

My stomach roiled, but I took a couple of deep breaths to calm myself. I stood and looked down at the cat.

"Where did you find it?"

Diesel stared up at me for a moment. He turned and walked over to the wardrobe, and I stepped closer to it. I pulled a handkerchief from my pocket and wrapped my hand in it. One door of the wardrobe stood open enough to admit my inquisitive cat's head and front paws. I pushed it farther open, and I found myself staring down at a pile of human bones.

How long have these been here?

Suddenly spooked, I backed away from the wardrobe and called Diesel to me. I threaded my way as hastily as I could through the piles of junk to the stairs. I lumbered down them, eager to get away from the sight of those pathetic, jumbled bones. I went straight to the sink to wash my hands, but after I did, I couldn't find a towel to use to dry them. I flapped them in the air for about thirty seconds while Diesel watched me, obviously confused by my actions.

"Dad, where are you?"

I had never been so happy to hear my son's voice. I hurried out into the hallway with Diesel to see Sean standing inside the front door.

"Thank the Lord you're here," I said.

"What's the matter?" Sean said, his tone sharp. He had obviously read the anxiety in my voice. He strode down the hallway toward us.

"Up in the attic," I said. "Diesel found some bones."

"Bones of what?" Sean sounded impatient.

"A person," I said tartly. "Look, I need to sit down for a minute. Let's go into the front parlor."

"Good grief, Dad," Sean said as he followed me back down the hall. "Is this some kind of joke?"

I didn't respond until I was seated in an old armchair in the parlor. Sean stood over me, looking down at me with an expression of concern.

"This is not some kind of joke." I knew I sounded testy, but the discovery of the bones had thrown me off balance. "There really are bones up there in the attic. In an old wardrobe at the back. Diesel found them. He knocked the skull out onto the floor; otherwise I might not have seen them."

"I'm going up to take a look myself," Sean said. "Where's the entrance to the attic?"

"Back of the kitchen. Last room to the right," I said.

Sean whirled away, and I heard the click of his booted heels on the wood floors as he hastened down the hall.

"We've got another mess on our hands," I told Diesel, and he meowed loudly. "But this time you're the one who found the body, not me." He meowed again. "Not that anyone will appreciate that distinction, of course. I'll still catch heck from Sean and Laura about it."

My son and daughter had grown increasingly worried about my involvement in murder cases, and I suspected this might prove to be another one. I tried to think of a logical explanation for why anyone would keep a skeleton in the attic. Maybe a medical specimen? Had a member of Martin Hale's family gone to medical school? Anything was possible, I supposed.

But there was dirt on the skull, and in that shocked, quick glance at the pile of bones in the wardrobe, I had seen more dirt.

I shivered and wished Sean hadn't left the room.

He returned a couple of minutes later. His grim expression told me he was not happy. "This is a mess," he said.

"I think that's obvious," I said peevishly. "Why don't you call the sheriff's department and get things rolling?"

"Already did," Sean replied tersely. He glanced around to find a seat and chose a high-backed sofa. "I wonder how old those bones are." His eyes narrowed. "If we're lucky, they'll turn out to be really old, an archaeological specimen maybe."

I brightened at the thought. "That might be." I also shared my idea that the bones could be a medical student's study aid.

Sean shrugged. "Possible, I guess. I don't know anything about the Hale family. Do you?"

I shook my head. "Haven't a clue, but of course the sheriff's department might know of them. And if all else fails, there's always Melba."

Sean snorted with sudden laughter. "Right."

My friend Melba Gilley, whom I'd known since childhood, appeared to know everyone in Athena, Mississippi, or if she didn't know someone personally, she could usually figure out whom to ask about them. She had been hugely helpful in the past when I was involved with murders, thanks to this knowledge of hers. I had a feeling she would be useful in this case, too.

"It's interesting," Sean said.

"What is?"

"Seeing the house that Granddad grew up in," Sean said. "And Aunt Dottie, too. I guess you don't remember much about it."

"More than I thought I would," I said. "I do have some fond memories of this house, most of them to do with my grandmother." I smiled briefly. "She would have adored you and Laura, and I hate that you never got to meet her."

"At least we had Granny and Granddad." Sean eyed me with blatant curiosity. "Why are you so sad? I can hear it in your voice."

"Memories of times lost," I said after a moment. "Sometimes I really miss my parents. There's a feeling of rootlessness without them to anchor me in the past, I suppose."

"I think I understand that," Sean said. "I know with Mom gone I feel like part of me is missing."

We looked at each other for a moment in silence, and then we tacitly changed the subject. Diesel chirped loudly. I knew he must be feeling uneasy because of the naked emotion in the room.

"I suppose we'll be locked out of the house while the sheriff's department investigates," I said. "I didn't really have much time to look around, but everything seems to be in good shape."

"Seems to be," Sean agreed. "How old is it?"

"Built in the late 1860s after the Civil War," I said. "There was an earlier house, but it got burned down during the war."

"So Harrises have owned this house and this land for over a hundred and fifty years," Sean said in a wondering tone. "That's amazing. This is really a part of who we are."

"Yes, it is." I heard footsteps on the porch, and a moment later there came a knock at the door.

Sean rose. "I'll go let them in." He strode from the room.

When my son returned, he brought with him Kanesha Berry, chief deputy of the Athena County Sheriff's Department, along with several others, including Haskell Bates, one of her deputies and also my good friend and tenant.

"Good morning, Charlie," Kanesha said. "I hear you've found another body."

Kanesha's dry tone was calculated to nettle me, but I refused to respond in kind. Instead, I said in my mildest tone, "Actually, Diesel found it, not me."

Hearing his name, the cat meowed loudly, and I would have sworn that I saw Kanesha's lips twitch ever so slightly.

"I'll be sure to include that in the report," Kanesha said. Behind her, Haskell, normally stone-faced while on duty, winked at me. "How do we get to the attic?"

"I'll show you," Sean said.

Kanesha and her team, with the exception of Haskell, followed Sean out of the parlor and down the hall toward the kitchen. Haskell seated himself in Sean's former place and took out a notebook and pen. "Tell me about it, Charlie."

I gave him a quick rundown of the events of the morning, trying to paint the full picture. Haskell nodded occasionally as he scribbled in his notebook, but he didn't interrupt me. When I'd finished, he flipped his notebook closed and put it away. "Thanks, Charlie, that's pretty thorough. Any idea who it might be?"

"I haven't a clue," I said. "This is the first time I've been in the house since I was about six years old, not long before my grandfather died. That's well over forty years ago. As I mentioned, I had no idea the house was still in the family. I thought my grandfather had sold it."

"Kind of a strange arrangement," Haskell commented.

"I thought so, too," I said. "But the Harris family has owned this house for so long, I suppose my grandfather didn't want to let it go even though my father had no interest in running the farm after him."

"Farming's not an easy life," Haskell said.

I remembered that Haskell had grown up on a farm, though he never talked about it much. "That's what my father told me," I replied. "I know my grandfather was disappointed, but he didn't try to stand in my father's way when he was determined to find a job in town."

"Same thing with my dad," Haskell said, "but my younger brother wanted to be a farmer, so my dad didn't kick up much that I wanted to be a cop."

I couldn't imagine Haskell as anything other than what he was, a good, hardworking, honest officer of the law. "I'm glad it worked out for you," I said.

Haskell nodded and pulled out his notebook again. "Go through your story once more for me. I want to make sure I've got it all down."

Suppressing a sigh, I did as Haskell had requested. I kept to the pertinent details, including my surprise at inheriting the house after having no idea that it still belonged to my grandfather. When I got to the discovery of the bones in the attic, a thought I had tried to keep out of my mind finally forced its way in.

Did that collection of bones belong to someone who had died in this house? What if that person was murdered here?

THREE

||||||||||||||||||||||||||||||||

I caught Haskell looking at me with some concern. "I'm okay," I said.

Haskell nodded. "Anything else to add?"

"No." I shrugged. "I didn't know Martin Hale personally. My parents might have mentioned him when I was much younger, but I don't think he was one of their friends."

Haskell flipped his notebook shut and tucked it away. "We'll ask you to come down to the sheriff's department and sign your statement later."

"Of course." My attention focused on the sound of approaching footsteps, several pairs of them. Moments later, Kanesha and Sean appeared in the doorway. Behind them lurked a couple of Kanesha's team.

Kanesha advanced into the room. A glance at Haskell brought him to his feet, and he joined his fellow officers behind her.

"Any conclusions?" I remained seated, Diesel beside me. He edged closer, and I rubbed his head. He felt my sudden tension, I knew.

"My best guess is that those bones were buried somewhere and then dug up and put in that wardrobe. When that was done, I don't have any idea," Kanesha said. "We're going to go over the property to look for signs of a grave, and in the meantime, I'm going to call in an expert to look at the bones."

"Who's the expert?" Sean asked.

"Professor at the college," Kanesha said. "Forensic anthropologist."

"Dewey Seton," I said. "Of course, I should have thought of him."

Kanesha nodded. "We've consulted him before. He's top-notch."

"I hope they turn out to be really old," I said, "though I hate the thought that someone might have desecrated a burial site."

"It happens," Kanesha said. "Tell me, does this house have a root cellar? Houses this old usually had one."

I started to answer that I wasn't aware of one, but then I remembered my grandmother taking me down into it to retrieve some canned goods she was giving us to take home.

"Yes, there is," I said slowly. "Or there was. I think the entrance was under the back porch."

Kanesha turned to two of the officers behind her and instructed them to check.

After a moment I understood the reason for her inquiry. The root cellar would have been a good place to bury a body. As I remembered it, the floor consisted of hard-packed earth, not concrete or wood flooring. Accessible for digging and burying.

I felt a sudden chill at that thought. I sent up a silent prayer that, wherever the body had originally lain, it wasn't in the root cellar beneath the house.

"You'll be treating the house as a crime scene." Sean stated it bluntly.

"Yes, we will," Kanesha said. "It will take a few days, until we know more about the bones, their likely age, and so on. Depends on how recently the person died."

"What's your best guess?" I asked.

Kanesha narrowed her eyes at me. "For what?"

"The age of the bones," I replied.

She shrugged. "I'm no expert. I haven't been called to a crime scene with potentially really old bones before."

That's not much help. I kept the words to myself. I wanted reassurance, but obviously Kanesha wasn't going to give it. I would have to be patient until the experts had time to investigate.

I stood. "Then I suppose we might as well go home." I dug the keys to the house out of my pocket and handed them to Kanesha. Haskell gave me a receipt for them.

"You go ahead, Dad," Sean said as he followed me to the front door. "I'm going to stick around a little longer to see whether they find anything in that root cellar. I'll call you right away."

"Thanks," I said. "Come on, Diesel, let's go home."

The cat had been silent all this time, but now he chirped happily. The atmosphere in the house had grown oppressive, or so it seemed to me, and no doubt it had affected my cat. On the porch I paused to take a couple of deep breaths and let my eyes adjust to the bright sunlight. I heard a rumble of distant thunder as we headed for the car. I remembered that possible thunderstorms had been forecast for the afternoon or early evening.

While I drove, my brain might as well have been a hamster on a wheel, the way various ideas spun, one after another. I shook my head at one point to try to clear it, and Diesel meowed loudly from the backseat.

"I'm going to concentrate on driving," I told him, and I did my best. I couldn't banish a mental picture of that skull on the attic floor. I had little doubt that I would be dreaming of it tonight and probably nights to come. Suddenly I recalled one of my favorite Nancy Drew books, *The Secret in the Old Attic*. Nancy had been looking for music manuscripts. No pile of old bones for her. *Lucky me*.

Traffic increased as I approached the outskirts of Athena, and I forced myself to pay more attention to driving. Athena was a relatively small town, but it was a busy one thanks to the college and a regional medical facility. From the city limits to my house in an older part of town the drive took only ten minutes, and soon Diesel and I climbed out of the car and went into the house from the garage.

An orange tabby fur ball attacked us the moment we stepped into the kitchen. Ramses, now nearly ten months old, had grown steadily more rambunctious. I looked forward to the day when he began to settle down a bit and stopped climbing my legs. Those sharp claws didn't feel good, but at least today I was wearing jeans.

He scampered up my leg and onto my shoulder so quickly I didn't have time to deflect him. He stuck his nose in my ear and licked. I had to laugh. I managed to get hold of him and pull him into my arms. He lay on his back like a baby and looked up at me with trusting eyes. I rubbed his stomach, and he purred.

At my feet Diesel warbled loudly. I knew he was jealous. I rarely picked him up and held him like this because of his size, but of course he didn't understand that Ramses weighed about thirty pounds less than he did.

I heard a chuckle and turned to see my housekeeper, Azalea Berry, entering from the hallway.

"You put that rascal down," she said. "He's so badly spoiled, he's about rotten, and that's not helping."

I laughed. "I'm not the only one who spoils him." Azalea had taken quite the shine to Ramses, and he sometimes went home with her on the weekends. He had a bad habit of hiding himself in her straw bag—the one she left conveniently accessible for him to crawl into whenever he wanted.

Bending down, I let Ramses slide gently out of my arms. He righted himself on the floor and immediately attacked Diesel. My Maine Coon glared disdainfully at the younger cat and batted him away easily with a large paw. Diesel looked at me and meowed before he ambled into the utility room. Ramses followed, a dinghy bobbing in the wake of an ocean liner.

Azalea stood at the stove, stirring the contents of one pot. Smelled to me like purple hull peas cooking in fatback. I sighed. Not exactly healthy, but one of my favorites. Nothing better than peas and fresh, hot buttered cornbread.

I pulled a glass from the cupboard and filled it with cold water from the fridge. After draining half the glass, I refilled it and took my usual seat at the table. "Azalea, did you ever know my grandparents? My dad's parents, I mean."

Her tone wry, Azalea replied, "Everybody in town knew Mr. Robert Harris, I reckon. He ran for sheriff a couple of times when I was a little girl. I remember my daddy talking about it. He was a tough man, but fair. Never got elected, but he stirred things up good."

That accorded with what my father had told me when I was a teenager and doing a family history project for school. "What about my grandmother?"

"Everyone said she was the sweetest lady they knew." Azalea opened the oven door to inspect whatever was inside. After a moment she shut the door and went back to the pots on the stove.

"I don't remember much about her," I said. "I was only about four when she died. What I do remember, though, is that she loved me."

"Why you thinking about your grandparents today?" Azalea asked. "Can't remember you ever talking about them before."

"I found out this morning that I've inherited my grandfather's house and property," I said. "I thought it was out of the family."

Azalea turned from the stove to stare at me. "I thought Mr. Martin Hale had bought all that from your grand-daddy years ago."

I shrugged. "That's what I thought, too, but Sean says otherwise. Apparently, my grandfather only leased the land to Mr. Hale for his lifetime, and on his death, the property reverted to my grandfather's heir. And that turns out to be me."

"Mr. Hale is dead?" Azalea frowned.

"Died in California a couple of months ago, Sean said. His family didn't let anyone here know until recently." My phone rang, and I pulled it from my pocket. Sean was calling.

"Excuse me. I need to take this." I got up from the table and headed out into the hall. Diesel and Ramses came running after me.

"What's the latest?" I asked after greeting my son.

"The root cellar is intact," Sean replied. "A fair amount of home-canned goods on the shelves. No sign of any digging, however. At least, not yet."

"Thank the Lord for that," I said with profound relief. "Anything else?"

"Not yet. I'm in the car on the way back to the office. Do you need anything right now?" Sean's concern was evident. "Don't worry too much about this, Dad. I'd be willing to bet that skeleton is really old, an archaeological specimen."

"Maybe so," I said, "but I find that upsetting. To think of someone disturbing a burial really bothers me."

"I see your point," Sean replied. "But let's wait until we know more, okay? No use worrying about things you can't control. Remember how you used to tell me that?"

I had to chuckle. "Yes, Dad, I do."

Sean snorted with laughter. "Later, dude." The call ended.

I knew Sean was right. Spending time agonizing over the origin and identity of the skeleton wouldn't be productive. I put my phone away and wandered back into the kitchen. Diesel and Ramses stayed hot on my trail. I noticed that Diesel made sure to put himself between Ramses and me.

Azalea was chopping iceberg lettuce by the sink. She turned as we entered. Her expression enigmatic, she asked, "What's going on? I can always tell when something's up."

I resumed my place at the table but twisted my chair around so I could face her. I gave her a brief description of the morning's activities at my grandfather's house. She appeared to be listening intently but remained focused on assembling the salad.

When I'd finished my story, Azalea didn't respond right away. She picked up a dishrag and wiped her hands before she turned to look at me. "I think I know who those bones used to be."

FOUR

Azalea's bald pronouncement startled me so much I nearly dropped my glass. I set it down. "How on earth would you know that?"

Her eyes narrowed. "Mr. Hale's wife was supposed to've ran off with another man about forty years ago. I never did think she was the kind of woman to do that. You mark my words, he got drunk one day and killed her and buried her somewhere on that farm."

"That's horrible," I said. "Was Mr. Hale an alcoholic?"

"He was bad to drink," Azalea replied. "My daddy worked for him for a while back when Kanesha was a baby. If it wasn't for old Mr. Hale's son, that farm would have sat there and gone to seed." She paused for a deep breath. "Then about twenty-five years ago, I reckon it was, Mr. Hale's son took him to a revival, and the preacher put the fear of the Lord into him. He gave up drinking right then and there. Took up working on the farm again and going to church."

"That's an amazing story," I said, still trying to take in the implications. If Azalea was correct about Mrs. Hale, this could be the end of the matter. Tragic, but with Mr. Hale dead, and presumably his son as well, there was nothing to do except give Mrs. Hale a proper burial.

"I suppose Mr. Hale's son is dead, too?" I asked.

"Killed in an accident on the farm nigh on twenty years ago," Azalea said. "His wife remarried and moved to California with her children. Left old Mr. Hale on his own. Word was she couldn't stand the old man."

"Did he start drinking again when his son was killed and his family left?"

Azalea shrugged. "Not that I ever heard." She turned back to her salad. "Mark my words, that's Mrs. Hale you found."

But who put her bones in the attic? And why?

I left those questions unspoken. Azalea couldn't answer them any more than I could. I decided to withdraw to the den. I filled my glass again, this time with chilled sweet tea, and called for the cats to come with me. Diesel stretched out beside my recliner, and Ramses hopped up on the footrest. He meowed in triumph as he looked down at Diesel, who was too large and heavy to lie on the footrest. Diesel ignored his little brother.

Kanesha needed to know about this possible lead to the skeleton's identity. I decided the easiest way to do it was to text her. All I said was that her mother had an idea about the identity of the remains and to call her as soon as she could. I laid the phone aside, satisfied that I had done what I should without being nosy and interfering. Kanesha might take it that way, but that was up to her.

I wondered whether I should share this news with Sean right away. No need to disturb him at the office, I decided after brief consideration. He had a busy schedule every day, and this news could wait.

The doorbell rang, and I gently nudged Ramses down from the footrest. Diesel sprang up and trotted out of the den, Ramses right behind him. I moved more slowly, and by the time I'd reached the hall, Azalea already stood at the door greeting my daughter, Laura, and my grandson, Charlie.

Upon seeing me, Charlie started chattering and trying to free himself from his mother's arms. Laura laughed and put the boy down. He tottered toward me still talking a mile a minute. The only word I understood was *Papa*, his name for me. I stepped forward and swung him up over my head. He giggled and clapped his hands. Then I brought him close to my chest and hugged him. He wrapped his arms around my neck and squeezed. He began talking again. His speech was becoming clearer now that he was thirteen months old, but the noises he emitted didn't sound much like words anyone but he knew.

"This is a pleasant surprise," I said as I walked forward to greet my daughter. I bent to kiss her cheek, and Charlie had to kiss her as well.

Laura laughed. "We were out and about, so I thought we'd drop by. After all, it's been nearly twenty-four hours since you and Azalea have seen us."

Diesel had been meowing the entire time. He considered Charlie his special charge, and whenever the baby was nearby, Diesel insisted on being close to him. I set Charlie down and he wrapped his arms around Diesel, chattering away. Diesel warbled, and Charlie answered.

Ramses sat and watched. He didn't appear to know what to make of this small human with the grabby hands.

I always kept an eye on Charlie and Diesel these days, because I knew the baby could easily hurt the cat without knowing what he was doing. So far, however, I had never seen him do it. Charlie seemed to have an instinct about how to treat Diesel, and Diesel certainly knew how to keep an eye on the baby.

"Y'all come on into the kitchen." Azalea led the way. "I know that baby is probably thirsty, and I've got some nice cold apple juice for him."

"Thank you, Azalea," Laura said. "That's perfect. I'll have some, too, if there's enough." She took Charlie's hand to lead him in the right direction. Diesel accompanied them, and Ramses trailed along.

"Were you running errands this morning?" I asked as we seated ourselves at the table.

"Doctor visit." Laura gave a mischievous smile.

"Was it already time for another checkup?" I glanced at my grandson. "He just saw the doctor a couple of weeks ago. Is there anything wrong?"

"No, Charlie's fine, Dad." Laura regarded me. "It was my turn to see my doctor."

"I hope nothing's wrong," I said. "Are you sick? You don't look it." In fact, she appeared to me to be glowing with health.

Azalea gave Laura a knowing look as she placed a glass of apple juice in front of her along with Charlie's sippy cup. The baby climbed into Laura's lap and she settled him with his cup.

"Miss Laura's going to have another baby." Azalea regarded me, one eyebrow raised.

Laura laughed at my expression. "She's right, Dad.

I've suspected it, but the obstetrician confirmed it. You're going to have another grandchild in about seven months."

I couldn't take in the news for a moment. I stared at Azalea. "She told you?"

Azalea snorted. "Didn't have to. I could see it by looking at her." Obviously, this was one of those mysterious things that only women knew. I didn't have a clue that my daughter was pregnant until she told me.

I turned back to my daughter. "Does Frank know?"

Laura smiled. "Of course. He was with me at the doctor's office, but he had to get back to campus once we were done."

Her husband, Frank Salisbury, was head of the theater department at Athena College, and Laura was an assistant professor there.

I got up from my chair to give my daughter a hug. "This is wonderful news. Are y'all ready for another baby?"

"Ready as we'll ever be," Laura said happily. "We wanted at least one sibling for Charlie, maybe a little sister to drive him crazy like I did Sean."

"A sweet little girl who looks just like her mama." Azalea beamed with joy as she came to hug Laura.

"Thank you," Laura said.

Charlie began to bounce in his mother's lap. He had evidently finished his apple juice and now wanted down. Laura eased him off her lap, and he immediately sat down to rub heads with Diesel. Ramses crawled into his lap.

Knowing that child and cats would be happily entertained for a few minutes, I told Laura about the morning's activities. Her eyes widened when I mentioned the bones in the attic. She gave a dramatic shiver and said, "How creepy." Then she motioned for me to continue.

Charlie, Diesel, and Ramses were crawling around on

the floor, all three making sounds of contentment and joy. I raised my voice as I went on to finish the story. I didn't include Azalea's potential identification of the body. There was no point in spreading that information for the moment.

"I hope they can find out who it is," Laura said. "The whole thing really is macabre. I think I'd have run screaming down the stairs if a skull had popped out at me like that." She glanced over at Diesel. "He had no idea what it was, of course."

"A potential toy," I said as the image returned, unbidden, to my mind. I suppressed a shiver.

"Nancy Drew never found anything like that," Laura said. "Even in the old attic book."

"No, she didn't," I said, "although at the age I first read the books, I would have been thrilled no end."

Laura laughed at that. "Me too, probably." She sobered. "Are you going to keep the house? I'd love to see it at some point."

"I honestly haven't thought much about it yet," I said. "Since I've only known about it a few hours now." I paused for a moment. "There's a part of me that is happy that it's back in the family because of the history of it. My grandparents lived there, and my father grew up there. But I don't honestly see myself living there. I'm perfectly comfortable here."

"What about Helen Louise?" Laura asked. "What are the two of you going to do after you're married? Live here? Or in her house?"

"We still haven't decided," I said, hoping to avoid further discussion of this issue. The truth was, Helen Louise and I had argued about this several times since I had asked her to marry me a few months ago. Neither one of us wanted to move to the other's house, and that presented a big problem. She grew up in her house, as had her father before her. I understood her attachment to the place, and I knew she understood my attachment to my house, left to me by my aunt Dottie.

Laura must have sensed I didn't want to discuss it. She didn't question me further. "I'm sure you'll have plenty of time to decide what to do with the house," she said. "This investigation could take months unless there are some lucky breaks."

I glanced at Azalea and frowned. I didn't want her to start talking about Mr. Hale and his possibly murdered wife, at least not until she had talked to Kanesha about it. Azalea stared back at me as if to say, *You think I don't have any sense?*

I wondered whether Kanesha had called her mother yet. In the excitement of Laura's arrival with Charlie, there had been no time to find out.

"I think you're probably right," I said in response to Laura's statement, though privately I hoped the situation would be resolved more quickly. I hoped that calling in Dewey Seton, the forensic anthropologist, would move things along at a more rapid pace.

Conversation turned to more domestic matters, and we three adults chatted for about a quarter hour while Charlie continued to play with the cats. Finally, he wore himself out and started to become fretful. Laura gathered him up, and I walked them to the car, leaving Diesel and Ramses to stretch out under the table for a nap. Charlie had exhausted them and himself.

Back in the kitchen I found that Azalea had set the

table for lunch. I checked my watch and was surprised to see that it was nearly twelve-thirty. I hadn't realized it was so late, but the morning had been full of incidents.

I gazed with happiness at the spread of food before me. Sliced Virginia ham, sweet-potato fluff, purple hull peas, salad, and hot, fresh cornbread. I helped myself and soon had a plate full of deliciousness. Azalea had set a fresh glass of sweet tea at my place, and I thanked her, as I always did, for the food she provided.

She nodded and left the kitchen. I never could get her to eat with me, and I had given up trying a few years ago. She had promised my aunt Dottie that she would look after the house as she had done for years, and make sure I was looked after, too. Thanks to a legacy from my aunt, Azalea really didn't need to work, but she wasn't the type to retire. As usual, she had cooked enough for four or five, but the food wouldn't go to waste. The leftovers would provide either dinner tonight or lunch tomorrow for me and my boarders, Stewart Delacorte and Haskell, his partner.

I heard the front door open and close, and moments later, Stewart appeared in the doorway, almost as if I had conjured him. He cast a hungry look at the table and smiled.

"Hey, Charlie. I'm starving. Looks like you've just started." He went to the cabinet for a plate, and then extracted silverware from the drawer. He set these at his place and poured himself a glass of sweet tea. After filling his plate with food, he settled in to eat. Diesel and Ramses left me and moved to sit on either side of Stewart's chair. He had frequently been known to share bits of his meal with them, and they weren't about to miss any opportunities.

"What have you been up to this morning?" Stewart asked after he had eaten several mouthfuls of food.

I gave him a shortened version of the story. When I reached the point of the discovery of the skull, he laughed. "Good heavens, Charlie, can't you go anywhere without finding a dead body? Well, in this case, skeletal remains." He took a bite of ham as he regarded me, eyes twinkling with mischief.

"I'm beginning to think I can't," I told him with a gloom not totally feigned. I finished the story without interruption.

At the conclusion Stewart put down his fork and reached for his glass. After a healthy swig of the tea, he said, "Dewey Seton is exactly the person to sort this out."

"I hope he can," I said. "Do you know him? I've read about him in campus publications, but I haven't met him."

Stewart nodded. "Nice guy, a bit younger than me. On the intense side, not much of a sense of humor, but you know these bone guys. They relate better to dead people than to live ones, at least in my experience." He chuckled.

Not having personally known any *bone guys*, as Stewart labeled them, I couldn't argue.

"He also has a cadaver dog," Stewart said. "Did you know that?"

I shook my head. I'd heard of cadaver dogs, but I didn't realize there were any in our area. I knew there was a group in Memphis who used them for search and rescue, but that was the closest area I knew about.

"They're amazing animals." Stewart gazed blandly at me as his hand slipped under the table, no doubt to dispense bites of ham to two starving felines. I pretended not to notice, but if either cat got sick, I decided I would insist that Stewart clean it up.

33

"Then the sooner Kanesha gets Dr. Seton and his dog on the case, the better," I said. "I want to know where those bones were before someone put them in the attic."

"I'm sure you do," Stewart said. "It's a bit spooky, isn't it? I wonder how long they were in the attic. I wonder if old man Hale put them there."

"Who knows?" I said. "We may never know the answer to that, but if we can find out who those bones were once upon a time, maybe we'll be able to find out how they got into the attic."

"For your sake I hope this isn't drawn out over months," Stewart said. "Or longer."

"Me too," I replied. "Azalea has a theory about those bones." I hadn't wanted Azalea to mention it in front of my daughter because I didn't want Laura upset by the story, not in her condition. I knew it wouldn't faze Stewart in the least.

"Really?" Stewart regarded me with an interrogative expression. "Do tell."

"She told me that Mr. Hale at one time was a mean drunk, and that he probably killed his wife. Then he put it about that she ran off with another man."

Stewart snorted. "Try running that by Haskell, why don't you?"

"What does Haskell have to do with it?" I asked, puzzled.

"Mrs. Hale was his mother's sister," Stewart said. "He never said anything to me about her running off with anybody."

FIVE

"Mrs. Hale was Haskell's aunt?" I shook my head. "When I saw Haskell earlier, he didn't mention any family connection with the Hales."

"I don't think it's one his family is proud of," Stewart said, his tone wry. "Old man Hale had a bad reputation as a nasty drunk for years, but at some point he must have seen a light on the road to Damascus, so to speak, because he gave up drinking and became holier-than-thou." He grinned. "Every bit as obnoxious as he'd always been but without the cusswords."

I couldn't help smiling at Stewart's insouciant description of Mr. Hale. "So, I take it Haskell's mother knows what happened to her sister? Is she alive and well somewhere?"

"I'm not really sure," Stewart said. "Haskell only mentioned her to me once, and that was a couple of years ago." He shrugged. "He's pretty buttoned up about any-thing to do with his family."

"I know he's not mentioned them often in my presence," I said. "I thought it was simply his natural reticence."

"Partly that, I suppose," Stewart said. "But I know that his relationship with his parents and his brother and sister hasn't been all that good since he came out to them when he was about twenty-five. He doesn't even talk about it much to me."

"Have you met any of his family?" This was rather nosy of me, but sometimes I couldn't help myself. Haskell was such a good man, I hated the idea of his having strained relations with his family.

"Only briefly, and not very happily." Stewart's face darkened with what I presumed was anger.

I didn't want to probe further, but I had to clamp down on my tongue to keep from asking him, *What happened?* Whatever had occurred at that meeting, it obviously hadn't been pleasant.

I waited for Stewart's emotions to level out again. Diesel meowed, aware that Stewart was upset. Ramses followed suit, always alert to whatever his big brother did. Stewart mustered a smile and rubbed the Maine Coon's head. Ramses stood on his hind legs to butt his head against the hand, and Stewart laughed, his good humor now restored.

"Families can be horrible," he said once he'd finished giving attention to the cats. "I suppose Haskell's isn't any worse than most. They're plain folks, farmers, and nothing wrong with that, of course." He shrugged. "Their worldview is rather limited, that's all."

"It's too bad they can't see Haskell for the good man he is," I said.

"I think they're proud of him, in their way." Stewart laughed, a tinge of bitterness in the sound. "It's me they have no use for, you see. I led him astray."

"Their loss," I said warmly, "and if they could only see how happy the two of you are together, they'd get over their prejudice . . ."

I trailed off because Stewart was shaking his head. "No point in discussing it further. I don't think they'll ever come around." He pushed back from the table as Azalea entered the room. He thanked her for lunch. "I'd better get upstairs and take my little demon out for a walk before he chews up anything else expensive."

His *little demon*, Dante the poodle, actually had a sweet and loving nature, but he did get bored up in Stewart's suite on the third floor. I had urged Stewart to let him have the run of the house, or at least the third floor, but Stewart seemed reluctant to do so. I thought he feared the dog would tear things up. He might do that, I reasoned, but with Diesel and Ramses to play with most of the time, he should stay busy enough to keep out of the worst mischief.

Azalea began to clear away Stewart's plate and utensils, after brushing off my offer to do it. Ramses meowed loudly. She glanced down at him and frowned. "Listen here, mister, you're not getting anything more off this here plate. I know Mr. Stewart slipped you food. You're getting fat."

Ramses meowed in protest, and I had to smother a laugh. Azalea used to stare at me when I talked to Diesel, her expression plainly revealing she thought I had lost my mind. I forbore these days to return the favor, now that she exhibited the same behavior with Ramses. I simply enjoyed the irony. She occasionally spoke to

Diesel, referring to him as *Mr. Cat*, but not as frequently as she chatted with Ramses.

Azalea ignored Ramses's further attempts to cajole food out of her. I finished the last few bites of food on my plate. Before I could push back my chair to dispose of my plate and utensils, Azalea picked them up and carried them to the sink. I thanked her for clearing, and she nodded.

"Did you know that Mrs. Hale was Haskell's aunt?" I asked. "Stewart told me that during lunch."

"I knew that." Azalea frowned. "Forgot to mention it to you. I reckon it doesn't change anything else about what I told you."

"Surely Haskell would have told Stewart that his aunt disappeared one day and was never seen again."

Azalea shrugged. "Maybe they don't like to talk about it, but it sure enough happened."

Ordinarily, I would have said that Azalea's word was utterly reliable, but unless Haskell had withheld the complete truth from Stewart, there was a big discrepancy here. I wondered whether I should bring up the subject with Haskell. He knew all too well that I was nosy when it came to suspicious deaths. Given that he had not talked much about his family to me before now, I decided that I had best leave well enough alone for once.

I wondered what Melba would have to say about all this. I debated calling her. She should be either at lunch or close to finishing it, so this would be as good a time as any to call her.

"I'll be in the den if anyone needs me for anything," I told Azalea. "Come along, boys, let's get out of the way."

Diesel chirped as I pushed back my chair, and Ramses

meowed. While Diesel followed me readily, Ramses looked back and forth between me and Azalea, no doubt hoping for more treats from his willing acolyte.

"You get on out of here," she told Ramses. "You ought to be ashamed, begging like you do. I declare you're more than a body can handle sometimes." She flashed a brief smile after she scolded the cat, and Ramses responded with a plaintive mew. Azalea flapped her apron at him, and he ran out of the room ahead of Diesel and me.

In the den I made myself comfortable in my recliner, and Ramses immediately hopped up into my lap, circled around several times, and then settled down for a nap. Diesel stretched out on the floor by the chair.

Melba answered after a couple of rings. "Hi, Charlie. How are you enjoying your day off?"

"It's an interesting day so far," I replied. "Do you have time to talk?"

"I do. Finished lunch a few minutes ago, and I don't have to be back at my desk for a bit. What's up?"

I gave her a quick rundown on my unexpected inheritance, and she was surprised and curious.

"I thought your daddy or your granddaddy had sold that house to old man Hale," she said. "I'm glad he didn't. Place like that ought to be in your family where it belongs."

"It's a bit of a shock, really. Not something I ever expected. I haven't given much thought to the place in years. I have to say that Mr. Hale kept the house in good condition." I paused. "But I did find something totally unexpected when I went through it this morning. Or, I should say, Diesel found it. In the attic, of all places."

"If you tell me you found a dead body in that house, I'm not going to believe you." Melba hooted with laughter. "Even you don't have that kind of bad luck."

"Well, you'd be wrong, then." My tart tone stopped the laughter.

"You found a dead body?" Melba fairly shrieked the words, and I jerked the phone briefly away from my ear. "You have got to be kidding me, Charlie. Who was it?"

"I don't know," I said. "I'm definitely not kidding you. All we found were bones. They were in an old wardrobe in the attic. Diesel was nosing around and knocked the skull out onto the floor."

"Just bones? That's interesting," Melba replied after a brief silence. "There wasn't anything with them?"

"I didn't go through them," I said. "We went back downstairs and found that Sean had arrived. He called the sheriff's department. I wasn't about to go messing around with anything. Kanesha would have had my head off if I'd disturbed anything."

"True," Melba said. "I wonder who it could be."

"Azalea thinks it's Mr. Hale's wife. She thinks Hale killed her and told everybody she ran off with another man. Apparently, at the time Hale was a mean, abusive drunk."

"He was, but after his wife was gone, he eventually got sober and got religion." Melba's tone evinced her disgust. "From one extreme to the other. He was an unpleasant man."

"When did all this happen?" I asked.

"Twenty-five years ago, maybe," Melba said, some uncertainty in her tone. "After you moved away, anyway. It's true about Mrs. Hale, that she sorta disappeared, that is. Nobody really knows what happened, except maybe her family, but they don't talk about it."

"Whatever happened, Kanesha and her team will eventually get to the bottom of it," I said. "They're going to call in Dewey Seton. He has a cadaver dog, and maybe the dog can find where the bones were originally. I suspect they were buried somewhere on the farm."

"What if the bones are older than that?" Melba asked. "What if they were buried while your grandfather was still alive?"

That was the question that had been haunting me ever since I first saw the skull on the attic floor.

SIX

||||||||||||

"I'll have to face that if it turns out to be what happened," I said after a long pause. "I didn't know my grandfather well. I was so young when he died, and my father didn't talk a lot about him, either, after his death. I don't know what kind of man he was, not the least whether he was actually capable of murder."

"I don't remember him, either," Melba said slowly. "I don't remember my mama or daddy talking about him much, other than him running for sheriff and not winning. Guess maybe they didn't really know him, although they knew your mama and daddy."

"A lot, at least in my mind, depends on where the body was buried," I said. "If they can find the burial site, maybe that will tell them something about the *who* and the *when*, if not the *why*."

"That's a good point," Melba said in an encouraging tone. "Old man Hale could have dug up those bones anywhere, anytime, and brought them home as a curiosity or some kind of weird souvenir. He was more than a little loopy, if you ask me."

"I'll take your word for it," I said, a bit dryly. A beep from my phone interrupted my train of thought. "Hang on a moment. I've got another call coming in." I checked the phone. Sean was calling, and I answered quickly. "On another call with Melba. Let me tell her I'll call her back."

Moments later I was back on the line with my son. "Any news?"

"A bit," Sean replied. "They got farther into the root cellar. Still no sign of digging in there so far, but it's full of all kinds of junk. It's going to take a while to clear it before they can check the floor. It's hard-packed earth."

That accorded with my own dim memory of the place.

"The good news is that Kanesha has spoken with that guy at the college, Dewey Seton," Sean continued. "He's going over with that dog of his right away to see whether she can pick up any kind of trail."

"That would be interesting to watch," I said.

"As the property owner, I don't see why you shouldn't be able to," Sean said. "If you like, I'll call Kanesha and ask about it."

I thought about it for a moment, rather tempted to be involved, but I decided against it. The less I forced my presence into this investigation, the better my relationship with Kanesha would remain. She had learned to tolerate my involvement in cases, but I suspected that her toleration frequently involved the gritting of teeth.

"Thanks, but I'll wait to hear officially from Kanesha what's going on," I said.

Sean chuckled. "Discretion being the better part of valor in this case."

"Now, don't *you* start quoting Shakespeare, too," I said, half-jokingly. My daughter, Laura, a trained actress, often shared apposite lines from the Bard of Avon in conversation.

"Talk to you later, Dad." Sean still sounded amused.

I put down the phone. Now I began to regret passing up the chance to witness the cadaver dog in action. I felt restless sitting at home with the cats and doing nothing constructive.

Helen Louise was in New Orleans for several days with two of her best friends from law school. She had invited me to come with her, but neither of her friends, both women, were bringing their partners. I declined with a smile, knowing that she would enjoy herself more without having to include me in conversations and other activities. I could call her, I knew, but I didn't want to interrupt whatever the trio was doing. We would talk tonight, and I'd bring her up to date on my most unusual discovery.

I wasn't in the mood to read, though I had several good books waiting, including newly reprinted Golden Age detective stories by E. C. R. Lorac, Anthony Gilbert, and George Bellairs. When I didn't feel like reading, I knew I was too restive to accomplish much.

Abruptly I decided that I would get on the computer and dig around to try to find information about the late Martin Hale and his family. I gently removed Ramses from my lap, held him to my chest until I was out of the chair, and deposited him in the vacated spot. Diesel raised his head to look an inquiry at me, while Ramses simply yawned and rubbed a paw over his nose before going back to sleep.

"I'm not going anywhere," I told Diesel in a low tone. I pulled out my desk chair and got comfortable. After waking my computer, I opened the browser to my favorite search engine and typed in Martin Hale's name along with the words *Mississippi* and *obituary*. I figured that, even though he had died in California, the local paper would have run a notice of his death.

Bingo. I clicked on the link to the recent obituary in our local paper. There was no picture of Martin Hale, but the obituary itself consisted of several paragraphs. I skimmed them rapidly, looking primarily for a mention of his wife. There was none that I found on this first perusal, so I went back through again, slowly this time.

No mention of his wife. That truly was strange, but I figured someone in his family had probably written the account or had at least given the salient facts to the newspaper's obit writer. There was obviously a mystery surrounding Mrs. Hale, and the Hales, whatever their reasons might be, had excluded her.

The obituary mentioned that Hale had lived on the old Harris farm, once owned by the late Robert Charles Harris of Athena County. Hale had retired from farming some ten years ago, but there was no mention of what became of the farm after his retirement. I would have to check with Sean about that. I assumed that Hale had rented the land to other farmers. Surely he hadn't let it all lie fallow. Small farmers probably didn't make a lot of money, and I figured Hale would have needed the income from rented land.

I realized that I had no idea how large the farm was. I knew my grandfather hadn't been wealthy, but I couldn't recall any signs of poverty in my memories of my grandparents. My father had never spoken to me of growing up poor, though I knew the Great Depression had not been easy for his family. My mother's family, on the other hand, had been below the poverty line thanks to her ne'er-do-well father.

I decided I needed to sit down with Sean and go over all the particulars he might have about the farm and its history since my grandfather's death. I thought about calling him right then but decided that conversation could wait. There were more pressing matters.

I searched the newspaper archives for any other mentions of Martin Hale or members of his family. Other than the occasional mention of a graduation of one of his grandchildren, there was nothing substantial except for the obituary of his son killed in the farm accident. Certainly nothing that could help a nosey parker like me dig more deeply into his life.

Another perusal of the obituary, however, revealed a few items of potential interest. Among them were the names of his son, Martin Horace Hale Jr., and his grandson, Martin Hale III. There was also a granddaughter, Alissa. The deceased's wife was named Suzanne, but as she had remarried and moved to California, I didn't think there was much point in trying to find out more about her. Sean might have contact information for the grandson, however, Martin Horace Hale III.

What reason would I have for getting in touch with the grandson? I supposed I could offer condolences on the death of his grandfather, if nothing else. For the first time, however, I thought about what the grandson could be feeling about the loss of a property he might naturally have thought he was due to inherit. As I recalled, I hadn't thought to ask Sean about the grandson's reaction to the news that the property hadn't belonged to his grandfather.

Might as well call Sean and ask, I decided. I pulled out my phone and speed-dialed my son. I hoped he wouldn't be too busy to talk to me. For some reason I felt a sense of urgency about the issue.

Sean answered quickly. "What's up, Dad?"

"I didn't think about it this morning when you told me about my grandfather's house," I said. "How did young Martin Hale, the grandson, feel about the fact that he didn't inherit the property?"

Sean expelled a breath into the phone. "I was hoping you'd forget to ask me anything like that."

My intuition had been correct. "He wasn't happy."

"No, he wasn't," Sean said in a flat tone. "He's threatening to sue for ownership of the house and all the farmland."

SEVEN

"I can't say I'm totally surprised," I said slowly. "Does he have legal grounds to succeed with this suit?"

"No," Sean said. "I found a copy of the original agreement between your grandfather and Mr. Hale in the files here. My father-in-law was meticulous in everything, and I doubt young Hale could come up with convincing grounds to break the agreement."

"Did the elder Mr. Hale leave a will? You mentioned that he handed over something to you?"

"It was a holograph will, witnessed by two men," Sean said. "It was simple, leaving everything that Hale owned to his heirs."

"Since he didn't own the property or the house," I said, "he couldn't leave them to anyone."

"Exactly," Sean said. "I explained that to young Mr. Hale, but he didn't want to hear it. He evidently needs money, and he wants to be able to sell the property." He paused. "He seems to be a very determined guy."

"How old is he?"

Sean expelled a breath into the phone. "Early thirties, I'd say. Nice-looking but scruffy, wearing clothes that look pretty shabby. I think he's an addict of some kind. He's nervous, can't keep still."

"That's not good," I said. "If he's desperate, no telling what he might try if he's in need of a fix."

"I agree. I've told Kanesha about him, and the sheriff's department is going to keep an eye on him as long as he remains in the area."

"Do you think there's a lawyer in town who'll take his case?"

"Most of them won't touch it," Sean said wryly, "because of my father-in-law's reputation. They know it would be a lost cause."

Q. C. Pendergrast had been known as one of the finest lawyers in the state of Mississippi, highly respected for his legal acumen and his staunch integrity.

"Still," Sean went on, "there are a couple of ethically challenged operators here who might be willing to take the case." He laughed suddenly. "I almost hope they do. I mentioned it to Alex a few minutes ago, and she says she wants to be the one to go to court if the case comes to pass."

Alexandra Pendergrast Harris, my daughter-in-law, could be as formidable in court as her late father had been, I knew. She wouldn't take lightly to someone attempting to overturn her father's work.

I chuckled. "I'll be in court to watch her, if it comes to that."

"I don't think it will get that far," Sean said. "Any lawyer worth his or her beans should be able to see that from the signed agreement. I gave you only the most important points this morning. It's incredibly detailed, and it's pretty ironclad as far as I can see."

I trusted my son and his legal know-how. I'd put him up against any lawyer in town, in the state, even.

"As long as I've got you on the phone," Sean continued, "there's more business to discuss. The farmland. Mr. Hale retired from farming about ten years ago, and even before then he was subleasing most of the land to a couple of other farmers. This is covered in the agreement your grandfather signed, so that's all fine. With Hale's death, however, those agreements are revoked."

"I had wondered about that since I'd read online he had retired. I don't know anything about farming," I said, "and at this point I'm too old to learn, even if I wanted to."

"Precisely my thinking," Sean replied. "With your permission I will talk to the two farmers and inform them of the situation. If you have no objection, I'll talk to them about continuance of their leases. I will of course make sure that the terms are favorable for all parties concerned."

"I have complete faith in you," I said. "You have my permission to go ahead."

"Thanks, Dad," Sean said. "This will take some time to settle, naturally, but I see no reason to stop these men from continuing to work the leased land."

"I agree. You do whatever you think best."

"And while I talk to them, I'll try to find out whether they know anything about those bones in the attic." He sounded smug.

"Do you think Kanesha will approve of your doing that?"

"Maybe. Maybe not." Sean chuckled. "I'm going to take my lead from how you do things and ask anyway. Talk to you later, Dad." He ended the call before I could respond.

I was tempted to call him right back and scold him the way he had scolded me in the past for my interference, as he labeled it. I knew it was pointless, however, and I didn't call back.

A sudden loud crash of thunder startled me, and I glanced out the den window to see that the sky had turned dark. Then came a flash of lightning, and I quickly powered down my computer and got up from my desk. I went over to the window for a better view of the weather conditions.

Sheets of rain pelted down, and I heard more thunder, followed in seconds by flashes of lightning. I moved away from the window. Ramses and Diesel, made jumpy by the loud sounds, had disappeared from view. I headed for the hallway, calling them as I went. "Come on, boys, it's okay."

The scrabbling of claws against the wood floor alerted me to the cats' presence behind me. I hurried into the kitchen to check on Azalea, who I knew disliked storms even more than I did. I also wanted to retrieve the weather radio. We never knew when storms like this might spawn heavy winds or even a tornado, and it paid to be prepared.

In the inside corner of the room, Azalea had the weather radio on, and I paused a few steps inside the kitchen to listen to the broadcast. Diesel and Ramses huddled by my legs as the thunder sounded again. Azalea turned up the volume, and we heard the announcement that the storm was traveling at a rate of fifteen miles an hour and would soon pass through the area. High winds were to be expected, but there were no signs so far of tornadic activity according to the weather radar.

"That's a relief," I said, and moved farther into the room toward Azalea, careful to stay away from the windows.

Azalea nodded. "Yes, thank the Lord." Her eyes closed, and her lips moved in what I knew was a silent prayer. I waited quietly until she'd finished, mentally adding words of my own to hers.

I pulled chairs from the table, and we sat with Diesel by my feet and Ramses curled up in Azalea's lap until the storm passed. Probably a matter of no more than fifteen minutes, but it seemed far longer as we listened to the wind and the rain lashing the house. When the wind and rain ceased, I got up from my chair and stretched. Diesel rubbed against my legs and meowed. Ramses climbed down and meowed along with his big brother.

I went to the window and looked out into the side yard. I spotted a few twigs and numerous leaves, but no large branches. "I'm going to take a look around," I said to Azalea.

After a circuit of the house, as I squelched through the sodden yard in my rubber boots, I was happy to see that there had been no hail to damage the roof. No large limbs, simply more twigs and leaves. Once the ground had dried, I could easily rake everything up in half an hour.

I remembered my grandfather's house—now my house, I reminded myself—and I wondered if there had been any damage there. So many trees, so much more opportunity for harm. I figured that the sheriff's department officers were there when the storm came through, and if they saw any significant damage, they would surely notify Sean.

Had the storm delayed the deployment of the cadaver dog? I thought it probably had, at least until the bad weather moved on. I was anxious to know where the bones had lain before someone unceremoniously dumped them in the attic.

Diesel started chattering the moment I came in the kitchen door, telling me in no uncertain terms that he hadn't appreciated being left inside. I patted his head and told him he should be thanking me for keeping his feet dry. Then, boots off and stowed away in the utility room, I gave Azalea the good news about the lack of damage.

"Thank the Lord," Azalea replied. "We are blessed. I called my neighbor, and she said the same thing about my house."

My phone rang, and I pulled it from my pocket. Sean responded quickly to my hello. "I just got off the phone with Kanesha," he said. "They had to take shelter in the house when the storm blew up. No damage to the house, but several trees are down nearby, including one over the driveway by that thing she said is a cattle gap. They're stuck there at the moment until they can get the tree moved."

"No vehicles damaged?" I asked.

"Not that she mentioned," Sean replied. "The forensic anthropologist didn't make it because of the storm. They're going to try tomorrow instead. Forecast calls for clear skies all day."

"That's good," I said. "Look, I changed my mind about being there while the cadaver dog is working. Can you talk to Kanesha about it for me?"

"I will," Sean said. "I'd already got her to agree to let

me be there to observe on your behalf, so I don't see why she would object to your presence."

Other than plain orneriness, I thought.

"If she does object, I won't push the matter," I said, trying not to sound disappointed. "It's probably more important that you're there to observe anyway, since you're the legal mastermind."

"Perry Mason on the job." Sean laughed. "Let me give Kanesha a call now, and I'll get back to you."

I thanked him and ended the call. I shared the news of the downed trees at the farm with Azalea, and she once again expressed her thanks to the Lord that no one was hurt.

"Let's go back to the den, boys," I said to the cats, and they followed me out of the kitchen.

We met Stewart coming down the stairs with Dante at his heels. The moment he spotted Diesel and Ramses, however, the little poodle scampered down as fast as he could and launched himself at Ramses. The two tussled right under my feet, and I had to grab the banister to keep from tripping over them. Diesel hissed at them, trying to bat them apart.

Stewart called out a sharp command to his dog. Dante ignored him. I clapped my hands loudly over the scuffling animals, and that caught their attention. They hadn't been fighting, only playing, but the yipping and growling noises were a bit much.

Stewart picked up Dante and cradled him in one arm. Ramses sat licking a paw, as innocently as if he and Dante hadn't been roughhousing. I laughed.

"That was a nasty storm while it lasted," Stewart said. "Any damage? I couldn't see any out of our windows on the third floor."

"Just some twigs and leaves blown loose," I said. "There was some damage on my grandfather's property." I shared with him the news Sean gave me.

"The county will soon have that tree out of the way. Nobody wants to get on Kanesha's bad side." Stewart laughed.

"I certainly don't," I said. "We were going to the den. Want to join us?"

"I will in a few," Stewart said. "I'm going to let Dante out in the backyard for a quick wee first."

"Okay." I moved down the hall to the den, aware that Diesel and Ramses had followed Stewart and Dante. I knew Stewart wouldn't let them out in the yard. Diesel didn't like getting his paws wet, nor did Ramses. Dante was every bit as finicky, so I wished Stewart luck in getting the dog to pee.

I settled into my recliner in the den and waited for Stewart and the beasties to join me. I closed my eyes for a moment, and I must have dozed off. Next thing I knew, a hand on my shoulder shook me gently, and I heard Stewart saying, "Charlie, wake up. Your phone is ringing."

I stared at him for a moment before his words sank in. I pulled my phone out and answered. "I'm here."

"Yes, I know that," Sean said, sounding stressed. "Listen, Dad, something freaky has happened out at the farm."

Now wide-awake, I said quickly, "Was someone hurt after all?"

"Worse," Sean said. "Martin Hale is dead."

EIGHT

"He's already dead," I said, confused.

"Not the old man," Sean said, biting off the words. "The grandson. One of Kanesha's officers found him on the edge of the woods, under a fallen tree."

"Oh my Lord," I said. "What was he doing out there in a storm?"

"Your guess is as good as mine," Sean said. "Maybe he was camping out there. He told me he'd had to borrow money to come here to see about his grandfather's property. Maybe he didn't have the money for a hotel room. I don't think he had any family here to take him in. At least that he'd have felt comfortable asking, I suppose."

"That's terrible," I said. "He could have stayed here, if I'd known he had nowhere to go."

"That's just like you, Dad. I don't think you'd have wanted him in the house, though, as jittery as he was. I wouldn't have trusted him, frankly."

"No point in judging him now," I said, still feeling sad and a little guilty about the young man's tragic death.

"No," Sean said, his tone finally softened. "Kanesha will be getting in touch with his family in California. I don't know whether anyone there will want to pursue the suit he intended to bring."

"We can face that if it happens," I said.

"Right," Sean replied. "Gotta go now." He rang off.

I put my phone away, the shock only slowly beginning to fade. I had forgotten Stewart's presence until he spoke and reminded me.

"Sounds like something bad happened," he said.

I nodded and shared what Sean had called to tell me.

Stewart frowned. "I wonder if Haskell has said anything to Kanesha about his relationship with the Hale family."

"Don't you think she'd know about it already?" I asked. "She must know about the backgrounds of everyone on her team. Haskell wouldn't have any reason to hide that from her, would he?"

"His family is pretty odd when it comes to that connection," Stewart said. "I think the whole thing's on the bizarre side. Every family has skeletons they'd rather keep hidden, but I don't get why this one is such a big deal."

I agreed with Stewart, but it was Haskell's family, and if they didn't want to acknowledge the connection, there wasn't much we could do about it. I was itching to ask Haskell about his aunt, though, and now that a cousin of his had been killed, it somehow seemed important to me to get to the bottom of this odd mystery.

Stewart voiced my thoughts. "Surely now he's got to talk about it, at least to his boss."

"Let's hope he does," I said. "I feel so bad for the

young man. Sean thinks he might have been camping in the woods because he didn't have the money for a hotel room."

"When the storm came up, why didn't he run to the house and ask for shelter?" Stewart asked. "They would have let him in. That doesn't make sense to me."

"Sean thinks he was an addict of some kind," I said. "He might have been in no condition to think rationally."

"True," Stewart said. "If he was really in need of a fix, he wouldn't have been thinking clearly." He gazed at me for a moment. "This wasn't your problem, Charlie. I know you feel bad about this young man, but he wasn't in any way your responsibility."

"I know," I said, a touch of regret in my tone. "I can't help feeling sorry for him, all the same."

Stewart smiled. "That's why you're such a good man. You have a deep well of compassion, more than anyone I've ever known."

I felt my face redden in embarrassment. Moments like this always threw me a little. I think I managed to mumble a hasty *thank you*.

Mercifully for my composure, Stewart changed the subject. "What are you going to do with the house, once everything is settled?"

"I don't know," I said. "It's part of my family history, one that I thought was lost and gone. It's going to take some time to figure it all out."

"I can't see you and Helen Louise moving out to the country," Stewart said.

Diesel chose that moment to meow loudly, and that caused Ramses and Dante to join in.

Stewart laughed. "I don't think Diesel wants to move, and I know Dante doesn't, either."

"Helen Louise also doesn't want to move," I said, somewhat morosely.

"Still no decision on where you'll live," Stewart said, his tone noncommittal. "And no wedding date."

"No to both statements," I said. "We're at a standstill, and I'm not sure what the next step is."

Diesel sat up on his hind legs and patted my arm. I rubbed his head, and he purred. I knew he had sensed my disquiet over this dilemma between Helen Louise and me.

"No need to rush to a decision," Stewart said. "You've got this situation to deal with. Let the other matters lie fallow for now."

"That's all I can do," I said. Suddenly I recalled that I had some good news to share. "Guess who's having a baby?"

Stewart's double take amused me. "Surely not Helen Louise?"

I laughed. "No, of course not. Laura and Frank."

"That's wonderful," Stewart said. "When's it due?"

"About seven months, Laura said."

"I bet they're hoping for a girl," Stewart said.

"They are," I replied, "but as long as the baby's healthy, nothing else matters."

My phone buzzed to alert me to an incoming text message. "From Laura," I announced to Stewart. "Her ears must have been burning." I peered at the screen. "She wants to tell Helen Louise herself once Helen Louise is home, so I have to remember not to let anything slip when I talk to her."

I texted back to assure her I'd keep quiet, and she thanked me. I put my phone away again. The text from Laura reminded me that I needed to concentrate on the good news and not fret so much about the bad news over which I had no control whatsoever. Cheered by this thought, I smiled.

Ramses startled me by jumping into my lap and butting his head against my chin. I rubbed his head for a moment. He turned around in my lap several times and finally settled down. Diesel watched this performance with what I would have called an expression of disdain on a human. I had to smile again.

Stewart scooped Dante into his arms and rose from his seat. "I've got work I've been putting off, and I can't ignore it any longer. I hope you don't mind, Charlie."

"Getting ready for the first day of classes?" Stewart was a professor of chemistry at Athena College, and the semester was starting the following week.

He nodded. "I've been doing this for over a quarter of a century, and you'd think it would get easier. For some reason, it never has." He shook his head.

"Because you've never become jaded with your profession," I said. "Unlike some tenured persons I've encountered at the college."

"Thanks," Stewart said with a quick grin. "I try to keep things fresh and interesting for all concerned. Here's hoping this year's crop of chemistry students is a good one." He waggled one of Dante's front paws in farewell as he left the room.

For Stewart's sake I hoped he did have promising new students. He could have insisted on teaching only upper-level courses, to seniors and graduate students, but he loved teaching freshmen, sparking their interest in chemistry. I admired his dedication.

I thought about Laura's news. A third grandchild would be wonderful. Sean and Alex had given me beautiful, sweet Charlotte Rose, my dear Rosie, and I wondered if they would have another child. Alex had suffered terribly from postpartum depression with Rosie, and I wouldn't want her to go through that again. Sean hadn't mentioned the possibility of another child, and I couldn't bring up the subject myself.

My thoughts drifted lazily as I imagined a baby girl who looked like Laura. What would they name her? Maybe Jacqueline after Laura's mother? Before long I dozed off, Ramses still in my lap, and Diesel on the floor beside my chair.

The next thing I knew, I heard Azalea calling my name. I surfaced to find her standing a foot away from my chair, frowning.

"Didn't want to bother you," she said, "but there's a person here to see you. He says it's important. He tried to give me a card, but I told him to hold on to it." She paused to eye me dubiously. "Are you awake enough to talk to him?"

I rubbed my eyes and yawned. "Sorry, yes, I suppose I am. Where is he?"

"In the living room," she said as she turned away. "I'll go tell him you're coming."

"Thank you," I called after her. Ramses had begun stirring when Azalea woke me, and now he hopped onto the floor and padded after her. No doubt he was hopeful for a snack.

I glanced at Diesel while I put down the footrest of the recliner. He gazed up at me and yawned. "Let's go see who this stranger is, boy." I rose from the chair, and he preceded me to the door.

Azalea crossed our path, her lips tightly pursed. Obviously, something about this unexpected caller had not sat well with her. Had he been rude? I followed her to the kitchen.

"Azalea, did this person do anything to upset you?"

Evidently surprised, Azalea turned around to gaze at me. "He was polite, if that's what you mean. I just got a bad feeling about him. Can't say more than that."

"Okay." I had a healthy respect for Azalea's *feelings*. Her impressions of people were almost always spot-on.

"Come on, Diesel." I headed back down the hall to the living room.

My visitor turned from looking out the front window when I entered. "Good afternoon. I'm Charlie Harris. You wanted to talk to me, I gather."

He stepped forward, hand extended. "Thank you for seeing me without any advance notice, Mr. Harris." After a quick handshake, he passed me his business card. "Marvin Watkins, with Watkins-Hightower Development."

The card revealed that he developed real estate. I judged him to be in his midthirties. He wore what was probably an expensive suit, well tailored to suit his tall, muscular frame. His brown hair had been expertly cut and slicked back, and his brown eyes were candid, his gaze and manner friendly.

I distrusted him immediately. I wasn't sure what had put Azalea off, but overall, he seemed, well, packaged, for want of a better term. Too slick for my taste.

I attempted to return his card, but he waved me away with a smile. "No, please keep it. I hope you'll find occasion to make use of the information."

Nodding, I tucked the card into my shirt pocket. Watkins appeared to notice Diesel for the first time. "Goodness, what kind of cat is that? I've never seen one that big before."

I gave my standard spiel about Maine Coons, and Watkins appeared to listen intently while he observed Diesel. I noticed that Diesel made no effort to approach the man's outstretched hand, not even to sniff his fingers.

Watkins laughed when I'd finished. "He's a big one, all right. Funny, though. Cats and dogs usually like me."

I didn't respond to that. Instead I said, "Please have a seat, Mr. Watkins, and let's talk about why you came to see me." I indicated one of the armchairs across from the sofa.

"Please, call me Marv," he said when he had seated himself. "'Mr. Watkins' is way too formal."

I nodded at him while Diesel stretched out on the sofa beside me. "Okay, Marv. What is it you want to talk about?"

"You're direct, Charlie," he said, again flashing a smile. "I like that. I'm direct myself. Saves time, doesn't it?" He paused. "I'm here about your farmland. My company is looking for country properties to develop, and yours sounds like exactly what we're looking for."

"How did you hear about my farmland?" I asked. I almost added that I'd only heard about it myself this very morning, but I held back.

"From a young man named Hale," Marv said. "He said it belonged to you, not to his family."

"When did you talk to Hale?" I asked.

"Had breakfast with him this morning at the Farrington House Hotel," Marv said. "He was staying there."

NINE

I itched to call Kanesha right away and tell her about this. Sean, too, because evidently he was off in his assessment of young Hale's finances. If he had been staying at the Farrington House Hotel, he had money.

"That's interesting," I said. "I've not met young Mr. Hale myself. May I ask why you were talking to him? About the farmland, I presume."

Marv flashed me his engaging smile again. "Got it in one, Charlie. He had contacted me a few days ago, said he had some land to sell here out in the county, and we arranged to meet this morning." His expression sobered. "That's when I found out the land wasn't his to sell. It would have been a complete waste of my time, but he told me you're the owner."

I wondered why it had taken him so long to get to me, if he was truly interested in the property. As far as I knew, he had made no attempt to contact me earlier today. "I see. Tell me, if you will, exactly what your plans are for this land, should I decide I want to sell."

Marv leaned back in the chair and regarded me with obvious pleasure. "Like I said, I like a man who is direct. I'm happy to talk about our plans with you. It's beautiful land, by the way. Absolutely charming, exactly the kind of landscape that we think our potential buyers will go for in a big way. Now, what we're thinking is that a lot of families these days want more space for themselves and their kids. No McMansions for them, you could say." He paused for a breath.

"So, you're wanting to provide larger lots with more privacy and the illusion of country living," I said.

Marv chuckled and slapped his knee. "Exactly. You're sharp. We're thinking of two-to-four-acre lots, depending on the buyers' needs, with houses starting at four hundred thousand, up to as much as three-quarters of a million. Perhaps even more."

I could almost see the dollar signs dancing in front of his eyes. The fervor of his tone as he mentioned the money was too blatant to ignore.

"Sounds impressive," I said, though I did not care for the idea at all.

"Isn't it?" Marv said, teeth bared in a wide grin.

I rose from the sofa, and I took some small satisfaction in seeing him disconcerted, although he hid it quickly. He rose also.

"Thank you, Marv." I moved toward the door into the hall. "You've given me a lot to think about. You'll understand, of course, that there are various legal formalities that have to take place before I can make any decisions on disposal of the land. You know how these things work, I'm sure. My lawyer is my son, Sean Harris. I'll make sure he has your card, and when I'm ready he will be the one to talk with you about it."

"Of course, Charlie," Marv said, no sign of disappointment in his expression or his body language. "I think I've met your son at some function, probably the Rotary meetings."

I nodded. "Very likely." I opened the door, but before he stepped out, I said, "I meant to ask you about young Hale. How was he at breakfast? Did he seem terribly upset about the land?"

Marv frowned. "I could tell he wasn't happy, but he seemed more philosophical about it than anything."

"I know it must have been a big disappointment to him," I said. "Well, nice talking to you."

With that, Marv walked out of the house, and I resisted the urge to shut the door rather firmly behind him. I looked down to see Diesel beside me. "We didn't like him, did we?"

Diesel trilled.

"I agree. Way too slick."

We went to the kitchen, where I poured myself a glass of sweet tea from the fridge. Azalea was not there, nor was Ramses. I took my usual place at the kitchen table and pulled out my phone. I might as well call Sean and let him know about Marv Watkins.

Luckily, I caught my son between appointments. "Hi, Dad. Yeah, I know the guy. Looks like he stepped out of a page from *GQ* magazine. He's got a reputation for sharp dealing. What did he want from you?"

I gave Sean a quick rundown of the conversation.

"What did you tell him?"

"That you would be the one to deal with him once all the legalities had been taken care of," I said.

"You're not seriously thinking of selling the land, are you?" Sean sounded annoyed.

"Not to him, that's for sure," I said. "I don't know what I want to do with the house and the land, to be honest. I've hardly had time to think about it."

"True," Sean said. "I'd hate to see it go out of the family, though."

"Me too," I admitted. "But there's a lot to think about."

"Yeah, I know. Look, you said he had breakfast with Hale this morning. At the Farrington House. I can't believe Hale was really staying there, he acted like he was stony broke."

"That's what Watkins said," I replied.

"I think I'm going to check on that," Sean said. "Then I'm going to call Kanesha. She'll want to interview Mr. Slick. Talk to you later, Dad."

I put my phone on the table. I felt restless, and I knew why. I wanted to know what was going on at my grandfather's house. Were Kanesha and her crew still there? Had they found anything? I was tempted to jump in the car and drive out there again, but I figured my reception would be chilly, to say the least. As the property owner, however, I had a right to know what was going on.

That sounded good. How would Kanesha answer that?

I started to rise but sank down again.

Did I really want to face Kanesha down over this?

No, I decided. Not right this minute.

Instead, I decided to call her. If she didn't answer, I would leave a message, telling her I'd like to know what was going on. I could do that much, at least.

I made the call. I was mentally preparing the message

I planned to leave, but after a few seconds, Kanesha answered.

"Yes, Charlie?" she said, her tone brusque.

"Hi, Kanesha. I'm calling to get a status update. Have you made any new discoveries? Sean just called and told me about Hale."

"I hear you had a visit from Marvin Watkins," she said as if I hadn't spoken.

"Yes, I did. But you didn't answer my question," I replied tersely.

"No, I didn't," Kanesha said. "Because there's nothing to report, other than that I'm back in town. You should be able to get back in the house by late tomorrow afternoon, at the latest. Now, if there's nothing else, I have calls to make. Starting with Marvin Watkins."

"No, that's all. Thanks," I said.

She ended the call. I'd gotten more out of her than I'd frankly expected. Not enough to satisfy my curiosity, but Kanesha knew that, of course. I couldn't blame her for wanting to run an investigation without any help—or interference—from me. I wouldn't be unhappy if situations like the present one stopped occurring in my life. I might be a bit bored, honestly, but not unhappy.

In order to distract myself from thinking about my grandfather's house and young Hale's untimely death, I decided to get out of the house and go visit the independent bookstore, the Athenaeum, on the town square. Helen Louise's French bistro was located nearby, and I could drop by and pick up some pastries to bring home. Not that my waistline needed any of the tasty delicacies from the bistro, but my taste buds would thank me.

"Come on, Diesel, we're going out." Diesel warbled, and I went into the hall and called out for Azalea. After a few seconds she appeared at the head of the stairs, and I let her know that Diesel and I were going to run some errands. She nodded to acknowledge that she'd heard before turning away. Ramses sat at the head of the stairs looking down at Diesel and me. For a moment he appeared undecided whether to scamper down to us, but evidently Azalea's allure was stronger. He ran after her.

Ten minutes later I found a parking spot in front of the bookstore. Diesel hopped out of the backseat, and he preceded me to the door. A bell jangled when I opened the door, and Diesel hurried inside. The owner of the store, Jordan Thompson, was a favorite of his, and he of hers. She always had a treat or two for him, plus she lavished praise and affection on him.

Today was no different. I waited while Jordan and Diesel had their conversation. Diesel trilled and chirped excitedly while Jordan talked to him. When they had finished, with Diesel chomping on a couple of treats, I greeted Jordan and made the usual inquiries about how she and the bookstore were doing.

"Fine." She turned to the shelves behind the counter and pulled a stack of seven books from a cubbyhole. "These are the books you requested, plus a couple I thought you'd find interesting."

I grinned. Jordan knew my reading tastes all too well, and I found it hard to resist the books she thought I'd find interesting. She was almost always right. "Thanks." I pulled the stack toward me and began examining them one by one.

Carolyn Hart's newest Bailey Ruth novel sat atop the stack. That would be coming home with me for sure. In addition, there were new books by Donna Andrews, Lindsey Davis, Anna Lee Huber, a new Inspector Varg book by Alexander McCall Smith, and two nonfiction titles on historical topics.

"Sold." I pushed the stack back to Jordan, and she laughed. "I know," I said. "I'm such an easy touch."

"I wouldn't put it that way," Jordan said, trying and failing to suppress another laugh. "You're a bibliophile like me and so many others in town, thank goodness."

"True." A sudden idea struck me. "I'm interested in some local history." I explained about my grandfather's house and farm. "Do you have anything that covers antebellum and post–Civil War life in this area?"

Jordan thought for a moment. "You know, I think I do have something. It's a self-published book by a local amateur historian. Hang on, and I'll get it for you."

She returned less than thirty seconds later with a small hardbound book with a plain cover, titled *Antebellum Life in Athena County, 1832–1865*. Esther Carraway was the author and publisher of the book.

I glanced through the book, pleased to find photographs of some of the well-known antebellum homes in town and in the county. I saw that Miss An'gel Ducote, who along with her sister, Miss Dickce, owned the magnificent Riverhill, had provided a foreword for the book. That was enough for me.

"I'll take it," I said.

"You saw that Miss An'gel wrote the foreword," Jordan said.

"If she was in any way involved, then it must be solid research," I said. The Ducote sisters were the last members of one of the most storied and distinguished families in Athena County. Neither of them would let their name be associated with anything unworthy.

Jordan rang up my books and bagged them. While I

extracted my credit card from my wallet, she managed to slip Diesel at least one more treat. I pretended not to notice.

Diesel and I bade Jordan farewell, and I stowed my bag in the car. I was eager to get home to delve into Ms. Carraway's book. I hadn't checked for any mentions of my family's farm, because I didn't think the Harrises had been among the wealthy planter class of antebellum days. If I found any mention, I would be pleasantly surprised.

My errand at the bistro took only a few minutes. Helen Louise's manager, Henry, greeted me and Diesel with a smile, and he picked out some choice items that he himself had baked that morning.

Loaded up with pastries and books, Diesel and I headed back home. I set the pastries on the kitchen counter and took the bag of books into my den. Diesel had disappeared into the utility room. He would soon join me.

Ramses appeared at the foot of the stairs, and he followed me to the den. He made himself comfortable in my lap while I pulled out the Carraway book to examine. I flipped through the book again before turning to the back to look for an index. To my surprise I found what looked like a thorough one, not something I had expected in a self-published book. I knew putting together an index was a time-consuming, even tedious, job.

I found the name *Harris* right away, with several pages referenced. I flipped to the first and started skimming.

A few minutes later, feeling stunned, I set the book down. The book revealed information about my family that I had never been told by my father.

With my paternal grandparents dying when I was so

young, I never really got the chance to know them well or to hear their stories of their own lives. I knew almost nothing about my great-grandparents other than their names. My strong interest in history had always involved England, rather than my own personal history. My father had not spoken much about his family and its past. I also hadn't asked many questions, now that I came to think of it. I knew some bare facts about my grandfather's house and that Harrises had farmed the land for over a hundred and fifty years. That was pretty much the extent of my knowledge.

I had assumed that the Harrises of generations past had been small farmers. Esther Carraway's book revealed a much different story. The first Harris in Athena County had opened a dry goods store in 1834 that soon thrived, and the business continued to grow. He built a modest house in town, married, and soon had a growing family.

The original Harris, also Robert like my father and grandfather, had sold his house in town in 1858 and bought some land in the country, where he built a new, larger house for his wife, who longed to live away from the noise of town. Then came the Civil War, and as time passed, the business suffered. My three-times great-grandfather turned to farming, hiring laborers instead of buying enslaved people. His wife had come from an ardent abolitionist family, and he had come to feel the same way.

When the Union army came through the area, they destroyed some buildings in the town, but they never made it as far as the area where my ancestor had built his house and begun farming.

The trilling woke me from my self-absorption. Diesel

sat on his hind legs, both his front paws on the arm of the chair, as he watched me. I knew he sensed my mental agitation. I scratched his head to reassure him. "I'm okay, boy," I told him. "Some unusual news, that's all. Nothing you would understand, but don't worry. Just a lot for me to process."

He chirped at me, and Ramses stirred, yawning. After a moment he reached out a paw to Diesel, but the big Maine Coon paid no attention. Diesel still eyed me, and I scratched his head again. This went on for several seconds, and I had to use my other hand to pet Ramses, until they both finally settled down.

I decided I would have to get in touch with Esther Carraway to find out how much more she knew about my family's history. For some reason neither my father nor my aunt Dottie had ever talked about the mercantile past of the family.

Lifting Ramses gently and setting him on the arm of the recliner, I got up to riffle through the bag of books I had brought home from the Athenaeum. After examining the choices, I settled on the latest book by Donna Andrews. I knew I could count on Meg, Michael, and their family to keep me entertained.

By the time Azalea came to inform me that dinner was ready, I had read half the book, chuckling out loud frequently. I laid the book aside, albeit reluctantly, and rose from the chair to go wash my hands. Ramses had departed some time ago, but Diesel had remained with me. He followed me to the first-floor washroom and waited while I made my ablutions. He scampered ahead into the kitchen, no doubt sniffing the delectable scents wafting our way.

Tonight's menu consisted of fried chicken, fresh biscuits, rice, cream gravy, and green beans. One of my favorite meals, made often by my late mother when I was growing up, and also by my late wife, who made biscuits as good as my mother's.

"Azalea, you're bound and determined to make me as broad as a barn," I said with a smile.

She shook her head as she set the platter of chicken on the table. "You worry too much," she said, turning back to retrieve a plate of biscuits and a tureen of gravy. Last to arrive were the bowls of rice and green beans. "You eat and enjoy yourself and let tomorrow take care of itself. The Lord will provide."

I nodded and began to help myself to the food. "Is Stewart going to be here for dinner?"

"No, he went out," Azalea said, "so you eat as much as you want."

I eyed the plate of biscuits. I counted a dozen. I loved them, but even I couldn't eat that many in one sitting, even with heaps of cream gravy. I tucked in. I didn't forget to offer Diesel and Ramses tidbits of fried chicken and even the occasional green bean. I was careful not to overdo it, however. I didn't want to wake up during the night to the sounds of a cat throwing up on my bed. Ramses had a habit of scarfing down his food too fast, and it inevitably came back up at the most inopportune time. That is, usually while I was sleeping.

Later that evening, I had a brief chat with Helen Louise. She owned to having a fabulous time with her friends, and I didn't want to distract her from that. I told her I had some news to share when she was home again, and she didn't press for details. I couldn't wait to see her, and she said simply, "I miss you, love. But I'll be home soon."

I propped up in bed to read more of the Donna Andrews book, but before I'd read a couple of pages, my phone rang. I laid the book aside and picked up the phone. It was rather late for Sean to be calling, and I prayed there was nothing wrong with the baby or Alex.

"Hi, Dad," he said. "Sorry to call this late, but I just got off the phone with Kanesha. I knew you'd want to hear what she told me." He paused, evidently to take a sip of a drink, then continued. "It's about young Mr. Hale, unfortunately."

"Why unfortunately?" I asked, feeling alarmed.

"His death was no accident," Sean said. "He was dead before the tree fell on him."

TEN

||||||||||||||||||||

"He was murdered?" I found it hard to take in. "Why would anyone kill him?"

"I don't have a clue," Sean said, "but someone shot him in the back a couple of times and apparently left him where he fell. Before the storm hit, of course, and the tree toppled in the storm and landed on him."

"When did they figure out he'd been shot?" I asked, the reality of the situation beginning to sink into my brain.

"Once they got the tree off him, they could see the holes in his shirt," Sean said. "The tree had fallen across his upper torso, according to what Kanesha told me. All trunk, no branches, so they knew the holes had been caused by something else. Once they got a close look, they knew he'd been shot."

"It doesn't make sense," I said. "Why would someone kill him? He didn't know anyone here, did he?"

"I don't know, Dad."

"Sorry, thinking out loud," I said. "I don't really expect you to have the answers. Thanks for calling and letting me know. I'm sure you've got work to get back to."

"That's okay," Sean said. "Take it easy, Dad. You don't have to get involved in this, okay?"

"Okay," I said, but only halfheartedly meaning it. How could I *not* get involved? The young man had been killed on my property. I ended the call before Sean could admonish me further.

When I was in my dotage and unable to make good decisions for myself, then I would let Sean and Laura decide for me. Or so I told myself. I was fully *compos mentis*, and if I wanted to see justice done in the matter of young Hale's death, I would. Not to mention justice in the death and identity of the bones found in the attic of my grandfather's house. I wouldn't rest easy until that was resolved.

At the moment, though, I couldn't come up with a constructive idea of what to do about either situation. With Helen Louise away, I didn't have anyone to consult who might be more sympathetic to my point of view.

Except for Melba.

Of course. I should have thought of her sooner.

I called her before I could reconsider. She answered right away. "What's up, Charlie? It's after ten o'clock."

I had forgotten the time. "I'm sorry to call so late. Do you feel like talking?"

"What do you think?" Melba said. "I'm awake."

I filled her in on the latest developments, skipping over, at least for now, my discoveries about my merchant-turned-farmer ancestor. When I'd finished, there was silence at the other end of the line. I waited a moment, then said, "Well? What do you think?"

"Hale must have been involved in something shady," Melba said slowly. "Otherwise he wouldn't have been killed. The question is exactly what it was. Something to do with the house and the land, most likely. But what? There's not oil or natural gas on the property, is there?"

"Not that I'm aware of," I said, surprised by the idea. "I'll have to ask Sean. He has the papers concerning the property, but surely he'd have mentioned mineral rights if they were important."

"Some of my cousins down in Grenada County had a gas company guy come sniffing around their land out in the country, looking for natural gas. They got all excited because they thought they were going to get rich," Melba said, the scorn in her tone obvious. "'Course it came to nothing. No natural gas there, but they sure were excited for a while. Got into all kinds of squabbles with each other over it, like who had a bigger claim."

"That must have caused some hard feelings," I said.

"Sure did," Melba replied. "But they finally got over it."

"Hale knew that his grandfather didn't have any rights to the property," I said, "other than the profits from the farming while he lived. All that ceased when the old man died."

"Just because he knew it doesn't mean he was going to abide by it," Melba said. "You can't be that naive."

I laughed. "No, I'm not. He told Sean he was going to take us to court to make a claim for the property. Sean told me he didn't have a case, but it could have made things sticky for a while."

"That would give you a motive for getting rid of him," Melba said.

"True, if I were desperate to get my hands on the house and the property," I replied. "I found out only this morning, however, that it was mine. Not much time to hunt the young man down and shoot him."

"Kanesha will have to consider you a suspect, though," Melba said. "She'll enjoy that."

"No doubt she will," I retorted. "She knows better, or she ought to, by now."

"You might ought to suggest to Sean that he should look into the mineral rights angle, just in case," Melba said. "You never know."

"And maybe I should go around the property with a metal detector looking for hidden Confederate gold," I said. "Maybe there's buried treasure on the farm, and Hale knew about it from his grandfather."

"Ha ha ha," Melba said, her tone dripping with sarcasm. "That sounds like the plot of a Nancy Drew book. If you're not going to be serious, I'm going to hang up and go back to bed."

"Sorry," I said. "I do think your idea about mineral rights is a good one, and I will pass it on to Sean. This whole thing is so out of left field. The murder, and discovering a skeleton in the attic, well, it's all so weird. I can't help but wonder if the two are connected somehow."

"Now, that *would* be a Nancy Drew book," Melba said. "I'll keep thinking about all this. If I come up with anything useful, I'll let you know."

"Thanks. I appreciate it. One thing that would be helpful is finding out whether there's anyone in the area connected with the Hales to talk to. Did the old man have any family nearby?"

"I don't think so," Melba said. "But I'll have to think

about it, maybe call a couple of people. I'll get back to you."

I thanked her again and ended the call. Haskell had a connection to the Hale family through his aunt, but I was hesitant to ask him about it. Stewart had said Haskell didn't talk about his family much, and I didn't want to upset him by being nosy. I had confidence in Melba, though. She had a network that rivaled the Internet when it came to unearthing information.

After yawning a couple of times, I decided to put my book aside and turn out the light. Diesel and Ramses had already fallen asleep on the bed with me. I thought I would have trouble falling asleep, thanks to the mental turmoil I'd been experiencing, but I dropped off quickly. The next thing I knew, my alarm sounded. Time to get up and start the day.

I was due at the archives at Athena today, but while I showered and dressed, I considered taking the day off. I felt restless, and in such a mood I often found it hard to concentrate on work. Over breakfast I contemplated calling Melba to tell her I wouldn't be in, but I remembered I wouldn't be able to get back in my grandfather's house until probably sometime in the afternoon. That settled it. I might as well go to work. When I got the all clear from Kanesha, I could leave early and go out to the house.

Diesel and I left Ramses with Azalea. I hadn't yet taken the younger cat to the office with me because he was still a little too unpredictable. He also didn't like walking on a leash, though it was too hot this time of year for either cat on the sidewalks. Diesel and I drove the few blocks to work.

We stopped to bid Melba good morning. She didn't have much time to talk because she had to accompany Andrea Taylor, the library director, to a meeting. She promised we would talk later.

Upstairs in the office, Diesel went immediately to his spot in the window behind my desk and made himself comfortable after inspecting the tree outside for birds and squirrels. I opened my e-mail and checked for new messages. There were several queries about materials in the archives, and I made appointments the following week for one professor and two students to come in to work with the materials they requested. That done, I had to consider what to focus on next. I always had books to catalog, thanks to the fact that my predecessor had loathed cataloging. I had diminished most of the huge backlog she left, but I still had more than enough to keep me busy the three days a week I worked.

Before I got busy cataloging, however, I pulled out the copy of Esther Carraway's book I had brought from home. Like any good historian she had included a bibliography, and a cursory examination of it revealed she had consulted the college archives, along with those of the county historical society. I figured I should try to examine any sources in the archives that mentioned my family before I called Mrs. Carraway for a meeting.

She hadn't included footnotes, but she did list resources by chapter. I turned to the list for the chapter in which she wrote about the Harris family but was chagrined to learn that everything she consulted belonged to the county historical society. I'd have to make an appointment to see those papers, and that put another hitch in my plans. The historical society had only volunteer workers, and their schedule was erratic. Maybe I should go ahead and call Mrs. Carraway without doing any research on my own first. That might be more time-effective in the long run.

I looked online for the phone number and quickly found it. I used my office phone to call in case she had caller ID. I figured she would be more likely to answer a call from Athena College than from a number she didn't know.

A sharp voice answered after four rings. "Who is it?"

Taken aback by the tone, I faltered. "Um, hi, this is Charlie Harris. Is this Mrs. Esther Carraway?"

"Who else would be answering my phone, I'd like to know?"

"Yes, ma'am, of course," I said. Before I could continue, she interrupted me.

"Charlie Harris, you say. The Charlie Harris that's the grandson of Robert Charles Harris? I've heard about you from An'gel Ducote."

"Yes, ma'am, I am that Charlie Harris."

"Have you got another murder to solve?" she asked, her tone less abrasive. "I've always been interested in murders. I could tell you some interesting stories about some of the goings-on here in Athena County that would curl your hair."

"I'd love to hear some of those stories," I said, more out of politeness at the moment than actual interest. "I have one of your books, and I found out information about my ancestors that was completely new to me. I'd really like to talk to you about all that if you have the time."

"I can't talk right this minute, I'm too busy," she said. "But you can come by my house tomorrow at noon, and I'll have time to talk then."

"That's great. I'll be there."

The call ended. She hadn't given me a chance to ask for her address, but the Internet provided that, too. She sounded like a character. I wondered if her phone manner was typical of her interactions all the time. She sounded to me like a woman who wouldn't tolerate anyone who attempted to waste her time. I thought I had better be prepared for my visit with her and not go into it without careful consideration of the questions I wanted to ask.

As I cataloged, I found my thoughts straying to potential questions. I knew I wanted to find out how detailed were the sources Mrs. Carraway had used for the information on my ancestors. Perhaps the historical society had papers belonging to my family. If that were the case, I thought it odd that neither my father, nor my aunt Dottie, had ever mentioned it to me. They knew my interest in history, though I had expressed far more interest in English history, I had to admit, than I had in American or Mississippi history.

I might also find out about other relatives, cousins of varying degrees from earlier branches of the family. That would be interesting. I knew there were other people named Harris in Athena, but it was a fairly common name, after all. My father had never talked about cousins, nor had my aunt Dottie. Thinking about it now, I found it rather odd. At the time I hadn't questioned it, but Southerners talked about family a lot. My mother had no family to speak of, with both her parents being only children, and she an only child herself. I really ought to look into her family tree along with my father's.

Why hadn't my father and my aunt talked about their family? Was there something they didn't want me to know? Something truly terrible that could explain those bones in my grandfather's attic?

ELEVEN

The next day I left the library a quarter hour before my appointment with Esther Carraway. Earlier in the day, Kanesha had let me know that she wasn't ready to let me back into my grandfather's house. They hadn't finished going over it yet. I therefore had plenty of time to visit with the local historian.

Mrs. Carraway lived near the campus, and Diesel and I arrived at her home with a few minutes to spare. I had debated dropping my cat off at home before I met with her, but he had often proved invaluable in breaking the ice with strangers. I hoped she wasn't an ailurophobe or allergic to cats.

I needn't have worried. The moment Mrs. Carraway opened the door and spotted the Maine Coon, she smiled broadly.

"I've heard about this fellow," she said, extending her hand for Diesel to sniff. He seemed to take to her right away, and he ambled beside her as she led us into her living room.

Mrs. Carraway indicated a straight-backed chair across from her position on the sofa. She invited Diesel to sit with her, and he accepted. As my hostess continued to pet the cat and murmur to him, I took stock of her and my surroundings.

I figured Mrs. Carraway to be in her seventies. Her short stature, perhaps a shade over five feet, was offset by her outsized jewelry, bracelets, rings, and several strands of large beads around her neck. Her hair owed everything to henna, and it framed her face like a helmet. I hadn't seen hair like it since the seventies. Her red dress clashed with the hair, as did her crimson lips, and the blue eye shadow reminded me of the seventies as well.

The room had floor-to-ceiling bookshelves along two walls, and books overflowed from them. The furnishings were eclectic, a mixture of antiques and more modern pieces, with a fine Aubusson carpet in the center of the room. An elderly office desk had pride of place near the front window, and atop it sat both an old manual typewriter and a newish-model computer.

Evidently not one to waste time on the social graces, Mrs. Carraway recalled my wandering thoughts with a sharp question.

"What do you want to know?"

When I didn't immediately respond, she said, "Don't be shy. You probably want to know about any scandals in the family. That's what most people come to see me about. You wouldn't believe the skeletons in some of the closets in this town, and in the county, too. Over the years I've had to leave out some pretty ripe stuff, let me tell you. I don't want to get sued, you know, so I'm telling you right now, I'm not going to write anything nasty about your family. You're not taking me to court." Her soft Mississippi drawl removed some of the tartness from her words, but enough remained to assure me of her sincerity.

Diesel warbled loudly, probably slightly alarmed by her tone. He shifted away from her, and she seemed to realize what she had done.

"You relax, you handsome boy, Aunt Esther isn't going to be ugly to anybody, I just have to get that out of the way first thing." She cooed to Diesel, and though he looked at her a bit oddly, he remained beside her.

I had dealt with eccentrics before, and I wasn't disturbed by Mrs. Carraway. Her defensiveness probably had roots in a court case somewhere in her past, I reckoned.

"I'm not interested in suing anyone," I said in a placatory tone. "No matter what shocking things you might have to tell me about my ancestors. My father and my aunt Dottie never talked about the family, so anything you can tell me besides what I've already read in your book would be gratefully accepted."

Mrs. Carraway eyed me, her head cocked to one side. "Have you done your genealogy?"

I shook my head. "I haven't, though with these recent revelations, I've decided I ought to." I explained about the sudden inheritance of my grandfather's farm. "I know little about the Harrises, or about my mother's family, either."

She shook her head. "That's downright sad, you know. They're the people who made you who you are, and you don't even know their names. They are your roots. I can't imagine what it's like, not wanting to know my own roots. That's how I got started writing local history. Began with my own family. Found out a lot that wasn't passed down, let me tell you. Some of it was scandalous, but that made it more interesting. You'll probably discover the same."

"I already have," I said. "I had no idea my ancestors were wealthy merchants. I knew only that my grandfather was a farmer, though he died when I was really young, but he wasn't rich."

"A lot of wealthy folk came down in the world after the Civil War," Mrs. Carraway said. "The Harrises among them, of course. They were never really poor after that, because Robert Harris had taken up farming before he lost the mercantile business. He also didn't get as rich as he had been before." She arched an eyebrow at me. "The Union army did him a big favor by bypassing his farm. The fact that he didn't have any enslaved people working on it was in his favor, of course."

"I'm very glad to hear that. I looked at your bibliographical notes in the book, and apparently your sources for my family history came from the historical society archives," I said.

"They did," she said. "They have some old ledgers belonging to the family, dating back to around the time the war ended. Plus a few letters, and I think there are a couple of portraits, if I'm not mistaken."

"I'll talk to the historical society and make an appointment to look at them," I said.

"You might have to dig around a bit to find anything." She shook her head. "I've been after them for years to get things organized, but I might as well have been talking to the air for all the good it did me."

"I'm the archivist at Athena College," I said. "I can

volunteer to help get the historical society papers organized."

"You'd be doing a fine thing," Mrs. Carraway said. "They're real territorial, though, so you'll have to go about it the right way. Don't go rushing in there like a bull in a new pasture."

I had to suppress a laugh. "I won't, I promise. Is there a family genealogy that you know of?" I asked. "I haven't signed up for one of those genealogy databases yet, but I obviously need to."

"There might be one," Mrs. Carraway said, her tone bland. "You can find information in the census records, and there are records at the courthouse, of course. I do know that over the generations, the Harrises weren't known for producing many children. Your grandfather had a sister, born when he was an adult. His father had only one sibling, a brother, and his mother had two sisters who died in infancy. If you're looking for a lot of long-lost cousins, I don't think they're out there."

"That's too bad." I felt regret at this news. "I was an only child, as was my late wife."

"I hear you're going with Helen Louise Brady," Mrs. Carraway said.

Taken aback, I stared at her for a moment. "Well, yes, we're actually engaged to be married."

"Good for you," she replied. "I hear you have two children, a son and a daughter."

"I do, and each of them has a child," I said. "I'm glad my grandchildren, at least, will have cousins to grow up with."

She nodded in evident approval. "I believe your son married the Pendergrast girl. That's quite a family. Her daddy's escapades alone are enough to fill several books, but that's a conversation for another time. Shame he never wrote his memoirs, but I guess he thought he'd best not stir up any hornet nests."

I had no reply to this, not that she really needed one. She swept on.

"You haven't told me why you suddenly decided to get interested in your family," Mrs. Carraway said.

I hadn't exactly had much of a chance, I thought, but I didn't say that to her. "Because I found out I inherited my grandfather's house and farm. I thought it was out of the family for good."

Mrs. Carraway frowned at me. "I thought he left all that to Martin Hale."

"No, ma'am." I explained the terms of the lease and my grandfather's will. When I'd finished, she regarded me thoughtfully for a full minute before she replied.

"If your son says it's legal, then I reckon it must be. Not the way Martin Hale told the story after your grand-daddy died, though." She shook her head. "He always wanted to be bigger than he was, couldn't be satisfied with being a farmer. All that drinking didn't help, either. Not a good citizen, that man, though I reckon he paid his taxes on time."

I thought about asking Mrs. Carraway whether she was related to Melba Gilley. Her fund of knowledge about local people seemed pretty deep and wide. But she might not get the joke, so I kept my mouth shut. I would certainly ask Melba, however.

"I really don't know much about Mr. Hale," I said, "other than that his death brought about this inheritance."

"Surely you've heard about his wife disappearing and nobody has any idea what happened to her?"

I nodded, debating whether I should tell her about the

bones that Diesel and I found in the attic. I was about to when she started talking again.

"Some people said she ran off with another man because she couldn't take his drinking and treating her like dirt. I've never had any use for men like that. I took a baseball bat to my husband the first time he lifted a hand to me. We got along fine after that."

I opened my mouth to speak, and to my surprise she remained quiet. "What happened to Mrs. Hale is still a mystery, as far as I know. Though Diesel and I found something in my grandfather's house that might be relevant."

"What, pray tell, did you find?" Mrs. Carraway leaned forward in anticipation.

"We found a skeleton in the attic. Actually, it was in an old wardrobe in the attic, and it looked like it had been there for years."

"Good heavens." Mrs. Carraway looked thunderstruck. "I never thought he would have killed her. He was too much of a coward for that, I'd have said. My goodness me, that poor woman. Why didn't her family put up a fuss and find her?"

"There's no proof whatsoever that the bones belong to Mrs. Hale," I said. "There was nothing with the remains to identify the person."

"Yes, well, still seems suspicious to me," Mrs. Carraway replied. Her brow furrowed, she stared at some point on the wall behind me. "Who else could it be?"

"The remains could be centuries old," I said. "Mr. Hale, or even my grandfather, might have discovered them somewhere on the farm. I'd hate to think that my grandfather desecrated a grave, though, and kept those bones as some kind of trophy."

Mrs. Carraway shook her head. "I knew your grandfather. He was an old man when I was a young bride, but I don't think he was the kind of person to do something like that." Her expression grew grim. "Martin Hale, on the other hand, I wouldn't put anything past him."

I was relieved to hear that, and I hoped that Mrs. Carraway was right about my grandfather. This was a mystery that might never be solved, however.

I decided I would go ahead and tell her about the death of Mr. Hale's grandson. It would probably be on the evening news anyway. "Mr. Hale's grandson, also named Martin, came to Athena."

"Yes, I know," Mrs. Carraway said. "He called me and asked if he could come talk to me. Supposed to be here yesterday afternoon." She shook her head. "He never showed up. I guess the storm put him off."

"Sadly, he won't be calling you again." I explained briefly about the young man's death.

Diesel chirped and looked up at Mrs. Carraway. Her face drained of all but artificial color, she looked suddenly much older. "That poor young man," she said, her voice soft. "Truly a cursed family, you might say." She sighed. "So much tragedy."

I didn't quite know what to say to try to comfort her. This sorrow seemed personal to her in some way that I didn't understand.

Perhaps she sensed my confusion. Mrs. Carraway offered me a weak smile. "Martin Hale's father and I shared a great-grandmother, so we were cousins. Our families weren't close, but the family connection was there. The Hales weren't particularly upstanding citizens, you see. The men in the family had a history of weakness—for alcohol, for gambling, for women. Martin's son was an exception, but then he was killed in that horrible accident. And now his son has been murdered. I wonder if the young man had any offspring?"

"I don't know," I said. "I'm sure the sheriff's office will be in touch with his family in California."

"Then I'll have to talk to Kanesha Berry," Mrs. Carraway said. "Now, you must excuse me. I have an appointment to get to." She rose, and Diesel meowed at her sudden movement. He climbed off the sofa and came to stand beside me.

I offered Mrs. Carraway my hand, and she took it briefly while I thanked her for her time. I had not asked many of the questions I had wanted to, but they would have to wait for another time.

Diesel and I headed for the front door. Mrs. Carraway trailed behind. I turned as I opened the door and caught her with a troubled expression as she regarded me.

"One thing I should tell you," she said. "Martin Hale had two of the family weaknesses. Alcohol and women. That combination is sometimes deadly."

I waited for her to expand on that statement, but she did not. After a moment, I nodded, and Diesel and I exited the house. The door closed quietly behind us.

TWELVE

I wondered why Mrs. Carraway had made a point of that final statement of hers. Was she giving me an obscure hint? Could what she said have something to do with the bones?

I couldn't come up with any other explanation during the short drive home. Hale had a history of violence against his wife. More than likely he had treated other women the same. Could he have killed one of them and hidden her remains all these years?

Surely someone would have noticed the woman had disappeared, I reasoned. Unless she had no family, no friends, no connections in Athena, that is. I was sure that Kanesha would consider this possibility. She no doubt knew more about Martin Hale and his history than I ever would. I wondered whether she would share any of that knowledge with me, or perhaps with Sean?

I decided I would put the question to my son. As a

legal professional, and as my representative in the case regarding the property, he had a better chance to get information from Kanesha. Whether he would act on my request was another thing entirely. He didn't like my getting involved in murders and was more than likely to tell me to keep my nose out of this.

My phone rang as I was turning into my driveway. I stopped the car and pulled out the phone. Kanesha Berry.

"Good afternoon, Charlie."

I returned her greeting. "What's up?"

"If you have time right now, I'd like you to meet me at your grandfather's house," she said. "I've asked Sean to come as well."

"I'm on my way." Before I could ask her anything, she ended the call. I gritted my teeth, but I was used to her by now. I reversed into the street, and Diesel warbled loudly from the backseat. He knew we had been almost home.

"Sorry, boy," I said. "We're going out to the country to see the house again. We'll come back home after that, okay?"

Diesel chirped, and I heard him shifting position on the seat. He chirped twice more and settled down while I drove.

Sean was just getting out of his car when Diesel and I pulled up in front of the house. He waited to greet the two of us, and we climbed the porch steps together. "Did Kanesha say anything to you when she called?" I asked.

Sean shook his head. "No. I assume they're done going through the house, though. But they could have found something. Who knows with her?"

My son opened the door and motioned Diesel and me into the house. This time I wasn't entering it wrapped in a haze of memories. I felt more able to look objectively at the house, and as I gazed around I could see the shabbiness of some of the furnishings and the need for paint for the walls and trim. If I kept the house, I'd certainly have to invest in brightening it up again.

Kanesha appeared in the hallway from one of the bedroom doors about thirty feet away. She beckoned to us. "Good afternoon. Thanks for coming. We found something I want to show you."

She waited by the doorway. As I recalled it, this particular room might have been my aunt's room before she got married. I said as much to Sean, and he nodded.

We stepped into the sparsely furnished room behind Kanesha. She pointed to a door in the opposite wall. "We found evidence of occupation in there."

"Isn't that a closet?" Sean asked, casting his eye around the space.

"No, it's another small chamber like this one," Kanesha said. "Fitted out as a bedroom."

As I surveyed the room, I realized that its proportions were smaller than I would have expected. There had been no closets in the house, I recalled, because the house had been built at a time when they were not common.

"A room within a room." Sean turned to me. "Do you remember this, Dad?"

"Not offhand," I said, "but that doesn't mean anything. I didn't ramble through the house as a child. I usually stayed wherever my grandmother was, and I really don't remember coming into this room."

Kanesha had opened the door to the inner chamber, and she motioned for us to approach and look inside. Diesel preceded Sean and me inside, and he began nosing around.

This space was about a third the size of the outer room, but it had decent proportions. Suitable for a small child, I mused.

A cast-iron bed frame with an old, stained mattress stood against the outer wall under the lone window, and a chair and small dresser completed the furnishings of the room. Rumpled bedclothes gave evidence that the bed had been slept in, and a few toiletries lay scattered atop the dresser. One drawer stood partially open, and I glimpsed articles of clothing, perhaps underwear, sticking out.

"Do you think the victim was living here?" Sean asked.

"Yes, he was," Kanesha said. "We found papers with his name on them in one of the drawers of the dresser. From what we can tell, he had been living here for several days, if not a week or more." She frowned. "Right now we don't know when he arrived in the county. I figure he flew into Memphis and probably rented a car, but so far there's no sign of a car."

"Could he have hitched a ride?" Sean asked.

Kanesha shrugged. "Possible, and we're looking into that, but it doesn't seem too likely."

"Or someone met him at the airport and drove him here," I said slowly. "What about Marvin Watkins? He apparently had business with young Hale."

"Watkins claims that he didn't meet Hale face-to-face until Hale was already here." She waved her hand to indicate the house. "I think it's possible that he's lying about that, but at present I don't have any evidence to contradict him."

"Didn't his grandfather have a truck or a car?" I asked. "Maybe Hale was using it."

"He had a pickup," Kanesha said. "But it's nowhere to be found. Hasn't turned up at the airport in Memphis so far. We know that the elder Hale flew out of there to California."

"Have you found anyone else in the area who had contact with Hale?" Sean asked.

"Not so far," Kanesha said.

I remembered that I had looked in the refrigerator during my visit yesterday. There had been no food in it then. "What was Hale doing for food?" I asked.

Kanesha shrugged. "We found a few snack items in this room, and several takeout containers in the garbage. He was getting food from someone or leaving the house to eat his meals. Without a car, though, he'd have to catch a ride with someone."

I recalled what Marvin Watkins had said about Hale's claim he was staying at the Farrington House. I mentioned this to Kanesha.

"No, he wasn't registered there," Kanesha said. "Watkins told me the same thing. Hale obviously lied, probably because he didn't want anyone to know he was living in this house."

"Someone had to know," Sean said. "He had to have transportation and food. I can't see him walking into town from here to buy food. It's a good fifteen miles or so, one way."

"I agree," Kanesha said. "I've got a couple of my officers canvassing this road to find out whether anyone saw Hale in this area in the past week. They haven't turned up anything so far, though."

I heard the note of frustration in her tone. At some point there had to be a break in this case, I figured. Hale hadn't been invisible. Someone had to have seen him.

"Once the news of the murder gets around," Sean said, "you might hear from people. Are you going to get the newspaper to run a picture of him?"

"The only picture we have isn't one that would do us any good in the newspaper," Kanesha said.

I winced. That meant only a photo of the corpse, and I doubted readers would want to be confronted with that over the breakfast table.

Kanesha went on. "We're trying to get a usable picture of him from his family in California. His sister will be arriving tomorrow, and I'm hopeful she'll have information to share with us."

"What about Dr. Seton?" I asked. "When is he going to be able to examine the bones? And hunt for the burial site?"

"He's still involved with a case in Memphis," Kanesha said, and I sensed more frustration. "I'm hoping he can focus on this case tomorrow or the next day. I'd like answers, and I'm not getting any. I need this investigation to move further along."

I was starting to share Kanesha's annoyance at these delays and the lack of information. I didn't dare suggest, however, that I should assist. Frankly, I wasn't sure I could.

"Do you think there's any connection between Hale's murder and the bones in the attic?" Sean asked.

"I don't honestly see how there can be," Kanesha said. "Until we know more about the bones and hopefully where they came from, the only thing connecting them to the present murder is this property."

She cut a sideways glance at me, and I figured I knew what she was thinking. Was my grandfather a murderer or a grave robber? Or both? I had no idea, but I sure as heck hoped he was neither.

"I've got to get back to the office," Kanesha said. "We're finished with the house, but I'd appreciate it if you didn't go wandering around the property yet. I'd rather you wait until Seton and his dog have had a chance to investigate. No sense in adding to whatever scents already exist out there."

I nodded. "I agree. I'll stick to the house." I hesitated. "I guess that means I should hold off on getting anyone in to check the structure or do any kind of repair work."

"Yes, you should," Kanesha said. "Until I know where those bones came from, I don't want any more people here than are necessary."

"That's not a problem." Sean nodded in my direction. "We won't do anything to interfere with your investigation."

I thought I saw Kanesha's lips twitch, but I decided I had imagined it. Before she departed the room, she said she would be in touch in the next day or two if there were any developments.

Sean waited until she was presumably out of hearing before he addressed me. "I meant what I said, Dad. We are not going to get involved in this investigation."

I frowned at him. "I do hope you didn't mean that to be as patronizing as it sounded."

He flushed slightly at my tone, but his stern expression didn't falter. "I'm sorry if I offended you, but I know your tendency to get involved in these things."

Diesel, who had been hiding under the bed, emerged to chirp loudly at Sean. I had forgotten he was there, and a quick glance informed me that he collected dust and cobwebs during his sortie.

While the cat continued to fuss at my son, I used my hands to brush away as much of the dirt as I could. Die-

sel stood patiently as I did it, but he continued to gaze at
Sean.

"Diesel is annoyed with me," Sean said.

"He didn't like your tone any more than I did," I said,
straightening. "I need to wash my hands. Let's go to the
kitchen."

Sean trailed after Diesel and me. At the moment I
concentrated on washing the dirt off and ignored my
son. I knew he meant well, but I wasn't a doddering old
fool who needed looking after. I didn't put myself in the
way of danger when I got involved in these cases. I remembered one notable exception, however, and felt a
sudden stab of guilt.

Sean waited in silence while I finished my cleanup. I
then used a rag I'd found to wipe the cat's feet. I would
have to brush Diesel thoroughly when we got home, but
I figured he was clean enough for the moment.

"I'm sorry, Dad," Sean said, and he did look contrite.
"I didn't mean to be patronizing. I know you usually
don't deliberately put yourself in dangerous situations,
but you did have one pretty close call." He paused. "We
all worry, the way you did when Laura and I were kids."

"I know that," I said, my tone gentler than before, but
still not yielding. "There'll be time enough for you two
to bicker over me when I'm in the nursing home."

Diesel meowed loudly and started toward the hall.
Moments later, a gruff voice called out, "What the hell
are you?"

THIRTEEN

The owner of the voice appeared in the kitchen doorway about five seconds later. Sean and I had apparently been too engrossed in our conversation to hear anyone enter the house. Diesel had heard the intruder, though.

The man, a stocky redhead about my own age, had sun-reddened skin and a mottled complexion. He stood several inches shorter than Sean and me, which made him about five nine, I reckoned. He wore scarred and stained cowboy boots with rounded toes, and his jeans matched his boots. His work shirt, a dull blue denim, was splotched with sweat, and he exuded the scent of a man who worked hard in the sun.

"Who are y'all?" he asked.

"We might ask you the same thing," I said stiffly. "Do you usually just walk into houses without knocking?"

"I did knock, but nobody heard me," the stranger replied. "I thought maybe ol' Martin was sick, and I came in to check on him." He gestured at Diesel. "When I saw that bobcat, I knew something was wrong."

"He's not a bobcat," I said. "He's a Maine Coon cat."

Sean took over. He thrust out his hand, and the stranger took it. "I'm afraid Mr. Hale is dead. He passed away while visiting his family in California." He nodded in my direction. "This is my father, Charlie Harris. He is the new owner of the house and the farmland."

"Harris, eh?" The man looked back and forth between Sean and me. "I reckon you're the grandson of ol' man Harris who owned this place when I was a kid."

"I am," I said. "You still haven't told us who you are."

Diesel warbled loudly. He hadn't approached the stranger, and I took that as a sign he didn't think the man was anyone he wanted to know.

The stranger grinned unexpectedly. He proffered his hand to me, and when I took it, he shook and said, "Sorry 'bout that, the ball and chain's always getting on me about my manners. Gil Jackson. My farm's just down the road a couple miles. I been leasing some of the land from ol' Martin for about fifteen years now. About six hundred acres."

"Good to meet you, Mr. Jackson," Sean said. "According to the terms of my great-grandfather's will, the house and land returned to his heir, my father, upon the death of Mr. Hale."

"That's a hell of a note," Jackson said. "Where does that leave me? I got crops on that land, and you're not going to tell me that they're yours now." His face had reddened in anger, and for a moment I thought he might strike Sean.

Sean remained cool and didn't back away. "There's a lot to sort out in this matter, Mr. Jackson. I don't see any reason why your lease can't continue. I represent my father." He reached into his pocket for his wallet. He withdrew a business card and handed it to the farmer. "Call my office in a couple of days and make an appointment. Bring your lease agreement, and we'll discuss this further."

Jackson appeared slightly mollified by this. I supposed I couldn't blame him. He had leased the land in good faith.

"Mr. Hale never told you that he held the land only for his lifetime?" I asked.

"No, he sure as hell didn't," Jackson said. "He always acted like it was his, and he talked about selling it and moving to California to live with his family, as a matter of fact."

"When was this?" Sean asked.

The farmer shrugged. "Probably first started talking about it a couple years ago. Told him I wanted first option on buying the land, and he told me I'd be welcome to have it." He looked hard at me. "I'm telling you the same thing. You don't look like a farmer, so I'm betting you want to get shed of it all. I'll make you a good offer."

"I only found out about this yesterday," I said. "I haven't had time to consider what I'm going to do. This land has been in my family since before the Civil War, after all."

"Fair enough, I guess," Jackson said. "As long as I can keep farming the land I got from Hale, I'll make do. I got a question, though. Couple times I drove by here, yesterday and today, I saw sheriff's department cars here. What's been going on?"

I left this one to my son.

Sean said, "They're investigating a suspicious death

on the property. They found a body in the woods under a tree brought down by that storm yesterday."

"What's suspicious about that?" Jackson asked. "If a man was fool enough to be in the woods during that storm, it's all on him."

"I don't recall mentioning that the body belonged to a man, Mr. Jackson," Sean said coolly. "What makes you think it was a man who was killed?"

Jackson rolled his eyes. "Ain't no woman I ever known stupid enough to get out in a thunderstorm like that." He shifted his weight from one leg to the other.

I could think of several reasons a woman might risk going out in dangerous weather, but I didn't think listing them would add to the conversation in any helpful way.

"Have you seen anybody coming in and out of this house in the past few days?" Sean asked.

I thought Jackson hesitated before he answered, but I could have been mistaken.

"Naw," he said in a firm tone. "Hadn't been down this way in several days. Just happened to go by yesterday and today, heading into town for the wife. That's when I saw the sheriff's cars." He shrugged. "Today I thought I'd check in on ol' Martin when I came back by and saw two cars still here."

Diesel rubbed himself against my legs, and I rubbed his head. He didn't like Jackson, and I didn't think I cared for the man, either. There was something about him that made me a bit uneasy. I didn't really buy his conscientious neighbor act, for one thing. Mr. Hale had been gone for a noticeable length of time, and it was only today that Jackson decided to check on him. I knew farmers worked hard this time of year, but had he been too busy to notice that Hale wasn't around?

Jackson glanced at the business card, still in his hand. He stuffed it in his shirt pocket. "I'll be giving you a call," he said. "I better get back to the field." He turned and walked out of the kitchen.

Sean stepped to the door and into the hall. I followed him. We watched Jackson's progress to the front door. He went out and closed the door behind him. We turned to look at each other.

"What did you make of him?" I respected my son's assessment of character. He had a lot of experience dealing with clients from various walks of life.

"Hard man," Sean said. "Will try to bulldoze anyone in his way, if he can." Suddenly he grinned. "Not going to work with me, though. You can count on me whatever you decide to do with the property."

"I know that, and I appreciate it," I said. "I have no idea what the property is worth."

"I was looking into that earlier today," Sean said. "I came up with an estimate for what a sale might bring." He pulled out his wallet again and extracted a folded piece of paper.

I accepted it from him and opened it. When I saw the seven-figure number written there, I almost fainted. "You've got to be kidding me."

Sean grinned and shook his head. "I was surprised, too. Didn't realize how much good farmland is worth. I checked the county tax office, and my estimate was actually a little under the appraised value."

"How would someone like Jackson ever raise that sum?" I asked. "Would a bank even lend that much to a small farmer?" I couldn't imagine trying to borrow that kind of money. I had a comfortable income between my pension from the city of Houston and income from my late aunt's investment, but I was not rich.

"We don't know that he's a small farmer," Sean said. "I'm going to investigate him, now that we know who he is. I think there's another lessee, but I haven't dug up the name yet. The few papers I have of the elder Mr. Hale's aren't that informative, unfortunately."

"Since Mr. Jackson turned up, maybe the other lessee will show up soon," I said. "I'm surprised that young Hale wasn't in contact with them, frankly."

"I suspect he was," Sean said. "Jackson impresses me as a sharp operator. If he had any contact with the grandson, I doubt he's going to admit it. I wish we knew what the grandson was up to. His grandfather surely ought to have known he couldn't get away with selling this house and the farmland. The deed is still in your grandfather's name. I checked."

"Maybe he just liked to talk big," I said. "I've known men and women who liked to present themselves as more than they are."

"Grandson may have inherited those tendencies," Sean said. "If he did, that might be what got him killed. He might have swindled someone out of a big sum of money, got found out, and the person killed him."

That scenario sounded possible to me. "I wonder what his sister will be like," I said. "Will she be honest about her brother and her grandfather? Or will she be like them?"

"We'll find out tomorrow," Sean said. "I need to get back to the office. Are you going to hang around here for a while?"

I thought about it, but I decided I wasn't in the mood

to examine the house for potential repairs. "No, I think Diesel and I will head home." Diesel warbled loudly to signify his approval.

We walked to the front door. Sean opened it and followed the cat and me onto the porch. I handed him my key to lock the door. A sound in the driveway caught my attention. "We've got more company," I said.

A battered pickup moved slowly up the driveway. Sean turned to watch with me. The driver, an elderly Black man, parked and extracted himself slowly from the cab. He used a stout stick for aid as he came toward us. He moved stiffly, and I decided it would be better if he didn't climb the steps to the porch. I met him in the yard in the shade of a huge oak.

"Good afternoon, sir," he said, his voice soft but roughened by the years. He glanced down at Diesel, who slowly approached him to sniff at his walking stick. "That's the biggest kitty I've ever seen." He returned his gaze to me and stuck out his free hand, his left. "Asa Luckney, and you must be Charlie Harris."

"Yes, I am," I said, taking his hand. "Nice to meet you, Mr. Luckney. This kitty is Diesel, and he's a Maine Coon."

The handshake finished, Luckney held out his gnarled fingers for Diesel to sniff. Then the cat butted his head against the elderly man's hand. Luckney smiled.

I noted that Diesel evidently liked Mr. Luckney, whereas he had remained aloof from Gil Jackson.

"This is my son, Sean, Mr. Luckney," I said. "He's a lawyer in town."

Sean shook hands while Luckney gazed at him appraisingly. "Look like your great-granddaddy, young man. I knew him as a boy, and you're the spittin' image of him." He moved his gaze to me. "And you look like your daddy," he said. "Lot of your granddaddy in you, but you got your grandmama's eyes. The sweetest lady I ever knew."

I felt the tears gather and hoped they wouldn't fall. "Thank you," I said, my voice a bit husky. "I loved her dearly."

Luckney chuckled. "Bet you don't remember the time I took you and my son fishing."

I started to shake my head, but a memory began to surface. I recalled a boy about my own age, slightly taller and huskier, showing me how to cast a fishing line. A picture of the adult with us began to emerge in my mind, and I started to smile.

"I do," I said. "I can't remember your son's name, but he was really patient with me. Even stopped me from falling in the pond a couple of times."

"Levon," Mr. Luckney said. "He's got grandkids of his own now. He loves to fish."

"It was the summer I stayed with my grandparents for a few weeks while my parents went on a trip," I said as more and more of the time came back to me. "I was about four years old."

"That sounds right," the elderly man replied. "You was a little bitty thing, but scrappy."

Sean laughed. "I like that word *scrappy*."

Luckney nodded. "He was getting into all kinds of mischief, and his grandmama asked me if I could take him off her hands one morning for a few hours. He like to have drove her crazy, trying to help with the housework."

I had to laugh as I remembered my *helpfulness*. "I created more work for her, I'm sure. She had to go behind me and clean up wherever I said I had been helping."

"She loved you, though. You was her one and only grandbaby, if I recall."

"Yes, sir," I said. "I never had any brothers or sisters."

There was a brief pause in the conversation. I didn't want to be blunt and ask Mr. Luckney if he had any other reason for stopping by other than to reminisce. I also wondered how he knew who I was, other than his recognition of my resemblance to my late father.

As if he had read my mind, Mr. Luckney said, "You gotta be wondering why I stopped by today. You see, my wife and Miz Azalea been friends since their school days. My wife, Oralee, spoke to Miz Azalea last night and found out about Mr. Hale's death and you getting the property back." His expression turned grim. "Also heard about what happened to the grandson. Why would somebody want to kill him? He was a stranger here, mostly."

"We don't know, sir," Sean said. "The sheriff's department is investigating. We discovered that someone, probably young Hale, had been living in this house for a few days, or maybe longer. Did you happen to notice anyone around here during the past week?"

Luckney shook his head. "Not that I recall. Don't come this way much." He nodded his head to the right, the opposite direction that Jackson had indicated earlier. "My farm's down that way. Didn't have much call to come this way, 'less it was to give Mr. Hale a check."

"You are leasing some of the land?" I asked.

"Yes, sir," Luckney said. "About a hundred and seventy-five acres. My son and I work it. Been doing so for twenty years, I guess. I wanted to talk to you about that."

"The leases will continue as they are for now," Sean said. "My father only found out about the property returning to the family yesterday. Until everything is settled with Mr. Hale's estate, and the investigation into his grandson's murder, we're not going to make any decisions about the property."

"Fair enough." Luckney nodded. "If you decide to sell, I hope you consider selling me what I've been farming all these years."

"I will definitely consider it," I said warmly. Mr. Luckney's pleasant manner and tone had impressed me, far more than Jackson's had.

"Thank you. It's good land for corn," Luckney said.

"Not cotton?" I asked.

Luckney smiled. "Not in this soil. Better for corn."

I laughed. "That shows you how much I know about farming. I don't even remember what my grandfather planted."

Sean extracted a business card and gave it to the farmer. "Here's my information, Mr. Luckney. If you'd like to talk more about all this, please give me a call and we can set up a meeting."

Luckney stowed the card in a pocket of his overalls. "Thank you kindly." He nodded in turn at Sean and me, and he once again offered his fingers to Diesel. The cat meowed and butted his hand. The farmer chuckled. "Miz Azalea told Oralee all about him."

"I'll bet she did." I grinned. "She probably told your wife about Ramses, too."

Luckney chuckled again. "Oralee can't believe Miz Azalea is taking that cat home with her. I've always been partial to dogs myself, but this fella here is pretty nice." He patted the cat's head. "I'm sure y'all have plenty to do, so I'll get on my way."

We bade him goodbye and watched his slow progress.

Luckney waved once he had climbed back into his pickup. He turned the truck and headed back down the drive.

"Nice man," Sean said.

"Much nicer than Gil Jackson," I said.

"Appears to be," Sean said. "But right now I don't think you should trust anybody connected to this property. Either one of them could have killed the grandson."

FOURTEEN

||||||||||||||||||||||||||||||||||||||||||||||||||||||||

After brief reflection, I had to admit that my son was correct. Even though Asa Luckney seemed like a nice man, I didn't know that he was any more trustworthy than Gil Jackson. I had taken a dislike to the latter man because of his brash manners. Both men obviously had a strong interest in the farmland that now belonged to me. But would they kill for it?

"Be sure and tell Kanesha about them," I said. "Unless you want me to do it." I opened the back door of my car, and Diesel climbed inside.

"I'll take care of it." Sean opened my door for me, and he closed it when I got into the car. I rolled down my window. "Love you, Dad."

"I love you, too, when you're not patronizing me." I gave him a big smile and rolled up my window. He stood there laughing while I backed the car around. I lost sight of him as I drove down to the road. I knew he'd be right behind me in a matter of moments.

He tailed me all the way into town, until the point came for him to turn down a street in the direction of his office. Diesel and I continued home. I checked the time on the clock on the dash. Azalea should still be there. I wanted to ask her about Mr. Luckney, and also about Gil Jackson. She might not know the latter man, but I was sure she could fill me in on her friend's husband.

Ramses greeted Diesel the moment we walked in the kitchen door, and he accompanied his big brother while Diesel headed for the litter box and water bowl. Azalea emerged from the pantry as I approached the fridge for a cold drink. We greeted each other, and I took my accustomed place at the table with the can of diet soda I had found.

"I met Mr. Asa Luckney this afternoon," I said. "He reminded me of a time when he and his son took me fishing when I was a little boy. I believe he said his son's name is Levon."

"Asa is a good man, and Oralee has been my friend since we were little girls," Azalea said.

"I found out he has been leasing some of the farmland that belonged to my grandfather. I also met another man who is leasing land, a man named Gil Jackson. Do you know him?"

"Only by reputation, and it's not a good one. You ask Miss Melba about him," Azalea said. "He's a hard man."

"Can't say I'm surprised at that, after meeting him. His manners are lacking." I sipped from the can, and the cold liquid felt good doing down.

Azalea snorted. "Manners ain't ever met that man, from what I heard."

"Mr. Luckney impressed me, though," I said. "A gentleman, I'd say."

"He is," Azalea replied. "Oralee picked out a good one. Too bad about Levon." She shook her head.

"What's wrong with Levon?" I asked, surprised.

"Bad to drink," Azalea said shortly. "Asa's lucky if he gets that boy to work two days out of seven. Levon's wife ran off years ago and left him with two teenagers, and one of them has two little ones now of her own. They all live there with Asa and Oralee."

"Goodness, that's sad about Levon's wife," I said. "So Mr. and Mrs. Luckney have to look after all those family members and provide for them?"

"Levon's son, Junior, is a good worker, and so is his daughter, Ashanti," Azalea said. "Their parents are no-account, but they turned out good despite that. Levon took after his granddaddy, Oralee's daddy. Seems to want to drink his life away."

"Did Levon have anything to do with old Mr. Hale in his drinking days?" I asked.

"Probably," Azalea said. "I might as well tell you, although I'm sure Miss Melba will tell you the same. Gil Jackson runs a still, or so people been saying for years. Martin Hale used to be one of his best customers until he found the Lord and dried out." She paused for breath. "I reckon Levon is one of his best customers now."

"I'm sorry to hear that," I said. "I can imagine how that must worry his parents." I couldn't fathom what it would be like to deal with an alcoholic child.

Laws on alcohol sales in Mississippi were strict and controlled by a state agency. Illicit stills no doubt existed in many counties around the state, as they had for decades. I was frankly shocked that Gil Jackson was rumored to be operating one. I'd better not find out he was doing it on any land belonging to my grandfather's estate. I'd have to tell Sean about this the next time we talked.

My brain shifted from this topic to the murder and the mysterious bones in my grandfather's attic. They might not be directly related, I thought, but there had to be a connection of some kind. I would simply have to trace the relationships of the people who were connected somehow to my grandfather's property through the years.

What would be of great help was a timeline starting with my grandfather's death. Then I would add in when Hale's wife disappeared, when he went on the wagon and got religious, when he leased out the farmland, and so on. Then, when there was more information on the bones in the attic, they might fit in somewhere. I also wanted to know exactly when Mr. Hale's son died and when his widow moved with her children to California. The grandson had spent his early years here, and he and his mother may have kept in touch with their connections here over the years.

"Did you hear me?" Azalea's voice broke through my abstraction.

"I'm sorry," I said. "I'm afraid I didn't. What did you say?"

She quirked an eyebrow at me, waited a moment, then spoke. "I was telling you about your dinner. Hamburger steak with onion gravy, green beans, mashed potatoes, and cornbread. Caramel cake for dessert. How does that sound to you?"

Diesel, who had by now returned with Ramses in tow, chirped loudly, and I glanced down to see Ramses rubbing himself against Azalea's legs.

"Sounds delicious to me," I said. "Do you know if Stewart and Haskell will be here for dinner?"

"They're going to be out until later," Azalea said. "There's plenty for them when they get home, if they want. If not, it'll keep until tomorrow." She looked down at Ramses and shook a finger in his face. "None of it's for you, you bad boy." She transferred her gaze to Diesel. "You either, Mr. Cat. You stick to eating your cat food for once."

I wondered what had brought on these admonitions about food. Ramses had been looking a bit plump lately, so maybe Azalea had put him on a diet. I decided not to ask, however.

"Come on, boys," I said, pushing back my chair and rising. "Let's go to the den and leave Azalea alone. No more pestering her."

"Yes," Azalea said firmly. "Dinner'll be ready in about an hour."

"Thanks." I made my way out of the kitchen with Diesel alongside me. Azalea had to shoo Ramses out of the room before he decided he had better follow us.

In the den I went to my desk, sat, and opened a side drawer in search of pen and paper. I found a blank sheet, took up a pen, and inscribed *Timeline* in the center at the top. For this initial effort I would have to rely on the vague figures given me by various people. Then I could work on finding the exact dates. I started with my grandfather's death and filled out the list, as follows:

45 yrs ago Grandfather's death
40 yrs ago Mrs. Hale runs off
25 yrs ago Hale Jr. killed in accident
23? yrs ago Widow remarries; moves to
    California

20 yrs ago Luckney leases land
15 yrs ago Jackson leases land
Present: Mr. Hale's death; grandson Hale's
    murder

That was the basic framework I established, subject to verification. Did the bones in the attic fit into this timeframe somewhere? Impossible to know until after the forensic anthropologist had examined them and the sheriff's department located their original site of deposit. If they did fit into this timeline, then there probably was a connection to the murder. Otherwise, the presence of the bones would be an odd coincidence.

Sean might be able to track down the exact dates more quickly than I could, like the exact dates for when Mr. Luckney and Jackson had leased farmland from Martin Hale. I figured I could find the date of Martin Hale Jr.'s death online in the local newspaper's obituaries. I decided now was as good a time as any to do that, so I turned to my laptop, woke it up, and connected to the public library's databases.

The local paper's archives had been digitized, thanks to a grant from the Ducote sisters, and the search engine was easy to use. I found the obituary within a couple of minutes. Martin Hale Jr. had died twenty-six years ago, leaving a widow and two young children, Martin III and Alissa. No ages were given for the children, but given the date of the father's death, they would be in their late twenties to early thirties now. Martin Hale Jr. had been only twenty-seven himself when he was killed.

I made the correction on my list of dates. I had a dandy new scanner that Sean had given me for my birthday a couple of months ago. I scanned my list and converted it to a pdf. Then I e-mailed it to Sean's work account. He was obsessive about checking his e-mail, and he called me about three minutes after I had sent the message.

"What is this for?" he asked.

"It's a timetable," I said.

"I can see that." He chuckled. "Now who's patronizing whom?"

"Point well taken. I thought it might help to set up a framework so we can understand the relationships of person to person and person to events. The answer to the murder of the grandson has to be somewhere amidst these connections."

Sean did not answer right away, and I knew he was considering what I had said. Finally, after what seemed like several minutes, he said, "I think you're probably right about that. This may not provide any answers about the bones in the attic, though, unless that person in life was connected in some way to this."

"I agree," I said. "We'll have to wait until the forensic anthropologist has had time to examine the bones. Who knows how long that will take, though? In the meantime, I think this will be helpful. Can you track down the dates of the land leases? And maybe get copies of birth certificates so we know how old various people are?"

"I'll get to work on it. I believe there's information on the subleases of the land in some of the papers from the elder Mr. Hale. Right now, I have to deal with another, more pressing matter, though. Talk to you soon."

Sean ended the call before I could ask whether he thought we should share this with Kanesha. Coming from him, she might not be as annoyed as she would if I shared it with her. With a sudden laugh, I thought about how I used to *help* my grandmother when I was small. My grandmother had been far more tolerant, although Kanesha did occasionally ask for my help. I didn't see her doing that in this case, however.

I glanced through the list of dates again. One of them stuck out—the date when Mrs. Hale left her husband and disappeared. How would we find the exact date when that happened? We had only an approximate one, and that might have to suffice. Kanesha might know what happened to Mrs. Hale, and I wondered whether she would be willing to share that particular bit of information. I was ambivalent about approaching Haskell on the matter, given what Stewart had told me. Haskell might not know anyway, as his relationship with his family was an uneasy one.

If the bones in the attic didn't belong to the missing Mrs. Hale, perhaps her disappearance had nothing to do with the present-day case. Until we knew more about the bones, though, I had the feeling the current case wouldn't get much further.

FIFTEEN

||||||||||||||||||||||||||||||||||||

The next day found Diesel and me in the archive office at the college. I hadn't heard anything more from Sean since I had talked to him last night. I knew he was busy with various clients, and I told myself I had to be patient.

Calling Kanesha wouldn't get me anywhere. Her usual attitude, unless she specifically asked for information or other help, was *hands off, Charlie.* I understood that, annoying as it was. I'd had an uneasy night, dreaming about those bones, worried that my grandfather was responsible in some way. I hoped Dewey Seton, the forensic anthropologist, had wrapped up what he was doing in Memphis and could now focus on this case.

Melba had been busy with our boss this morning when Diesel and I arrived, and that provided another test to my patience. I e-mailed her to tell her that I had some questions for her when she had time to talk. I'd been at work cataloging books for two hours now, and not a peep from downstairs yet. I looked up from my work and glanced at the window behind me where Diesel liked to sprawl. He had an excellent vantage point there to keep an eye on dastardly squirrels and evil birds who might attempt to get into the office. He sat up, yawned, and then climbed down from the window. He walked around my desk and sat in front of it.

Moments later I heard footsteps in the hall, and Melba appeared in the doorway. Diesel went to greet her, and she fussed over him, rubbing his head and scratching down his spine. He meowed happily and followed his friend when she came over and took the seat in front of my desk.

"Good morning," she said. "What's up? Any developments? I read about the murder in the paper this morning."

"No, nothing yet," I replied. "I'm hoping you can help me fill in some blanks, though." I handed over the piece of paper with my chronology on it. She scanned it but handed it back to me.

"I don't know specific dates for any of this," she said. "Some of those things happened when we were kids." She shrugged. "You found out when Martin Hale's son was killed in that accident, I'm guessing from the newspaper archive online. But there's not going to be anything in the paper about Mrs. Hale running off, or the son's widow marrying and moving to California."

"You're right," I said. "I was hoping it might spark some memories; maybe you've heard things over the years that could tie in to all this." I explained my idea about the chronology helping to figure out who killed young Hale and why. "It's the connections I need."

"I can tell you a little about one person, at least I think

so. Is the Jackson you've got listed there Gil Jackson by any chance?"

"Yes, it is," I replied.

Melba's lip curled in disdain. "He's a jackass. He's another one whose wife ran away because she couldn't put up with him. Whenever I saw her, she had a bruise or two. They didn't have any children, and one day she managed to get away from him and hop a bus north. I don't know where she ended up."

I couldn't say that Melba's news shocked me. "There's no current Mrs. Jackson?" I asked.

Melba shook her head. "He's had a couple of live-ins since then, but no one permanent. They don't put up with his crap for long."

"Do you know how long ago Mrs. Jackson left him?"

Melba considered this for a moment. "About twenty years ago, maybe."

"That makes two women connected to the men in this case who have disappeared," I said.

"You don't think those bones belong to Mrs. Jackson, surely?" Melba looked incredulous. "I know two people who saw her get on that bus."

I shrugged. "That's as may be. She could have come back without anybody knowing about it. Jackson could have beaten her up again and gone too far."

"Why would he dig her up years later and hide her bones in your grandfather's house?" She shook her head again. "That doesn't make any sense."

"It's far-fetched, I agree, but I'm simply exploring the possibilities," I said.

Diesel trilled, and Melba resumed her attentions to him. She had been too engrossed in our conversation to minister to his needs for affection. "When are they going to look at those bones and figure out how old they are?"

"Hopefully today or tomorrow. Dr. Seton has been working on a case in Memphis, but he should be back soon," I replied.

"What's Kanesha's take on all this? Is she talking to you?"

"No, not in any detail," I said. "She did discover that young Hale was apparently living in the house. There was no sign of a car, however. They don't know how he was getting back and forth into town."

"Somebody was giving him rides," Melba said.

I nodded. "The question is, who?"

"Whoever had the most to gain from associating with him," Melba replied.

"Yes, but I have no idea who that is at the moment," I said.

"I'd start looking at Gil Jackson," Melba said. "If there's anything shady going on, he's probably at the back of it. Have you heard about him and his bootlegging operation?"

"Azalea told me about it last night," I said. "I met him yesterday. I didn't take to him."

Melba nodded. "What was that other name on your list? The other person who leased land."

"Asa Luckney," I replied. "His wife, Oralee, is a good friend of Azalea's."

"I don't know him or his wife, but I know about their son, Levon," Melba said.

I could tell from her tone that what she knew was evidently not that good. "Azalea said he's an alcoholic, or in her words, *bad to drink*."

"He's been kicked out of every bar in town," Melba said. "He's a mean drunk. I heard that he's involved in Jackson's bootlegging operation. I imagine he gets paid in moonshine."

"His poor parents," I said.

"And his poor kids," Melba replied. "Their mother is long gone, and their daddy's a drunk. If it weren't for their grandparents, they'd be on the streets begging."

Azalea had told me last night about Levon Luckney's wife, and I hadn't really registered the potential significance of it. Now I did.

"That's the third wife who ran off," I said. "Do you know where she went, and when?"

"I can't remember who told me," Melba said. "Better ask Azalea, since you said she's friends with Levon's mama."

"I will. She told me last night, but at the time it didn't really click. Those bones could belong to Mrs. Hale, Mrs. Jackson, or Mrs. Luckney. Potentially," I added.

"Maybe you'd better talk to Kanesha about this," Melba said, rising from the chair. "I'd better get back."

"Thanks for your help," I said.

Melba waved and turned toward the door. Diesel followed her into the hallway, and I heard her talking to him briefly. Then he returned to the office and resumed his spot in the window.

I picked up my phone, intent on calling Kanesha's office number. Then I paused. Would it do any good? She probably already knew about all three of these women. She worked with Mrs. Hale's nephew, after all. And her mother's good friend was the mother-in-law of another. Finally, she was probably well acquainted with

Gil Jackson and his history, if the rumors about his boot-legging operation were true.

I put the phone down. Then I picked it up again and dialed Kanesha. Maybe if I shared this information with her, she might at least tell me what she knew about these women and their present whereabouts.

Kanesha answered after two rings and identified herself.

"Good morning," I said. "This is Charlie Harris."

"I recognized the number," she responded coolly. "What do you want?"

"I've found out that three women who are connected to the farm all disappeared at some point. All three of them left abusive or drunken husbands, and I think those bones could belong to one of them," I said. "You're probably aware of this, but I thought I ought to tell you anyway."

"Thanks," Kanesha said. "Yes, I'm aware. We're investigating the whereabouts of all three women, but I don't have any satisfactory answers yet. Does that satisfy your curiosity?"

"For now," I said. "And thank *you*."

Kanesha ended the call, and I set my phone down. At least Kanesha and I were thinking along the same lines, I thought. She had the machinery that could produce answers more quickly than I could, and I hoped she found those answers soon.

I went back to my cataloging and worked at it for about half an hour before my phone rang. Sean was calling.

"Hello, Son, what's up?"

"Hi, Dad," he said. "How would you feel about letting Mr. Hale's granddaughter stay at the house? I don't think there's much money in that family, and she might not be able to afford a hotel for an extended stay."

"In my house?" I asked. "I guess so, I have plenty of room, and I suppose it would be a nice gesture, given everything that's happened."

"That's what I thought," Sean said. "Plus it will give you a chance to find out more about the Hale family. She might be more forthcoming with you than she would be with the sheriff's department."

"Oh, really?" I asked. "How come you're suddenly wanting me involved in this? I thought I was supposed to stay out of it."

"I know you too well," Sean said wryly. "You're not going to stay out of it, no matter what I say, or Laura, either, so I might as well help you."

So you can keep an eye on me, I thought.

"All right," I said. "I'll call Azalea and ask her—"

Sean interrupted me. "No need. I've already talked to her. Ms. Hale should be in Athena around six o'clock tonight. You can expect her then." He ended the call.

I was tempted to call him right back and express myself over his high-handedness, but then I saw the humor in the situation and laughed at myself.

The clock informed me it was close enough to lunchtime for me and Diesel to head home for our meals. "Come on, boy, time to eat."

Diesel knew those words well enough, and he was at the door into the hallway before I was halfway out of my chair. We headed down the stairs and through the back door into the small parking lot. The archive and the library's administrative offices occupied a restored antebellum home on the edge of the college campus. The much more modern library building stood next door. I opened the car doors to let out the built-up heat, and Diesel hopped inside.

A few minutes later we were walking into the kitchen from the garage. Ramses greeted us. He always seemed to know when we arrived home. I supposed he learned the sound of the car and the garage door opening. Azalea must be upstairs seeing about a room for Ms. Hale.

Lunch stood ready on the table. Slices of recently baked ham, potato salad, and a fresh garden salad. While Diesel went to water himself and take care of other needs, I served myself, watched carefully by Ramses. I cut off several small bits of ham and gave them to him, and he gobbled them down.

I had almost finished eating by the time Azalea appeared in the kitchen. "Thanks for having lunch ready," I said. "That ham is delicious."

"How much of it did Ramses and Mr. Cat have?" Azalea asked, sounding stern.

"Only a little," I said. "You know how they beg, and it's hard to resist them."

Azalea chuckled as her expression softened. "I sure do."

"Sean told me we could expect Ms. Hale around six," I said.

"Everything's ready for her," Azalea replied.

I was about to thank her, but she spoke again.

"I been thinking about something," she said, and I could see she appeared troubled now. "You remember I told you that Levon Luckney's wife ran off."

"I do, and I also found out that Gil Jackson's wife did the same thing."

Azalea nodded. "That man's a pig. Ain't no good woman ever gonna take up with him now. But I'm talking about Levon's wife. Her name was Janelle. She didn't have much family to speak of, and they've all died since she ran off."

"Do you have any idea where she is now?"

Azalea shook her head. "That's the trouble. Nobody knows. I'm thinking now those bones in your grand-daddy's attic might be hers."

SIXTEEN

"How long ago did she leave?" I asked.

Azalea considered for a moment. "About fifteen years ago, maybe. Her children were small, and I couldn't understand her up and leaving them like that, even as bad as Levon was."

"She might have been desperate," I said, though privately I agreed with Azalea. I could never have abandoned my children, but then, I hadn't been in Janelle Luckney's position, living her life.

"Did she say anything to anybody about her plans?" I asked.

"Not that I ever heard. I knew her mama. Her daddy'd been dead for a few years by that time, and her brother moved to Detroit a long time ago. He was about fifteen years older than her."

"Nobody saw her leave?"

Azalea sighed. "Oralee told me they woke up one

morning and she was gone. Not a word, even for her babies. She kissed them good night, like she always did. In the morning she was gone."

"No one ever suspected she could have been murdered or kidnapped, I suppose."

"No, I don't think so. Oralee knew how rough Levon was. She and Asa tried everything they could, but Levon wouldn't listen. He even struck his daddy down once, but he wouldn't raise a hand to his mama."

"Kanesha is probably aware of all this," I said.

"Janelle was a couple of years ahead of her in school, and they were friends," Azalea replied. "They didn't keep in touch after Janelle started with Levon. He wanted her to himself."

That was never a good sign for a relationship, I thought. That behavior was typical of abusers who wanted to isolate their victims from any friends or family.

"Did Levon and Janelle live with his parents?" I asked.

"On their property," Azalea said. "Asa and Levon built a small house at the back of the yard for them."

"Let's hope that Janelle is alive and well somewhere," I said.

"Yes, praise the Lord she is," Azalea said.

I couldn't think of anything to ask her, and by now it was time for me to be back in the office. I rounded up Diesel, gave a firm no to the supplicant Ramses, and the big cat and I drove back to the office.

Melba reappeared during the afternoon, and I shared what Azalea had told me about the missing Janelle Luckney. Melba frowned. "Isn't it strange that three women can just disappear like that and nobody makes a fuss about it?"

"I agree, but there's probably more to each of those stories than we know. The families may know more than they're willing to share with outsiders."

"That's true, I guess," Melba said, "but I still think it's odd. The one thing in common is that they all lived out in the county, away from town. Nobody close by to see what was going on, or what could have happened to them."

I hadn't thought of the situation in quite those terms, but now that Melba had voiced it, I found it chilling. Those farms were probably several miles apart, making it much too easy for bad things to happen without any external witnesses.

Melba and I exchanged glances, and Diesel must have sensed our mutual unease. From his position on the floor beside Melba, he meowed loudly. Melba stroked his head to assure him we were fine. After he quieted, she rose. "Back to work again. I guess y'all will be leaving soon." She pointed to her watch. "It's nearly three-thirty."

I nodded. "A couple of small things to finish here, and then we'll head out. Have a good weekend, if I don't see you before then."

She waved goodbye and departed. I finished with the book I'd been working on when Melba came in and made a last check of my e-mail for the day before packing up and leaving.

On the short drive home, I thought about the isolation of those farms. I hadn't considered that before. I grew up in town and had always lived in town. Other than brief stays with my grandparents when I was very young, I hadn't lived on a farm with neighbors who might live several miles away. Would I, as an adult now, find spending nights in my grandfather's house spooky at all?

I figured I should test myself at some point. I couldn't make an informed decision until I had spent time in the house. I might find I liked the quiet of country living. The odds of that were small, I admitted, but I wouldn't know until I tried. Maybe when Helen Louise returned from her New Orleans vacation, I would suggest we spend a long weekend there. I knew she would be interested in seeing the house. Before we spent even a night there, however, I wanted someone to go through it and clean it thoroughly. All the bed linens needed to be replaced, for one thing. I didn't like the idea of using sheets that had belonged to someone else for who knew how long.

Diesel and I greeted Azalea and Ramses in the kitchen, and the cats padded into the utility room. Struck by a question that hadn't really occurred to me before, I asked Azalea.

"I can't remember, did Aunt Dottie get any of my grandparents' furniture or other effects when my grandfather died? I'm wondering if any of the things in the house might have been left there for the Hales to use."

Azalea nodded. "I was working for Miss Dottie when your granddaddy died, but she told me later on about the pieces she took for this house. There's a list somewhere. She was real organized about it."

"Then I'll look for the list," I said.

"Anything that looks old," Azalea said, "is probably from your granddaddy's house. I know this kitchen table was there, and some of the pieces in the living room." She thought for a moment. "I reckon there's a few things stored in the attic, too, that she didn't want to leave but couldn't find a place for here. She didn't like to put anything delicate in the boarders' rooms. Young men aren't careful about things."

For years my late aunt had rented rooms to college students and gave them two meals a day for modest fees. She liked having young men about the house, but I understood why she wouldn't want them using prized family possessions. When I inherited the house, I had continued per her wishes, but after my last college-student boarder graduated, I hadn't kept up. For one thing, there hadn't been any new applicants, and I decided the idea had run its course.

I texted Sean a quick question about the contents of my grandfather's house. He ought to have information on that. I would have to work on the assumption that everything there belonged to the Hale heirs now. I wondered if Alissa Hale would be prepared to make decisions about the disposal of the items.

She would probably not be in a frame of mind to deal with all that at the moment, I realized. She would no doubt still be in shock over her brother's murder. I wouldn't bring up the subject unless she did.

Sean responded a few minutes later with a phone call. "Hi, Dad. I thought I had told you when we met the other day about the furniture and other effects in the house."

"No, you didn't, not that I can recall," I said. "Surely I would have remembered if you had. Azalea told me that Aunt Dottie took some of it when my grandfather died. There's a list somewhere. I guess anything she left out there became Hale's by default."

"I'll have to go through the lease agreement again," Sean said. "Depends on the wording, of course. I seem to remember a clause in you grandfather's will about all this. I'll check that, too. Didn't your parents take anything from the house?"

"Offhand, I don't remember," I said. After my parents' deaths, I had sold their house in Athena, not thinking I would ever return here to live. I had kept a few small things of sentimental value, but I didn't recall that my parents had any valuable antiques. I sold the furnishings as a lot rather than put it all in storage. I used the proceeds from that and from the house sale to fund my children's college educations. I knew my parents would have approved. My education had been important to them, and they would have wanted their grandchildren to go to college, too.

"See if you can find your aunt's list," Sean said. "In the meantime, I'll be working on this end. Can't get to it right away, because I've got a court date tomorrow morning. After that, I'll be able to clear some time for it."

"Thanks, I appreciate it. Good luck in court tomorrow." I put my phone down. Where could that list of my aunt's be? I had her desk in my bedroom, but I had been through the contents numerous times and was pretty sure no such list was there.

Probably in the room where most of her book collection was stored, I decided. The closet in that rarely used bedroom was filled with boxes of her things. I decided I would start my search there, but I cautioned myself not to get distracted by my aunt's books.

"We're going up to check the closet with Aunt Dottie's boxes," I told Azalea, and she nodded.

Ramses scampered up the steps along with Diesel and me. My pace was far more sedate, however. I paused for a moment before I opened the door of the bedroom. I always felt my aunt's presence in this room. She had shared my love of mysteries and had always encouraged me to read whatever I wanted to from her library.

What a library it was, too. All the classic children's

mystery series: Nancy Drew, the Hardy Boys, Judy Bolton, and many others. As she grew older she began collecting adult mysteries from the Golden Age: Agatha Christie, Margery Allingham, and Dorothy L. Sayers, among many others whose names were far less well known these days. I could spend hours in this room looking at the books and riffling their pages, dipping in to read a paragraph or two, or a chapter or three.

I opened the door and walked in. I glanced at the wall covered with books, smiled, then turned my attention toward the closet with my aunt's boxes. Some of them bore markings with broad categories of contents. There were at least three that simply said *papers*. I might have to go through all three of them before I found that list.

I located one of the boxes and carried it to the bed. I sat beside it, sideways, and opened the lid. Ramses had already hopped on the bed, and he immediately wanted to climb in the box. There was no room, though, and I gently dissuaded him from his intent. Diesel joined us on the bed, and he engaged the younger cat in play while I began to examine the contents of the box.

I had no idea of the time as I went through loose papers and folders. The latter were thankfully marked, and I could put those aside quickly in many cases. Eventually I placed everything back in the box and replaced the lid. I set the box on the floor beside the closet and extracted another one.

This time I didn't have to dig far before I found a folder helpfully labeled *property lists*. I opened it to find a mixture of invoices—all marked paid, with check numbers included—and lists. Toward the end of the file, I found what I had been seeking, a three-page, stapled list marked *items from Robert's house*.

I returned everything else to the box and then put both boxes back in the closet. I made sure that the cats were in sight before the door clicked shut. I hated the thought of locking one of them inside a dark closet.

Back on the bed I began to scan the list. I recognized each piece. Several had the annotation *attic* beside them, and I presumed that meant she had placed them in her attic here, rather than the attic in my grandfather's house. I'd have to check that to be sure, though. I hadn't been in the attic in this house since I had moved back to Athena several years ago. I couldn't remember what was up there. No telling how dusty it would be by now. I should go up there regularly to clean and sort stuff out. Surely there was plenty that might be of use to someone.

On the last page Aunt Dottie had noted certain items that she had decided to leave behind. I recognized two of them. One was the settee in the front parlor. The other was one of the rocking chairs on the front porch. It had belonged to my grandfather. The one I sat in on my visit the other day. The others didn't sound familiar at all.

I heard Azalea calling me, probably from the foot of the stairs. "Come on, boys," I said, trying to herd the cats off the bed. "Let's go see what Azalea wants."

For once they actually did what I asked, instead of continuing to wrestle. Diesel hopped down and scampered out the door, and Ramses bolted after him. I turned off the light and shut the door.

When I reached the landing, I glanced down into the hall below. To my surprise, I saw Kanesha standing there with Azalea.

"I have news," Kanesha said. "Dr. Seton has done a preliminary examination of the bones."

I hurried down the stairs to join her. Azalea left us,

and Ramses followed her into the kitchen. Diesel remained with me after greeting Kanesha. She patted his
head but continued to stare at me.

"What's the news?" I asked, a little breathless from
my rapid descent.

"The skeleton isn't complete," Kanesha said. "I already knew that, of course, but he confirmed something
I only suspected."

"What's that?"

"The feet and hands were amputated. They're missing."

SEVENTEEN

||||||||||||||||||||||||||||||||||||||||||||||||||||

"I never noticed," I said. "After I got a look at the skull, I didn't really examine the rest of the bones. What was the killer trying to hide, do you think?"

"I don't know," Kanesha said. "The most obvious reason is to stop us from identifying the corpse, if the body had been found before complete decomposition. I'm betting on that cadaver dog to turn up something for us, though. Maybe the missing body parts were buried close to where the body was originally hidden."

"Do you think that's why the bones were put in the attic? To conceal the original burial spot?"

Kanesha nodded. "I think that's as good a reason as any. The other would be to incriminate someone in the house, either your grandfather or Mr. Hale, depending on when this person died."

"Maybe for both those reasons," I said. "Sounds to

me that you think foul play had to be involved in this death, too."

"I can't think of any other reason for the hands and feet to be amputated," Kanesha replied, an edge to her tone. "Unless it was a freak accident, and I'm not buying that."

"Maybe the bones are really old," I said. "Has Dr. Seton said anything about the potential age of the bones?"

"He says they're from a female, an adult probably in her sixties or older. That's from a quick examination. He's going to do a more thorough one tomorrow," she replied.

"Okay, but actually I meant how old the bones might be."

Kanesha nodded. "His best guess is less than a hundred years, but that's all he would say until he's had time for tests. I've got to go. I just stopped by on the way out to your grandfather's house. I'm meeting Dr. Seton there with his dog in about twenty minutes."

"I don't suppose I could come, too?" I asked.

Kanesha shook her head. "No, you can't. I can't have any extraneous persons on hand for this. If we find anything significant, you'll be informed. That's all I can tell you for now."

I accepted defeat. "Thank you for stopping by. I wish Dr. Seton and his dog the best of luck today."

"I'll pass that along," Kanesha said before she turned to leave.

Diesel and I escorted her to the door and saw her out. I watched her hurry to her car before I shut the door.

I found her news unsettling. The thought of those amputations disturbed me. The whole thing sounded so grisly. I wondered if Dr. Seton would be able to determine *when* the hands and feet were amputated; before or after death? For the sake of the victim, I hoped it had been after. I shuddered. Scenarios like this were the reason I didn't watch graphic movies or read books with graphic details of autopsies or murders. My imagination was bad enough without having visual or written descriptions to stimulate it.

Tantalizing aromas wafted my way from the kitchen, and I followed them, Diesel at my heels. Azalea stood at the stove, tending pots. Ramses sat near her feet, watching her carefully in hopes of dropped tidbits.

"Smells good in here." I was determined to banish my recent thoughts from my mind. I'd never be able to do justice to Azalea's meal if I let myself think about the news Kanesha had just delivered.

"Fried chicken, rice, gravy, biscuits, and butter beans," Azalea replied, her back to me. "I thought you might enjoy some of your favorites tonight."

"I certainly will," I said, mentally adding up the pounds I would gain from such a meal. I had no resistance when it came to fried chicken, biscuits, gravy, and rice. Butter beans I could take or leave.

"Stewart said he'd be here for dinner," Azalea said. "I reckon Mr. Haskell is working with Kanesha."

"I imagine so," I replied. "They're going to be searching my grandfather's property with a cadaver dog."

Azalea turned to look at me, her expression puzzled. "I heard Kanesha talk about one of them a while back. What exactly does it do?"

"These dogs are specially trained to find dead bodies, or, in this case, places where a dead body might have been put in the ground." I told her the little I knew about dogs who had been able to find burial sites even hundreds or thousands of years old. "It's pretty incredible to me. I knew dogs had amazing senses of smell, but this is crazy."

Azalea sniffed and turned back to the stove. "Sure sounds crazy to me. But that's my daughter's job, not mine. I wouldn't want to go traipsing around all over the Lord's creation after a dog, looking for dead bodies or their graves."

Normally I wouldn't, either, I thought, but in this case I'd make an exception. I had seen and touched the skull of the person in this case, and I felt a sense of connection, odd as that might sound.

"How long until dinner?" I asked.

"Should be ready in about twenty minutes," she replied.

"I'm going to wash up. Do you think Stewart will be here soon?"

"Said he would."

Diesel came with me upstairs. I hadn't changed out of my work clothes yet, and I wanted to be more comfortable for dinner. For one thing, I wanted to put on my sandals and get rid of my socks and shoes so my feet could breathe.

Back downstairs a good ten minutes later, I walked into the kitchen to find Stewart chatting with Azalea. We exchanged greetings, and I asked how his day had gone.

"Fine," he said. "The usual academic claptrap. The one thing I won't miss about my job when I retire is the committee meetings. We never can seem to have an organized one. People are invariably going off on tangents, and I want to stand up and scream."

"Why don't you?" I asked, jokingly.

Stewart pinned me with his gaze. "Don't think I might not do that, one of these days." Then he grinned. "I'm going to get Dante and let him out in the backyard to run around for a bit. I'll be back with you in about ten minutes."

"Is there anything I can do?" I asked Azalea, knowing it was futile. I felt I had to ask occasionally, however.

"Not a thing, unless you want to take this rascal here and lock him up somewhere." Azalea pointed to Ramses, who meowed plaintively at the gesture.

"He hasn't eaten in days," I said. "The poor mistreated little thing."

Azalea snorted. "That's what he thinks, anyway. He's a pester-box, that's for sure."

"Come here, Ramses." I took my chair and held out my hands. Ramses trotted over and let me pick him up. I stroked him and scratched his head. He started purring. Diesel sat beside my chair and stared at me, no doubt disgusted at my attentions to his annoying little brother. "I know," I said to my big baby. "You'd rather I were doing this for you, but he deserves some attention, too."

Diesel did not appear to agree with me. He warbled once before he lay down, his back to me.

By the time Stewart returned, Dante with him, dinner was on the table. Azalea gathered her things, ready to leave. Stewart and I assured her we would clean up her kitchen, and she bade us goodbye. Dante darted back and forth between the cats, trying to engage them in play. Diesel ignored him, but Ramses batted at him playfully.

After we had helped ourselves to the food and taken a few bites, Stewart sat back in his chair, fork down. "Okay, what's the latest? Any big news about the bones in the attic?"

I figured if I didn't tell him, Haskell probably would. "Yes, the skeleton is probably female, adult, around sixty or older. But the hands and feet are missing."

Stewart made a moue of distaste. "That's grisly."

"I agree," I said. "And the less said about that while we eat, the better."

Stewart nodded emphatically. "Okay by me."

I filled him in on other new bits of information, including the names of the three runaway women. "I don't suppose Haskell has said anything to you about his aunt since the last time we talked."

"No, he hasn't," Stewart said. "I haven't asked. I'll bring up the two other women, though, and see if he volunteers anything about Mrs. Hale."

"He and Kanesha may already know her whereabouts, and whether she's still alive. I reckon she'd be in her late seventies, maybe eighty by now."

"Sounds about right," Stewart replied. "Haskell's mother is seventy-four, and I think the aunt was her older sister."

"Do you know either Gil Jackson or Levon Luckney?"

"No, not that I recall," Stewart said. "I don't move much in farming circles, other than the occasional tense meal with Haskell's family." He grimaced.

We resumed eating, and silence reigned for a brief period. Silence, that is, except for the occasional sorrowful meow or pitiful whine, the latter from Dante. Stewart and I both succumbed and doled out bites of biscuit, chicken, and the occasional butter bean. Oddly enough, Diesel really liked them. Because Diesel ate them, Ramses did, too. Even Dante had a couple.

"I'm sure Haskell knows both those men you mentioned," Stewart said. "Jackson and—what was the other name?"

"Luckney," I said. "You mean because he's from a farming family?"

"Yes, he knows a lot of the people out in that part of the county, since he grew up there," Stewart replied.

"One thing I didn't tell you about Gil Jackson," I said, "was that he's rumored to be a moonshiner."

Stewart slapped a hand on the table, and I almost jumped.

"*That's* who that guy is." Stewart apparently hadn't noticed my reaction. "I thought the name sounded slightly familiar. Haskell has talked about a moonshiner out that way, but they've never been able to catch him. Every time they go out there to shut him down, his still is gone."

"Sounds to me like somebody is tipping him off," I said.

"Haskell thinks so, too," Stewart replied. "Kanesha's been trying to find out, but so far they haven't had any luck." He grinned suddenly. "I think it's the sheriff myself. He's fond of his liquor."

Given what I knew of our sheriff, I wouldn't be surprised if Stewart was right. Kanesha wouldn't have much luck, in that case, putting Jackson out of business.

We finished our meals, and then we began to clear the table. Our three helpers, after they realized there were no more tidbits forthcoming, got out of our way while we moved around.

"Too bad Haskell isn't here to eat this fresh," I said. "He's been putting in long hours."

"Always, it seems." Stewart shook his head. "I worry that he's not getting enough rest, but if I bring up the subject, he turns it off and tells me not to worry."

In the brief silence that followed, we both tensed when we heard a sound at the front door. There was a knock, and then someone rang the bell.

"Who on earth could that be?" Stewart asked.

I felt like an idiot when I recalled that Alissa Hale was coming tonight. I glanced at my watch. The time was now nearly six-thirty.

"I'll explain in a moment, but it's young Hale's sister. She's going to stay here," I said before I hurried to open the door.

When I did, I found a harassed-looking deputy, a young woman I didn't recognize, standing there. "Good evening, Deputy."

"Are you Mr. Harris?" she asked.

"I am. Do you have Ms. Hale with you? She's supposed to come stay with me."

"I have her," the deputy said, her tone grim. "But she says she's not staying in this house. She insists on going to her grandfather's house."

EIGHTEEN

|||||||||||||||||||||||||||||||||||||||||||||||||||||||||||||||||||

"It's not her grandfather's house," I said, somewhat blankly. "It's my house."

The young deputy shrugged. "I'm just repeating what she said, Mr. Harris. I told her it was arranged for her to stay here, but she won't get out of the car. Would you like to come talk to her?"

"I guess I'll have to," I said, stepping out into the sultry evening. The sun wouldn't be setting for a couple of hours yet, and the heat beat down on me. I made Diesel remain in the house.

I followed the deputy down the walk to the car. The deputy suggested I get in the backseat with Ms. Hale, and I demurred at first. Then I decided being inside an air-conditioned vehicle was a smarter choice than arguing with a stranger inside one while I stood in the heat. I nodded agreement.

The officer opened the door, and I climbed into the

car next to my intransigent would-be guest. "Good evening, Ms. Hale. I'm Charlie Harris. I really am very sorry about your recent losses. I didn't know your grandfather or your brother."

She was short. Her feet didn't touch the floorboard. I estimated she was barely five feet, if that. Her hair had been streaked blond, but the roots were dark. Her makeup, applied heavily, had that look of having traveled a long distance without much touch-up. She also emitted a rather strong scent, a mixture of sweat and patchouli. I would end up with a splitting headache if I had to stay in this car with her for more than a couple minutes.

Ms. Hale regarded me with hostile suspicion. "How do I know you're not the one who murdered my brother? He said you were trying to steal the house from my family."

"First off, I never met your brother. I have no idea what he looked like, and I had no earthly reason to kill him. Second, the house never belonged to your grandfather. My son, who is a lawyer, can explain it better than I can. Your grandfather had a lease from my grandfather that allowed him to live there during his lifetime. When your grandfather died, the property reverted to my grandfather's heir. I am that heir."

Her expression had turned mulish before I was even halfway through my explanation. "I don't believe you. Marty said he was going to take you to court, and we would win. A lawyer told him so."

I put a firm grip on my temper and held on for dear life. "I don't know who that lawyer was, but he was wrong, Ms. Hale. Now, I have offered you a room in my house here, and it's a lot more comfortable than the house in the country. Besides, your brother was killed there. Do you really think it's a good idea for you to be out there alone? Have you ever been out in the country during the nighttime?"

That got through to her.

"No, I haven't." Her hand trembled as she rubbed it down her jean-clad thigh.

"Also, a deputy in the sheriff's department has an apartment in my house. If you're frightened at any time, he'll be glad to protect you." I didn't mention that the deputy was not at present in the house, but maybe she wouldn't insist on meeting him right now.

"I still think you're lying about my grandfather's house, but I don't want to be out in the country all alone." She took a couple of deep breaths. "Are there bears out there?"

I suppressed a smile. "Not that I've heard. They're mostly gone from this area now."

"That's good," she said, still not making any move to exit the patrol car.

"Have you had dinner yet?" I asked.

She nodded. "On the plane. It was okay."

"If you're hungry, I can heat up some leftovers for you that my housekeeper cooked. Or my boarder Stewart is an excellent cook."

"Okay, I guess I'll stay here. I don't have enough money to go anyplace decent." She opened her door and got out of the car.

The deputy and I exchanged glances as I exited my side. The deputy popped the trunk, and I took out a medium-sized rolling suitcase and a small duffel bag. "Thank you, Deputy," I said.

Now that I had a better look at Alissa Hale, I decided that, despite her small size and childlike behavior, she was probably in her late twenties. There was a hard look to her face, and I wondered whether her life in California was an easy one. Somehow, I reckoned, it probably wasn't.

"Your mother wasn't able to come," I said.

"She couldn't," Alissa said, her face obscured by her long hair and downcast head. "She made me come instead."

And you didn't want to, I thought. Was she really that frightened of me? Or simply resentful of the situation and trying to exert some kind of control over it?

I set her bags on the stoop before I opened the door. I figured I had better let her know about the animal occupants of the house, in case she was afraid of them. "I have two cats. One of them is large. There's also a dog that lives here, a small poodle. They're very friendly and won't hurt you."

She turned to me, smiling. "I love animals. People who love animals are good people, I think."

"I think so, too." I should have opened with that, I thought as I turned the doorknob and ushered her inside.

Diesel and Ramses gave her a loud welcome, and Dante added to the clamor. Laughing, she dropped to the floor and let them crawl over her or, in Dante's case, stand by her and bark. I set her bags inside and shut the door.

Stewart came out from the kitchen and grinned when he saw the jumble of animals and young woman. Diesel sneezed a couple of times. Ramses didn't seem bothered by the patchouli, nor did Dante. The dog was now sticking his nose under her arm. I might have to give her a subtle hint about wearing it in my house. Or else I'd have to stand ten feet away from her all the time.

Having Diesel accept her so quickly eased my mind. Alissa seemed genuinely fond of animals, and I hoped she wouldn't prove to be a problem. I really did think she was better off here. Given what had happened to her brother, I didn't like the odds for her safety if she stayed alone at my grandfather's house.

"Let me show you where your room is," I said. "I'm sure you'd like to freshen up before you have anything to eat."

Alissa got slowly to her feet. Diesel looked even larger standing beside her. She rubbed his head. "Will you come with me, boy?"

Diesel meowed, Dante barked, and Ramses curled around her legs. Laughing, she took the duffel bag from me and followed me up the stairs to the second floor. Azalea had prepared the room that Laura used before her marriage to Frank Salisbury. Comfortable, and furnished in a more feminine style, it should suit Alissa fairly well.

"This is really nice," she said after she looked around the room. She dropped her bag and went to the door of the en suite bathroom. "This is *really* nice." She turned to me with a shy smile. "Thank you."

"You're welcome." I placed her suitcase by the four-poster bed. "Come downstairs when you're ready. The kitchen is to the right of the stairs. Come along, boys." I herded cats and dog out of the room and shut the door behind me. A moment later I heard the key turn in the lock.

Stewart stood impatiently tapping his right foot when I entered the kitchen. "Okay, give, what is all this about?"

"As I told you, she's the victim's sister. Her mother

sent her here to deal with everything, which I think is pretty shabby myself, but I don't know the woman. She has very little money, and I agreed to let her stay here."

Stewart smiled. "Sometimes you're too kind for your own good."

I shrugged. "I haven't said this to anyone yet, but I do feel a bit guilty that they lost their grandfather's home to a stranger."

"No, we're not doing that," Stewart said. "It's not your fault if they were deliberately misled into thinking their grandfather owned the property. He was either senile when he told them he did, or he deliberately lied for some reason." He thought for a moment. "Probably wanted to make them think he had a lot more money than he did."

"I don't have any idea how much he had," I said. "Unless he spent recklessly, he should have saved a significant amount over the years. But I don't know anything about the economics of farming. He could have been simply scraping by."

"Sean will find out," Stewart said. "Now, is Ms. Hale coming back downstairs?"

"I believe so. I offered her food, although she ate on the plane. You know what airplane food is like, though. I think she'd appreciate something better to eat, or at least to snack on."

Stewart took my cue without any prompting. "I'll have a look around and see what there is. I can fix her something or heat up some of the leftovers." He glanced down at Dante, sitting expectantly at his feet. "Nothing for you, though, you little pig." Dante barked.

"Ms. Hale loves animals, so you may have to put him

upstairs if you don't want him eating anything else," I said. "She'll probably try to feed them."

"I'll take that chance," Stewart said. "Maybe playing with the boys will wear Dante out by the time we go back upstairs."

We resumed our seats at the table after refreshing our glasses of sweet tea. Desultory chat occupied our time until roughly half an hour had passed, and Alissa Hale walked into the kitchen.

She presented a stark contrast to the young woman from the taxi. Her face, devoid of the heavy makeup, looked younger than her years. Her hair, now pulled back in a ponytail, enhanced that impression. She smiled shyly at Stewart, who rose and extended a hand.

"I'm Alissa," she said.

"Stewart," he replied, and released her hand. "Why don't you have a seat? Can I get you something to eat and drink?"

"I'd love some mineral water, if you have it," she replied as she pulled out a chair.

"Would you like it over ice?" Stewart asked.

"As long as it's cold, that's not necessary."

"It's cold." Stewart pulled a bottle from the refrigerator and passed it over to her. I hated the stuff myself, but Stewart loved it, so Azalea made sure it stayed stocked in the fridge. "How about something to eat? I could make you an omelet, if you like. Ham and cheese."

Alissa shook her head. "Thank you, but if you have cheese and crackers, and maybe some fruit, that's all I need."

"Coming right up." Stewart started preparing the snack for her.

Alissa sipped her mineral water, absently stroking in turn each of the animals crowded next to her chair.

"Tell them to stop if they bother you," I said. "They understand that word."

"No, they're fine," she replied. "I'm sorry about earlier." She sighed. "We should have known it was all just my grandfather's big talk, trying to make himself sound important."

"I didn't know your grandfather at all," I said.

"I barely knew him myself, other than what my mother told us about him," Alissa said. "I was only two when we moved to California. I was born a few months before Daddy was killed."

"I'm so sorry," I said, thinking how awful it was that she had to grow up without knowing her father.

"It's okay," she replied. "My stepfather was a good man. He died several years ago." She turned to me. "You reminded me a lot of him, when you talked to me in the car. That's mainly why I decided to trust you."

"Thank you," I said. "I'm sorry for your loss. I know you must miss him."

She nodded. "My mother, Marty, and I have been on our own since he died, and he didn't have much to leave us. Mother is disabled, and Marty had trouble holding a job, so I was working two jobs." She took another sip from her water. "When my grandfather showed up out of the blue, he was shocked when he saw the apartment we live in."

"Is that when he started talking about the house here?" I asked.

Stewart slid a plate of sliced cheese, crackers, red grapes, and a banana in front of her, and Alissa thanked him again. Stewart resumed his seat. He patted her hand. "Enjoy."

Alissa had several bites of cheese and cracker, then popped a couple of grapes in her mouth. She looked straight ahead the whole time, not glancing at either one of us.

I was about to repeat my question when she responded. "He told us about his farmhouse, and how long it had been there. Made it sound like a mansion. He told us we should all move back to Mississippi and live with him. He had enough money to take care of us. He even gave my mother a couple thousand bucks."

Stewart and I exchanged glances. Had Martin Hale been wealthy? Had he been giving them false hope?

"The house isn't a mansion," I told her. "It's a farmhouse. It's a nice one and a good size, but not what it probably sounded like."

"Figures," Alissa said. "My mother told Marty and me one night after my grandfather had gone to bed more about the old man. She warned us not to take him seriously, but Marty did, and he had me believing, too."

"How long had your grandfather been with you when he died?" Stewart asked.

"Only about ten days," Alissa said, her face clouded. "It was awful."

"What happened?" I asked. "If you feel like talking about it. Otherwise, we can talk about something else."

"I don't mind," she replied. "We already knew he was a bigot, anyway."

"What did that have to do with his death?" Stewart asked.

"Marty's boyfriend came to dinner the night my

grandfather had passed away in front of us," Alissa said. "He thought it was bad enough that Marty was gay, but when he found out Marty's boyfriend is Black, he went nuts, screaming and making a big fuss." She paused for a sip of water. "That's when he had the stroke and died."

NINETEEN

‖‖‖‖‖‖‖‖‖‖‖‖‖‖‖‖‖‖‖‖‖‖‖‖‖‖‖‖‖‖‖‖‖‖‖

"That must have been horrible," I said, appalled by the situation she had described.

"He wasn't a nice man," Alissa said. "I loved my brother, and so did my mother. Marty was Marty. I figure that he was a lot like our grandfather. Marty liked to talk big, and act like he was something more than he was, but he wasn't a racist or a bigot."

"Your grandfather sounds like a lot of men his age in this area. They can't accept that the world is moving on from these outdated attitudes," Stewart said.

"You're gay, aren't you?" Alissa asked.

"Yes," Stewart said with a smile. "So is my boyfriend."

Alissa giggled at that. "I'm glad to hear it. He's a cop, isn't he?"

"A deputy in the sheriff's department. He's working on your brother's case," Stewart said. "His boss is a woman named Kanesha Berry. You'll probably be seeing them tonight or first thing tomorrow morning."

"You'll also meet Kanesha's mother, Azalea Berry, in the morning. She's my housekeeper," I said.

Alissa gazed back and forth between Stewart and me. "I guess this really is the safest place for me to be, after all."

Stewart's phone buzzed, and he pulled it out. After a moment he said, "Haskell texted. He and Kanesha will be here in a few minutes." He put the phone away. "Haskell Bates is my partner," he explained.

Alissa took a deep breath. "I don't want to talk to them by myself. Do you think I'll have to?"

"I don't know," Stewart said. "Kanesha might let Charlie stay in the room. He's helped with cases before."

"Are you a private eye?" Alissa asked. "I love those books."

"No, strictly an amateur," I said.

Alissa nodded. "Like Miss Marple." She ate more grapes.

Stewart chortled with laughter. "More than you know."

I rolled my eyes at him, and that only made him laugh harder. Alissa giggled again. Her sudden tension had eased, I realized. Good for Stewart.

Diesel meowed for attention, and that set Ramses and Dante off. Stewart pushed back from the table and stood. "I'd better get Dante upstairs. He'll have a fit when Haskell gets here. I think he likes Haskell better than he does me." He scooped up the dog and headed upstairs.

If Kanesha didn't let me stay while she interviewed Alissa, I decided to make sure Diesel did. Having the cat with her would help keep her calm. I felt bad for her. She was about the same age as Laura, but in some ways, she seemed a good bit younger.

"Would you like more mineral water?" I noticed her bottle was empty.

"Thank you," she said. "That would be great."

I retrieved it for her and set it on the table. I heard sounds of entry from the front hall. Moments later Haskell and Kanesha strode into the room. They both looked tired. I hoped Haskell would be able to stay when Kanesha was done.

I introduced the deputies to Alissa and stood, irresolute, waiting to be dismissed.

Kanesha said, "I'm sorry for your losses, Ms. Hale. I know this is a terrible time for you, but it would really help us if we could talk to you and ask a few questions."

"That's okay," Alissa said. "I want Charlie, Mr. Harris, to stay with me. All right?"

Kanesha shot me a grim look. I kept my expression bland. "Would you like some coffee? Or water?"

"I'll make some coffee," Haskell said. "I could use it."

Kanesha didn't respond to that. Instead she looked down at Alissa. "If you really want Mr. Harris here, I'll allow him to stay, as long as he remains quiet unless I ask him a question."

Alissa glanced my way, and I smiled in reassurance. "I promise I'll be quiet." I resumed my seat at the table, and Kanesha took the chair across the table from Alissa. Haskell busied himself preparing the coffeemaker.

"Before I start the interview," Kanesha said, "I need you to come tomorrow to the morgue to identify your brother. We need a formal identification by someone who knew him well."

Alissa's eyes widened, and she looked alarmed. Then she nodded. "I'll do it."

"Thank you," Kanesha said. "I know it's hard, but we have to be certain."

"I understand," Alissa replied. "Nobody here knew my brother."

Haskell joined us at the table and drew out his note-book and a pen. He found a blank page and prepared to take notes.

"Why did your brother come here, Ms. Hale?" Kanesha asked.

"He thought he'd inherited my grandfather's prop-erty," Alissa said. "He wanted to see about it. He thought maybe we could move here. Him, my mother, and me."

"He was not aware of the fact that your grandfather had leased the land and didn't own it?"

"Not when he left California," Alissa said.

"But he found out after he got here?"

Alissa nodded. "He called me four days ago and told me. He was really angry with our grandfather. Marty was all set to be a big man like our grandfather claimed to be, inheriting land and money."

"Did he tell you what his plans were then?"

"He said he'd found a lawyer who was going to get the land for him. Said he had a good case."

Kanesha glanced at me, and I nodded to indicate that I was aware of this.

"Did he mention talking to Sean Harris, Mr. Harris's son, who is also a lawyer?"

"He mentioned another lawyer but didn't tell me his name." Alissa shot me an apologetic glance. "Marty said this guy was a slick operator, and he didn't really trust him."

"How did you respond to all this when you talked with your brother?" Kanesha asked.

"I believed him, at first," Alissa said. "I always believed him, at first. He always had some scheme or other going, trying to make money without working for it." Her tone turned bitter. "I was the one working two jobs and keeping food on the table and getting the rent paid."

"When did you begin to think your brother was wrong about the ownership of the property?" Kanesha said. "Did you talk to your brother again after that conversation?"

I wondered why Kanesha was so focused on this. I supposed she was trying to ascertain whatever she could about Marty Hale's actions by what he shared with his sister.

"That was the last time I talked to him," Alissa said. "I tried calling him a couple of times, but he didn't answer. To answer your first question, I thought he might be wrong, because my mother always said you couldn't rely on what my grandfather told us." She paused. "I guess I just really wanted to believe him. I hate my life, and I wanted a new start somewhere." The anguish in her tone saddened me.

My heart ached for her. I was no longer surprised she had been so hostile toward me when she first arrived. Her hopes for a new life had crashed all around her, and her brother had been murdered. I wanted to reach out and pat her hand, but I kept still.

"We found out that your brother arrived in this area nine days ago, yet he didn't talk to either lawyer until earlier this week. Did you talk to him often after he arrived here?"

Alissa shook her head. "Only two other times before the last call."

Kanesha said, "Did your brother mention anyone he knew here, other than the two lawyers he talked about? You see, as far as we've been able to ascertain, your brother didn't have a vehicle to use, unless it was your grandfather's truck."

Alissa frowned. "My grandfather said he lent his truck while he was gone to the man who drove him to the airport. I don't remember him mentioning a name, though."

"We haven't found the truck," Kanesha said. "I guess the man who borrowed it still has it." She nodded at Haskell, and he rose and walked out into the hall. I heard him talking after a few seconds, and I reckoned he was communicating with the sheriff's department to put out an alert for the truck.

"Did your brother tell you anything about how he was getting around?" Kanesha asked.

"He said he met a guy in town. He took a bus from Memphis to get to the town, he told me. This guy he met offered to give him rides when he found out who he was."

"I don't suppose your brother mentioned his name," Kanesha said.

"Not that I recall," Alissa replied. "Marty never had any problem picking up guys. He was really handsome."

Kanesha blinked at that. "So your brother was gay."

Alissa nodded.

Kanesha pondered that for a moment. I knew she was assessing whether that could have had anything to with his murder. I hoped it didn't.

"Marty did mention one other guy," Alissa said, sounding pleased. "No name, but he said the guy was a farmer who knew our grandfather."

"Did he give you any other information about this

farmer?" Kanesha asked. The elder Martin Hale had probably been known to many farmers in the area.

"No, he didn't," Alissa said. "Marty was pretty cagey about things. He always liked knowing more than anyone else."

The picture Alissa was painting of her brother's character was not a particularly appealing one. I was curious to see a snapshot of him, wondering if he was really as handsome as she seemed to think. Sean had told me he thought the young man was an addict of some sort because of his nervous behavior.

I raised my hand, and Kanesha fixed me with her basilisk gaze. "Yes, what is it?"

"I have a question for Alissa, based on something Sean told me about Marty Hale," I said.

Kanesha nodded slowly. "All right, go ahead."

I turned to Alissa. "Marty came to see my son, Sean, a few days ago about the property. Sean mentioned that Marty seemed really nervous, almost edgy." I hesitated. "Sean wondered if your brother might be an addict of some kind."

Alissa frowned. "I don't think he was, but I actually didn't see him that often back home. I work two shifts during the day, and by the time I get home, I'm ready for bed. Marty was never up in the morning, and he usually came in after I was in bed. While my grandfather was with him, I saw him a few times, and he seemed fine then."

"You can't say for sure that he wasn't?" Kanesha asked.

"No, I can't." Alissa sounded unhappy. "I always thought he was too smart for that. My mother wouldn't have liquor in the house, even beer. She said it was because of my grandfather."

"Did your mother ever talk about your grandmother?" I asked, hoping that Kanesha wouldn't smack me down.

Kanesha shot me a look but didn't speak.

Alissa appeared confused. "My grandmother died before I was born, before my father was killed. I don't think my mother could have known her very well."

Interesting, I thought. Had Alissa's mother lied to her children? Or did she really think her mother-in-law had died?

TWENTY

IIIIIIIIIIIIIIIIIIIIIIIIIIIIIIIIIIIIIIIIII

I watched Kanesha intently to see how she reacted to Alissa's statement. I had speculated that Kanesha knew the truth about Mrs. Hale's disappearance, but she gave no sign of it. I should have expected that. The woman could be the Sphinx incarnate when she chose.

Too bad Haskell was out of the room when Alissa answered the question. He might have given something away, although he had an exceptionally good stone-face himself. My curiosity remained unsatisfied.

Haskell chose that moment to return. He caught Kanesha's eye and nodded before he resumed his seat. Alissa glanced at him curiously but did not speak.

"Your brother mentioned a farmer during one conversation," Kanesha said. "Did he say anything at all about the man?"

Alissa considered this for a moment. "I think Marty said he was old, but that was it." She shrugged. "To

Marty, anyone over forty was old, even though he was thirty-two, almost thirty-three."

He could have been talking about either Gil Jackson or Asa Luckney, I thought. They probably would have seemed old to him.

"Can you think of anything else your brother might have told you that could give us a clue to what he was doing while he was here?"

"We didn't usually talk for very long," Alissa said. "Marty didn't like talking on the phone, and his connection was kinda spotty. He said reception out there wasn't that good." She thought for a moment, then frowned. "He did say that he had seen some interesting stuff while he was out walking around the farm, but he wouldn't say what that was."

I wondered if he had stumbled across Gil Jackson's still. That would qualify as something interesting, I thought. I figured Kanesha and Haskell would agree with me.

"If you think of anything else, I'd appreciate it if you'd write it down," Kanesha said. "We don't have any strong leads at the moment into your brother's death, so anything you can tell us might help."

"I will," Alissa said. "I want whoever did this to be caught and go to jail. Marty could be annoying as hell, but he was the only brother I had." She rubbed away the sudden tears that had begun to fall. I pulled out my handkerchief and handed it to her. She gave me a tremulous smile when she accepted it to dab at her eyes.

Kanesha rose, and Haskell followed suit. "One of my officers will come by in the morning to pick you up at nine to drive you to the morgue. I'll meet you there for the formal identification."

"All right," Alissa said. "I'll be ready." Diesel, who had not left her side during the interview, rubbed his head against her thigh and warbled softly. Ramses had tried a couple of times to crawl into her lap, but each time Diesel had swatted him down. Alissa hadn't appeared to notice.

Haskell followed Kanesha to the front door, but he returned to the kitchen after he saw her out.

"Are you done for tonight?" I asked as Haskell finally poured himself a cup of coffee from the pot he'd made.

He settled in his chair and leaned back. "I am."

"Are you hungry?" I asked. "There's plenty of food. Stewart said he'd fix you anything you wanted."

"Yes, I did," Stewart announced from the doorway. He walked over to his partner and laid a hand lightly on Haskell's shoulder. "What would you like?"

Haskell looked up at him and smiled. "Whatever's handy. I'd eat a pickled ox about now."

Stewart laughed. "No pickled ox, but I can warm up the fried chicken, biscuits, and rice. I know you don't want any butter beans."

Haskell grimaced. "No butter beans. Can't stand 'em. We had them all the time when I was a kid. Everything else sounds great."

"How about you? Are you ready for something other than a snack?" Stewart nodded at Alissa.

"No, thank you." She rose from the table. "If you don't mind," she said to me, "I'm going upstairs. It's been a long day."

"You go right ahead and get some rest. If you need anything during the night, ask me. My room is the first one by the landing on the side opposite yours."

She thanked me, smiled at Stewart and Haskell, and

left the room. Diesel stared after her, and I told him he could go with her. He padded after her, but Ramses, perhaps hopeful that more food would be forthcoming, stayed in the kitchen.

While Stewart worked on warming up the food for his partner, Haskell sipped his coffee and eyed me warily. I wanted to ask him questions about the case, but I also knew he was tired and probably didn't want to talk about it. I also wondered why he hadn't mentioned to Alissa that they were cousins. He must have his reasons.

Haskell surprised me by saying, "Go ahead, Charlie. I know you're dying to ask me questions. I don't mind."

"If you're sure," I said, and he nodded. "Okay, then, there's one that I've been really curious about."

"My aunt," Haskell said before I could frame my question.

I nodded.

"The answer is, I don't know what happened to her. I was maybe five at the time. All I was told was that she left her husband," Haskell said. "I told my mother about the bones in the attic, and she just shook her head. All she said was, '*Not my sister.*' That's all I could get out of her. My dad didn't say anything at all. I tried to question them further but got nowhere."

"That must have been really difficult for you," I said.

Haskell shrugged. "I'm used to difficult when it comes to my parents." There was a faint tinge of bitterness to his words, and I could understand that.

"I'm sure if your mother had any thought those bones belonged to her sister, she would speak up," I said. "I guess we'll have to take her word for it. Those bones belonged to someone else. Possibly the wife of either Gil Jackson or Levon Luckney."

"Or even yet another runaway of some kind," Stewart said as he refilled Haskell's coffee. "Almost done with the warm-up," he added.

Haskell flashed him a smile, and I marveled again at how perfectly these two seemed to go together. Haskell, normally taciturn around most people, appeared to blossom when Stewart was near, and Stewart treated Haskell with such loving care he had to know he was cherished. In these ways they reminded me very much of Helen Louise and me and our relationship, although neither of us could ever be described as taciturn. I almost laughed aloud at the thought.

"We're checking on the whereabouts of Mrs. Jackson and Mrs. Luckney," Haskell said. "The trail is pretty cold for both of them, though. If anyone saw them leave, or knew where they intended to go, they're not saying."

"That's really frustrating," I said. "It would be helpful at least to be able to rule one or the other of them out."

Stewart set a plate in front of Haskell, and Haskell sighed happily. "Perfect. God bless Azalea."

"Amen to that," Stewart said. "My fried chicken is good, but hers is always better, even warmed up." He sat and picked up his tea.

"I suppose there's a chance those bones could have been in the ground long before either of these two wives disappeared," I said. "Has the dog been used yet?"

"She worked in the area around the house," Haskell said. "A few acres. Didn't turn up anything. Seton's going to have another go tomorrow. Weather should be fine."

"I really wish I could see her in action," I said. "Kanesha said I couldn't, though."

Haskell put down a drumstick devoid of any meat and said, "You can't follow around with the dog, but there's

169

no reason you can't be in the house while she's working. I imagine you need to take Ms. Hale out there to see the place." He picked up a thigh.

"I think you're right," I said.

Stewart grinned. "Just don't tell Kanesha he said that to you."

I put my hand over my heart. "I swear. I'll make her think it was my idea."

"She'll believe that," Stewart said.

Haskell nodded and helped himself to a forkful of biscuit and gravy. Watching him eat biscuits and gravy made me feel hungry again, but I knew the feeling would pass. I was still stuffed from my own meal.

Haskell dropped a few bites of chicken for Ramses, until Stewart shook his head at his partner. Thereafter Ramses sat watching Haskell forlornly, uttering the occasional sad meow.

"Was there anything around the murder scene to give any clues?" I asked.

"Footprints," Haskell said. "Boots, by the look of them, but the way the tree fell on the area, they were badly disturbed."

"Not really usable," I said, disappointed.

Haskell shook his head and reached for his coffee.

"You don't have much to go on," Stewart said. "This could be one that won't get solved."

"Maybe," Haskell said. "It's early days, though. We've still got a lot of canvassing to do. We need to find whoever was giving Hale rides back and forth to town. That road isn't a busy one, but people do drive it on a regular basis. We're hoping someone will come forward with the sighting of a vehicle turning in there or in the yard. Or seeing Hale in town with someone."

"People might not have thought anything much about it," I said. "Did anyone know Mr. Hale had gone to California? Or that he died there?"

"They might not have known he was out of town, but after his obituary ran in the paper, they would have probably seen it," Haskell said.

"Provided that they take the paper," Stewart said.

"You're forgetting the county grapevine," Haskell said with a brief smile. "The minute one person finds out about a death, the news starts spreading. Same as here in town. Just ask my mother. She spends half her life on the phone talking to somebody."

"You're right," Stewart said. "Should have realized."

"What if the person who was giving Hale rides is the one who killed him?" I asked.

"That's entirely possible," Haskell replied. "But not certain."

"What about the real estate guy? Marvin Watkins," I said.

"Hard to come up with a motive for him, I should think," Stewart said.

"Hale may have led him on about the property, which Watkins seems to want pretty badly," I said. "When he found out Hale had no rights to it, Watkins might have killed him in anger."

"Not if it meant getting one of his three-thousand-dollar suits wet." Stewart laughed. "Marv, as he insists you call him, goes to our gym. He's a slave to his wardrobe."

"I can't see him killing Hale out in the woods," Haskell said. "Stewart's right. Watkins is one of the most fastidious guys I've met." He glanced at Stewart. "Even more so than this one."

Stewart rolled his eyes. "Just because I like things neat doesn't mean I'm *fastidious*." He pronounced the word as if it were a nasty insult.

"Sure," Haskell said.

"It's far-fetched, I know," I said, ignoring this byplay, "and he did seem like the fussy type. He was also a little too pushy. I didn't care for him, so I find it easy to cast him as the murderer."

"Remind me never to get on your bad side," Stewart said.

I looked at Haskell. "I think the word is *facetious*, not fastidious."

Haskell laughed, something I rarely saw him do. "That too," he said.

Stewart, in mock annoyance, snatched up Haskell's plate and took it to the sink. "Really," he said. He grinned at us.

Haskell pushed back his chair and took his mug and silverware to the sink. He set them down and wrapped his arm around Stewart. He whispered something, and Stewart replied.

Haskell released Stewart and bade me good night. "Seems like days since I had a full night's sleep."

"Rest well," I said, and he nodded as he walked into the hall.

"I'll finish with that," I told Stewart. "You go on upstairs."

Stewart flashed me a grateful smile. "You're a prince, Charlie. See you in the morning."

He hurried after his partner.

I scraped the chicken bones and bits of rice and congealing gravy into the garbage beneath the sink, and then I rinsed the plate before putting it into the dishwasher. I took care of the mug and the silverware and made sure the coffeemaker was off.

Ramses watched me the entire time. He was ever hopeful, I thought.

"Come along, you little beggar," I said to him as I turned off the lights in the kitchen. "Let's go upstairs and get in bed. I'm going to read, and you can do whatever you like."

He raced up the stairs ahead of me, but to my surprise he wasn't in my room when I got there. I suspected he had gone in search of Diesel, now that there was no food on offer. Alissa must have left her door lightly ajar, because I didn't hear Ramses scratching at it.

After my nightly ablutions, I picked up the Donna Andrews book, intent on finishing it before I turned out the light. I had read about twenty more pages before my phone rang. It was Sean.

"Hi, Son, what's up?"

"I found out the name of the lawyer that Hale consulted about trying to sue to keep the estate," Sean said. "She had the nerve to call me today and ask if I knew how to contact Hale's mother."

TWENTY-ONE

"Good grief," I said. "Is this person anyone you know?"

Sean laughed. "Unfortunately, yes. She's one of the ethically challenged attorneys I alluded to the other day. Gloria Batson. She runs after every ambulance she sees."

"Not good," I said. "I'm sure you brushed her off."

"Tried to," Sean replied. "She's the limpet kind, however. Did Hale's sister arrive? Is she there with you?"

"She's here. At first she was hostile, insisted on going out to the farmhouse, but I managed to calm her down. Diesel, Ramses, and Dante did the rest. She loves animals." I laughed a little self-consciously. "Apparently, I remind her of her stepfather, whom she loved."

"That's good," Sean said. "That means she'll talk to you. Have you managed to find out anything useful?"

I told him about the conversation I'd had with her and

Stewart, then went on to give him a summary of the interview with Kanesha and Haskell.

When I had finished, Sean said, "That doesn't give us much to go on. Before I forget, I looked at your grandfather's will again for the names of his witnesses. I didn't recognize them. I'll see if I can track the men down, but they could well be dead by now, if they were contemporaries of your grandfather."

"I'll give Miss An'gel and Miss Dickce a call. Melba too. Maybe they can come up with somebody who knew my grandfather pretty well all those years ago."

"Good idea," Sean said. "I've got to go, Dad. I'm getting reminded that it's time for me to help Alex with the dishes. Talk to you tomorrow."

"Give Alex my love," I said before he ended the call.

I set the phone aside and picked up my book. I read until Helen Louise called me around ten. We talked for about fifteen minutes, until she declared her intention of getting into bed before midnight at least one night during her vacation. I still hadn't mentioned the murder, because I didn't want to distract her from her time with her friends. She'd be home on Sunday. I could tell her everything then.

Time for lights-out, I decided. I turned onto my left side, and Ramses, who had appeared a few minutes ago, wiggled into position by my stomach. This was his favorite place to sleep lately. Before long we were both asleep.

When I woke the next morning, I found Ramses still curled up next to me. Diesel had joined us at some point during the night. He lay stretched out near Ramses, his head on his pillow. I smiled at the sight of them, one so large and the other much smaller in comparison. Ramses would soon be a year old, yet he looked a mere kitten next to his big brother.

Downstairs a quarter of an hour later, accompanied by the cats, I smelled the welcome scents of coffee and bacon wafting from the kitchen. To my surprise, I found Alissa seated at the table chatting to Azalea. The young woman had a mug of coffee in front of her.

"Good morning, ladies," I said during a brief pause in their conversation. I helped myself to coffee, had a few sips, then set my mug on the table. "I'm going to get the paper."

Diesel and Ramses remained in the kitchen, their attention devoted to Azalea and Alissa.

Out in the morning sunshine on what already promised to be another hot, muggy August day, I found the newspaper next to one of the flower beds along the front of the house. I opened the paper and scanned the headlines on the front page. As I had expected, there was another article about young Martin Hale's murder. I perused it quickly as I made my way back inside, out of the heat.

Nothing new. There was no mention of the bones Diesel and I had found in the attic this time. I supposed the paper considered the murder more important. There wouldn't have been anything new to write about, though. Evidently Kanesha had not released the news about the missing body parts to the press. Not until Dewey Seton and his cadaver dog managed to discover something, I figured.

I took my seat at the table and laid the paper aside.

Alissa looked at it for a moment. "Is there anything in it about Marty?"

"Yes, there's an article on the front page," I said. "You're welcome to the paper."

She nodded and reached for it. I watched her with concern while she read. I hoped there wouldn't be anything in it to upset her, other than the fact of her brother's death.

Her expression remained impassive, however. She set the paper aside and picked up her apple. Then I saw her wipe a tear away.

"Are you okay?" I asked.

Diesel meowed and placed a paw on her leg. Alissa nodded. "It just makes it so real, seeing it in the paper. Last night I dreamed about Marty, and we were laughing and having fun. At the beach we liked to go to sometimes."

"That's what you think about," Azalea said, turning from the stove. "You think about the good things. Don't let the bad stuff in. I'll be praying for you."

"Thank you, ma'am," Alissa said. "I'll do that."

Azalea set a plate of scrambled eggs, bacon, and buttered toast in front of me. I waited for her to do the same for Alissa, but she didn't.

Alissa noticed that I wasn't eating, and she frowned. "Oh, I don't ever eat much for breakfast. Especially not today." Her face clouded. "I don't want to be sick. You know."

"Yes, I know. Would you like me to go with you?"

"No, I'll be okay. I have to do this for Marty," she said. "But maybe afterward, we could go out to the farm? I really don't remember it, but I'd like to see it."

"I'll be glad to take you," I said.

While I ate breakfast, doling out bits of bacon to the cats, I listened to Azalea chatting with the young woman about California. Azalea had never been there and was curious about it. Alissa lived in the central part of the state, not far from San Luis Obispo, where her stepfather had worked on one of the ranches. This surprised me, because when I thought of California, it was always of Los Angeles or the Bay Area.

I remembered that a terrific series of mysteries that I loved, the Benni Harper books by Earlene Fowler, were set in that area, and I asked Alissa if she had read them.

"Every one of them. It's fun to read about places you know," she said, smiling. "I met the author one time when she came to the library, and she was so nice. I love to read, but these days I don't have much time because of work. I haven't been to the library in over a year."

"That's too bad," I said.

Alissa shrugged. "One of these days, things will be better."

Azalea and I exchanged glances. The sympathy in her gaze no doubt mirrored mine. I felt so bad for this young woman, who seemed to have a life of drudgery back in California.

"Aren't you going to the library today?" Azalea asked me.

"No, remember, it's one of my off days." A couple of months ago, after my grandson's first birthday, I had decided to cut back my volunteer hours at the public library. I wanted more time to see my grandchildren. Instead of working every Friday, I now worked the first and third Fridays of the month. Today was the fourth Friday.

"Maybe we could go to the library, too?" Alissa looked hopefully at me.

"We can," I said, "but if you're looking for books to read, I practically have a library myself. You're welcome to go through it and find a book to read."

I pushed my chair back, although I hadn't quite finished breakfast. "Come with me."

Azalea picked up my plate and set it on the stove to keep it warm, and Alissa, along with the cats, followed me down the hall to the den. Alissa took one look at the overflowing shelves that covered two walls, and she gasped.

"You must be rich to have all these books," she said.

"No, not rich, but I've been collecting books since before I was your age. I'm a librarian, too, and I've always loved books and reading. Look around and see if there's anything you'd like to read." I pointed to the mysteries. "You might want to start there."

She turned shining eyes in my direction. "Thank you," she whispered. "Can I do it now?"

"Go right ahead," I said. "I'm going back to finish my breakfast." I checked my watch. "You still have over an hour before a deputy will be here to pick you up."

I watched her for a moment. She gently ran a hand along the spines of the books on one shelf. I smiled again and left her to her exploration.

Azalea replaced my plate when I sat, and I thanked her for keeping it warm. "She may be in there awhile. She seemed entranced by all the books."

"That poor child has been telling me about her family. That mother of hers ought to whipped, if you ask me. I don't think there's anything wrong with her but selfishness. She's bone-deep lazy. And her brother wasn't much better. Putting all the burden on this child." Azalea rarely got angry, but she was now.

"While she's here, we'll take good care of her," I said. I reserved judgment on Alissa's mother, because I didn't know the particulars of her case. She could well be in no condition to hold down a job. In the late Marty's case, Azalea was probably right. I had known men like him before.

Alissa hadn't returned by the time I finished eating. I went back upstairs to shower and dress for the day. When I came back to the kitchen for more coffee, it was a quarter to nine. Alissa sat at the table, engrossed in an old paperback whose cover I couldn't see. Ramses and Diesel lay stretched out on either side of her chair. There was no sign of Azalea.

I watched Alissa as I refilled my mug. She didn't seem to notice me, not even when I sat at the table. I continued to observe her as I sipped my coffee. A few minutes later the doorbell rang, and she flinched and looked up. Her eyes widened in alarm.

"That must be for me." She laid the book carefully aside, and I saw that it was an older novel by Elizabeth Peters, the second Amelia Peabody book. Alissa certainly had good taste.

"I'll answer the door," I said, rising. "You wait here."

The deputy waiting on the stoop was the same young woman who had delivered Alissa last night. I invited her to step inside, but she declined politely.

"If Ms. Hale is ready," she said, "I'll wait for her here."

"She'll be right out." I closed the door and walked back to the kitchen.

"It is for you. The same deputy as last night," I said.

Alissa drew a deep breath and stood. "That's good. She was nice to me."

"Are you sure you don't want me to come along?" I had no wish to visit the morgue, but I felt protective of the young woman, so obviously dreading the coming encounter with her brother's corpse.

Alissa shook her head. "No, I'll be okay." She gave me a brief, trembling smile, then resolutely headed for the door. I remained in the kitchen.

Now would be a good time to give Miss An'gel and Miss Dickce a call, I decided. They were early risers, and I wanted to catch them before they left home. They had many obligations around town, owing to the various charities they supported and the organizations to which they devoted their time.

I always called Miss An'gel. As the elder sister, she assumed it as her right to be the one who everyone talked to first. I knew the proper protocol.

"Good morning," I said. We exchanged the usual pleasantries, then, "Do you have a few minutes to chat?"

"Yes, I do," Miss An'gel replied. "I assume you have questions for me."

I chuckled, and I knew Miss An'gel would be smiling. "You know me too well. I do. Sean and I are trying to track down anyone in the area who might have been a friend of my grandfather's. I know it's a long shot, but it would help if we could ask friends of his a few questions."

"Have you run across Asa Luckney yet?" Miss An'gel said.

"I met him yesterday, as a matter of fact," I replied, somewhat startled.

"Asa worked on your grandfather's farm from the

181

time he was a boy, and your grandfather took a great interest in him," Miss An'gel said. "He probably knew your grandfather as well as anyone. If your grandfather had any secrets, Asa probably knew them."

"I had no idea that Mr. Luckney knew my grandfather so well. He's been leasing land from Martin Hale for about twenty years, he told me."

"I always found it odd that your grandfather gave Hale a life lease to the property," Miss An'gel said. "I really expected he would have done that for Asa, or at least have left him some of the land outright, once your father made it clear he didn't want to farm."

"That doesn't sound good," I said.

"I know," Miss An'gel said. "People at the time thought it strange. Martin Hale went strutting around town, telling everyone he met about it. He was always puffing himself up like that."

"He worked for my grandfather, didn't he?" I asked.

"Yes. Your grandfather kept him on, despite Hale's drunken escapades. He felt sorry for Hale's family. He respected Hale's father and felt sorry for Hale's wife and son."

"You said my grandfather took a great interest in Mr. Luckney," I said. "Why would he favor Hale over Mr. Luckney, do you think?"

"I don't know," Miss An'gel said. "I hesitate to say it, but somehow I think Hale must have talked your grandfather into it."

"Or else he threatened my grandfather in some way if he didn't," I said slowly.

"That's possible. I'm sorry, Charlie. I know this must be hard for you."

Neither of us mentioned the bones in the attic, but I knew she must be thinking of them as much as I was. Hale's hold over my grandfather might have had something to do with those bones.

Was my grandfather a killer after all?

TWENTY-TWO

I decided that if my grandfather had been responsible for those bones, I would have to face up to it. He couldn't have been the one to put them in the attic, though, surely? That must have been done long after he died.

I had my hopes pinned on Dewey Seton and his dog for finding the original resting place of the person whose bones they were. I prayed that today's search would yield clues that would lead to the truth.

Belatedly, I remembered that Miss An'gel was still on the call with me. "I'm sorry, I spaced out for a moment."

"No need to apologize," Miss An'gel replied warmly. "I understand what you must be thinking about. Don't make up your mind yet. There is still so much that's unknown. Remember that."

"I will, thank you." I took a calming breath. "Is there anyone besides Mr. Luckney that I could talk to?"

"I'll have to think about that, and I'll ask Sister to as

well," Miss An'gel replied. "That was a long time ago, after all."

"I appreciate anyone you might come up with," I said. "I'll let you go now."

"Take care, Charlie," Miss An'gel said.

I set the phone down. I wanted to find Asa Luckney and talk to him right away, but I knew Kanesha would not want me to do that. At least, not until she had thoroughly questioned him herself. Then she might not mind if I talked to him about my grandfather.

Had she talked to him at all about any of this? Would he have spoken with her openly? Would he open up more to me because I was his mentor's grandson? Maybe I should suggest that to Kanesha.

Too many questions crowded my brain, making me restless and wanting action. The lack of progress frustrated the heck out of me. Kanesha might have made progress, though, that I hadn't heard about, and that added to my irritation. I hated being kept in the dark, even though I realized I didn't have any official status in this investigation.

Time to get my thoughts channeled in a slightly different direction. Alissa might return soon, and then we would drive out to the farm. I hadn't yet called the historical society to see about examining any papers in their collection relevant to my family. I went to the den and got on the computer to look up their number. The website had only minimal information, but it did include a phone number.

I was pleasantly surprised when a woman answered. I identified myself, mentioned that I was a librarian, and that I wanted to look at items relating to my family history.

She identified herself as Aleta Boudreaux, and I recognized the name. She was a public library patron, and I had chatted with her a few times there.

"I didn't know you're a member of the historical society," I said.

"One of the faithful few," she said cheerfully. "I try to volunteer a few hours every week."

"That's great," I said. "I was told that the society has irregular hours for the museum and archive."

"Yes, that's unfortunately true," she said. "If we could afford a full-time paid employee, we could at least be open regular hours during the week. But our budget barely covers the utility bills."

"That's not good." I wished I had the money to do something about the situation, but that kind of money was beyond my means. Unless I sold the farm, I thought. I would have to think about that.

"When were you thinking about coming to do your research?" Aleta said.

"Will anyone be there later this afternoon?" I asked.

Aleta sounded regretful when she replied. "No, I'm here only until noon. Could you possibly come by this morning?"

I could, but only if I disappointed Alissa. And myself, I realized, because I wanted to be on the scene, as it were, in case Dr. Seton and his dog found anything of significance.

"I'm afraid not," I said. "Perhaps sometime next week?"

"I'll be here on Wednesday from nine to noon," Aleta replied. "Will that work?"

"Yes, that will be fine. I'll plan to see you then." We exchanged final pleasantries, and I ended the call.

Wednesday was one of my days to work at the college, but since I worked only part-time, the library director didn't mind if I occasionally switched days. I would let her know on Monday that I planned to work Tuesday instead of Wednesday next week. There shouldn't be a problem. I was eager to get a look at the historical society's archives. I would like to confirm what Mrs. Carraway had written about the Harris family in her book.

I should join the historical society, I decided. Once I did, I could broach the idea of volunteering to get their archive organized. Perhaps a few hours once a month? That wouldn't cut too deeply into my free time. Now that I was going to be a grandfather for the third time, I didn't want to overcommit myself and cut into potential grandchild playtime.

Diesel interrupted my musings by warbling loudly, and I glanced down at him. Then I heard the doorbell ring. He had heard someone arrive before I did.

"Come with me, then." I realized Ramses hadn't joined us. He was no doubt *helping* Azalea somewhere in the house.

Alissa appeared haggard when I opened the door to her. I knew that having to view her brother's corpse must have been a harrowing experience.

"Come on in, and let's get you more coffee. You need a hot, sweet drink, and you'll feel better."

She let me shepherd her into the kitchen. Diesel walked beside her, uttering anxious chirps. Alissa didn't speak until she'd had a few sips of the hot coffee I prepared for her.

"Thank you," she said, her color back to normal now. "I knew it would be terrible, but it was horrible seeing poor Marty there." She sniffed, and I thought she was going to cry. She drew a deep breath and stiffened her back. "At least his face wasn't hurt," she said.

"I'm sorry you had to do that. I can only imagine how difficult it was for you."

She smiled at me. "Thanks. I think you really do understand." She returned to her coffee.

"When you're ready we'll drive out to the farm. Diesel will come with us. I take him almost everywhere with me."

"That's really awesome," Alissa said as she stroked the cat's large head. "He's the sweetest cat I've ever met."

"Is there anything else you need before we go?" I asked, thinking she might be a bit hungry, now that the worst was over.

She shook her head. "I'm fine. I couldn't eat anything right now." She grimaced. "Maybe by lunchtime." She drained her coffee and refused a refill. "I'm ready."

"Then off we go," I said. Diesel preceded us to the kitchen door and into the garage. I opened the passenger door for Alissa, then the back door for Diesel. Alissa turned in her seat to look at him. "He doesn't mind riding in a car?"

I laughed. "Not at all. He is used to it, but even when I first got him, he didn't seem to mind. He's always gone with me when I leave the house, except to church and the grocery store."

That wasn't completely true, but it was close enough for the moment.

"He really likes people, doesn't he?" Alissa said, still watching Diesel stretched out comfortably on the backseat.

"He does," I said. "But he doesn't like everybody. If he doesn't like someone, I always treat that person warily. He's seldom wrong."

"Dogs are like that, too," Alissa said, finally turning back to face forward. "We had a dog like that when I was little. He was the best. Just a mutt, but I loved him."

I encouraged her to talk about the dog on the drive out to the farm. Anything to keep her mind off the horror of her morning.

Once I'd turned off the highway onto the road that ran past the farm, she broke off her reminiscences. "Is it far now?"

"No, we'll be there in less than five minutes." I saw that she had tensed, her body stiff. "Do you remember the house at all?"

"Not really," she said, her voice low. "I was so little when we left. I don't recall anything right now."

Her reaction was interesting. I wondered if it was unconscious memory of her experiences in the house making her feel this way. I had expected her to be more relaxed, plain curious, if nothing else.

A few minutes later I slowed the car to turn into the driveway. I glanced at Alissa a couple of times, and her grip on the door handle looked tight. I braked the car and cut the engine. "Here we are." I had expected to see several vehicles here, official ones from the sheriff's department. If they were out working with the dog, they hadn't parked at the house.

Alissa stared through the windshield at the front of the house. She relaxed enough to loosen her grip on the door. Diesel meowed, wanting out. Once we arrived, he didn't like staying in the vehicle.

I opened my door, and Diesel leaped into my seat as soon as I stepped out of the car. Alissa hadn't opened her door yet. I went around to her side of the car and opened the door for her.

"Come on. I know something's bothering you, but I'm here, and nothing's going to harm you," I said.

She looked up at me warily. "I didn't think I remembered anything." She bit her lip. "I don't, much, I just got this scared feeling when I saw the house."

"There's nothing in there now that can hurt you. Let's go sit on the porch for a few minutes. We'll take it slow, okay?" I held out a hand.

Alissa grasped my hand and climbed out of the car. Diesel meowed at her and rubbed against her legs. "You'll stay with me, won't you, big boy?" The cat trilled, and Alissa smiled.

We walked across the yard and mounted the steps to the porch. I motioned Alissa to one of the rocking chairs, and I took the other, about six feet away. Diesel settled beside Alissa's rocker.

Slowly she began to rock, seemingly impervious to the humid air. I was already starting to sweat, and I hoped we could go inside soon.

"Looking out that way," she said, gesturing to the yard and beyond, "it looks so peaceful and so quiet. It's really pretty out here." She continued to rock and gaze out at the vista before her.

I agreed silently. It was peaceful and quiet here. Not much traffic, only the sounds of birds now and then, and a faint rumble of farm machinery in the distance. It would be easy to fall asleep here if it weren't so warm.

After ten minutes had passed, I'd had enough of the humidity. I stood and looked down at Alissa. "Why don't we go inside now? The longer you put it off, the worse it will seem."

The rocking stopped. Alissa stared up at me, and I

could see she was calmer now, but still afraid. "Diesel won't let anything harm you."

I realized that my words could be interpreted to mean that there were malevolent spirits in the house, if Alissa were at all worried about paranormal phenomena. I hadn't felt anything of the kind in my previous two visits here. Was she actually afraid of ghosts?

I didn't voice these thoughts. I went to the door and unlocked it. Holding it open, I gestured for Alissa and Diesel to enter the house. Diesel complied right away, but Alissa moved slowly. She paused on the threshold, and I patted her shoulder.

She took a couple of deep breaths and then stepped inside the house. I closed the door behind us, grateful to be inside with some cooler air. Alissa looked around and began to relax. Whatever she was worried about, this area appeared to be fine.

We began to explore the house, and I told her what I remembered from the time my grandparents lived here. "I was young when my grandparents died, and that's when your grandfather took over. My father didn't want to be a farmer, you see, and my grandfather wanted someone to run the farm. I think he hoped eventually either I or my children would want to live here. That's why he only leased the land to your grandfather."

"Are you going to be a farmer?" Alissa asked.

"No, not at my age," I said. "My son is a lawyer, and my daughter is a college professor. Neither of them wants to be a farmer, I'm sure. For now, I'll continue to lease out the farmland, but keep the house in the family."

Alissa nodded, and we progressed down the hall. "I'll

show you where your brother was living while he was here."

"Okay," she said.

I opened the door of the outer bedroom, and she walked slowly in. I could see that she had tensed a little, probably bracing herself for seeing her brother's belongings.

"It's that door over there." I pointed to the opposite wall. "There's another, smaller room behind it." I walked toward the door, Alissa slowly following.

I opened the door and turned on the light. Alissa stepped forward to peek inside. Her color drained, and she shrank back. Her expression wild, she said hoarsely, "That's where she always was. I'm not going in there."

She turned and ran out into the hall.

TWENTY-THREE

Startled, I stood there for a moment. Diesel bolted after Alissa, and I went after him. I found her at the front door, her hand trembling on the knob. Diesel was rubbing against her legs and warbling.

"What's wrong? A bad memory?" I asked. She still looked ashen, and I feared she might faint.

I opened the door and led her back to the rocking chair. She subsided into it and began to rock. Diesel and I continued to watch her in some anxiety. Apparently, the motion calmed her, though, because her breathing slowed and her color came back.

I pulled the other chair closer to hers and sat, waiting for her to speak.

"I'm okay, now," she said. "I don't know what it was, but I couldn't go in that room. Did I say anything?" She stared hard at me.

"You did." I repeated her words to her, and she frowned.

"Any idea who the woman was in that room? Or why you were afraid of her?" I asked.

Obviously bewildered, Alissa shook her head. "I don't know. I don't really even remember anyone, but I know I was afraid of whatever was in that room."

I considered that for a moment. She'd been a toddler when her mother took her and her brother to California with the woman's new husband. I never had clear memories of my life at that age, and I didn't imagine most children did, at least after they reached adulthood. Perhaps it was a repressed memory, brought back by the sight of that room. After all, it might not have changed much since she lived in the house.

"Your grandmother was gone, and the only other woman in the house was your mother, right?"

Alissa nodded. "I think that's right. I don't know who this other woman could have been."

"Maybe she was a maid, or a nanny who was helping your mother with you and your brother," I said.

"Could be," Alissa said. "I'll have to ask my mom about that. I don't have to go back in there, do I?"

"Of course not." I was glad now that I had persuaded her to stay at my house rather than staying here by herself. If she had gone into the room and had the same reaction while she was here by herself, well, I didn't like to think about the outcome of that scenario.

"You sit here with Diesel. I'm going back into the house for a look around." I rose from my chair.

Alissa shot me an anxious glance but didn't try to stop me. Diesel sat beside her chair, watching.

I entered the house and walked back down the hall to

the room that had frightened Alissa so badly. I stepped inside and looked around. I felt nothing, other than my own curiosity. Nothing malevolent here that I could detect.

Yet something had obviously happened in this room to frighten the toddler Alissa. Had the woman who occupied the room at the time been mean to her? Perhaps she had spanked, or even beaten, the child. I hated the thought of that, but it would account for Alissa's terrified reaction.

I would ask Asa Luckney about this when I saw him. Surely he would know who this woman was and her role in the household. This was the first I'd heard of her. I wondered if Kanesha knew about her, or Azalea? Surely Azalea would have said something if she did.

Could the bones belong to this mysterious woman? Could she have been one of the so-called missing women in this case? I thought it far more likely, though, that she was an unknown quantity. Other scenarios from my experience with Gothic fiction came fleetingly to mind, but they were too bizarre to contemplate in this setting.

I went back to the porch to check on Alissa.

"I'm glad I didn't stay here," Alissa said suddenly, before I had a chance to speak. "I would have lost my mind if I'd opened that door all by myself."

"I'm glad you didn't, either," I said. "Whatever you experienced in that room, it was obviously traumatic for you."

The sound of approaching vehicles alerted me to the arrival of the sheriff's department. I looked down the driveway. Along with two patrol cars, I saw a large pickup, the kind with a backseat. That must be Dr. Seton and his dog.

Once parked, the people alit from their vehicles, and Kanesha strode forward and onto the porch. Not far behind her was a small, wiry man in boots and work clothes accompanied by a beautiful dog. A Belgian Malinois, I recalled. I had never seen one before, but this one must be a perfect specimen of the breed.

"Good morning," Kanesha said. "Ms. Hale, Mr. Harris, this is Dr. Dewey Seton and his dog, Fleur."

I rose to shake the man's hand, and Fleur held out her paw as well. I shook it as I looked around for Diesel. He had not moved from Alissa's side, but he was staring curiously at the dog.

Dr. Seton nodded at my cat. "Maine Coon, I hear. Beautiful animal. Is he used to dogs?"

"A poodle," I said. "Neither he nor I have ever seen a Belgian Malinois before. She's gorgeous."

"Thank you." Seton smiled up at me. He couldn't have been more than about five five, I decided. His bright red hair and light dusting of freckles reminded me of a boyhood friend whose name had long slipped from my memory.

Seton chuckled. "You don't remember me, do you?"

I shook my head. "I don't recall that we ever met before."

"We used to live next to you and your parents for a couple of years," he said. "Then my father got a job at Cornell, and we moved to New York State."

"That was you?" I remembered the boy next door had been about three years younger than I, but we had played together often. That had been over forty years ago, so it was no wonder I hadn't recognized him.

"Yep, that was me." He chuckled again. "As you can see, I didn't grow much. You certainly did."

Diesel had emerged from his spot by Alissa to investigate the dog. Cat and dog stood almost nose to nose. Diesel didn't hiss or try to swipe at Fleur, and she stared curiously at the cat. Diesel meowed and turned to walk away, back to Alissa.

"It's good to see you again. I thought you looked a bit familiar, like a boy I knew when I was a kid, but I couldn't remember your name," I said. "It's been a long time."

"Sure has. When the job came open at the college, I had the urge to move back South," Seton replied. "I was getting tired of the cold Northeast in the winter. This is much better, and everyone here has been really welcoming."

"I know the authorities here"—I nodded to indicate Kanesha—"are delighted to have your expertise, and Fleur's, to help them."

"We are," Kanesha said. "Now, Dr. Seton, we really need to get moving on this search. Are you and Fleur ready?"

"We are," Seton replied. "Let me give Fleur the scent again, and we'll follow where she leads." He glanced at me. "Catch up with you later, Charlie."

I nodded. He, Fleur, and Kanesha exited the porch and joined her officers in the yard. Seton and Fleur went to the truck. Seton extracted something for the dog to sniff, then waited for her to start tracking. She stood still for a moment, then, when Seton called out "Seek," she started moving.

I wanted so badly to follow along, but I knew Kanesha would send me right back. I resumed my seat in the rocker and took stock of Alissa. She hadn't spoken, only nodded to acknowledge Kanesha and Seton.

"What is that dog doing?" she asked.

"She's a cadaver dog," I replied. "She's trained to find dead bodies."

"Who else is dead?" she asked, puzzled. "I mean, they already found Marty."

I realized that she didn't know about the bones that Diesel and I had discovered in the attic here. I told her about it.

She shivered in the heat. "That's so creepy. Who was it?"

"We don't know. Fleur is looking for where the bones were originally interred," I said. "Once we find the burial place, we may find clues to her identity."

"Her?" Alissa said sharply. "You know it was a woman."

"Yes, Dr. Seton is a forensic anthropologist. He studies old bones, and he had a preliminary look at the skeleton. He thinks she was an adult woman around sixty, give or take a few years."

"Do you think she could be the woman in that room?" Alissa's eyes widened in fear.

I patted her shoulder in reassurance. "It's possible, but there are several women connected to your grandfather and mine who disappeared many years ago. It could be any one of them, or someone else entirely. The bones could have come from a really old burial, for example. My family has lived on this land since before the Civil War, and the Native Americans before that."

Alissa appeared reassured by this. I wished I felt that. There were too many unanswered questions.

"How about something to drink?" I asked. "Azalea put together some drinks and snacks in a cooler. I'll go get it."

Alissa nodded, and Diesel came with me back to the car. I extracted the cooler from the trunk. Inside the cooler I found several bottles of mineral water and a couple of the still water I preferred. Another container held fruit, cheese, and crackers.

I handed her a bottle of mineral water. She declined the food, and I put it back inside the cooler for later.

We sipped at our water in silence. I left the porch briefly to find a bowl in the kitchen so I could give Diesel water as well. When I returned, I found Alissa standing at the top of the porch steps, craning her neck in the direction that Seton, the dog, and the sheriff's deputies had gone.

"See anything?" I called out. Setting down the bowl I had rinsed out in the kitchen, I poured water into it. Diesel came immediately to lap at it.

Alissa came back to her rocker. "No, they must have gone into those woods back there. I couldn't spot them." She paused for a breath. "That's where Marty died, isn't it?"

I nodded. "Yes, somewhere in there."

"I don't want to see the place," Alissa said. "I don't want to think of him there, and if I see it, I'll never forget it."

"Good decision," I said. "Would you like another bottle?"

"No, thank you," she said.

We rocked in silence for a while. The water had cooled me down briefly, but now I was starting to sweat again. "Do you think you'd be okay back in the house, maybe in the front parlor?"

She looked at me and frowned. "You're sweating, aren't you? I'm sorry. I'm used to heat, and it doesn't bother me. I'll go in with you. As long as I don't go near that room, I'll be okay, I think."

"Thank you." I picked up the cooler. Alissa opened the door for us, and the three of us went into the parlor. I felt better right away. I set the cooler on the floor near the settee, and Alissa sat there with Diesel at her feet. I chose a chair a few feet across from her.

"I don't remember this room at all," Alissa said as she surveyed it.

"I remember it, vaguely, from when my grandparents lived here. I think that settee was here then. My great-aunt left it behind after my grandfather died. She took some of the family pieces to her house, and my parents chose a few as well."

"Does that mean the rest of this belonged to my grandfather?" Alissa frowned.

"I believe so," I said. "We'll have to check with Sean. I don't know the contents of your grandfather's will, but I imagine he left everything to you and your brother. You can probably sell it all if you want to."

"I don't know anything about antiques," Alissa said. "I have no idea how to sell this stuff."

"Don't worry about it now," I said. "Time enough for that later. There are reputable furniture dealers in town who can advise you."

She nodded. "That sounds good."

My phone rang, and I saw Sean was calling. "Hello, Son, what's up?"

"Where are you, Dad? At home?"

"No, I'm at the farm. I brought Alissa out here to see it."

"Are you going to be there awhile?" he asked.

"Probably. Dr. Seton and his dog are here with Kanesha and some deputies. They're out in the woods, I think, searching."

"Okay. I'm going to run out. I have Mr. Hale's will,

and I need to talk to Alissa about it. Now's as good a time as any." He ended the call.

"My son," I explained as I put away my phone. "He's coming out here to talk to you about your grandfather's will."

"Okay," Alissa said. "Marty mentioned a will, but he wouldn't tell me what was in it."

I heard steps on the porch. After a few seconds, a knock sounded on the door. I called out, "Come in."

Kanesha appeared in the parlor doorway. "We found the burial site in the woods."

TWENTY-FOUR

‖‖‖

My heart started beating faster after Kanesha's announcement. "Where in the woods? Near the house?"

"Several hundred yards into the woods," Kanesha replied. "Dr. Seton is examining the area right now. I hope he's able to find something that will help us, besides the site itself." She turned to leave.

"There wasn't a marker of any kind?" I asked.

Kanesha turned back to face us. "A large stone that had been knocked over at some point stood at one end. It might have been a marker, but there's nothing inscribed on it."

"Maybe this will turn out to be a very old burial," I said.

"We don't know yet. The dog identified it as the place where the bones had lain, but the dog can't tell us how long they were there. I don't know if there's any way to figure out when the bones were removed, but if there is,

I have confidence Dr. Seton will do it." She turned to leave, and this time I didn't call her back.

"That's really sad," Alissa remarked. "Nothing to tell anybody who you were."

"It is," I said. Finding the grave was a step forward, but that it was an unmarked burial didn't get us much further.

I heard footsteps on the porch again, and moments later Sean walked into the parlor. I introduced him to Alissa, and they shook hands. Diesel came forward for a scratch of the head, then Sean gave me a searching look.

"What's the matter, Dad? You're pretty pale," he said.

"Unsettling thoughts," I said. "I'll explain later. I do have news, though. Dr. Seton's dog tracked down the burial site of the bones I found."

Sean took a seat in the other chair across from the settee. "Did that tell us anything?"

"No, it wasn't marked, except for a large stone that was there."

Sean frowned. "That doesn't help much. Maybe this anthropologist guy will pick up clues that mean nothing to the rest of us."

"I believe Kanesha is pinning her hopes on that," I said. "I believe you wanted to talk to Alissa about her grandfather's will." I rose. "I'll go into the room across the hall so you can discuss this privately."

"No," Alissa said. "I mean, please don't. Stay with me. I don't mind if you hear it."

"I'm happy to stay if you want me to, and Sean doesn't think I shouldn't."

"It's okay, Dad," Sean said. "Ms. Hale, Alissa, your grandfather didn't name any particular lawyer to oversee the distribution of his estate. Your brother turned the will over to me, though I expected him to ask for it back. Since he has died, may I act for you in this matter?"

"Sure," she said. "I don't know anybody here, but your father is a nice man. I'm going to trust you."

Sean smiled briefly. "Thank you. Your grandfather made what is called a holograph will. That means he wrote it by hand. It's attested by two witnesses, neither of whom I've been able to locate yet. I will continue to try to find them, however, in case questions arise."

"Okay," Alissa said. "What does the will say?"

Sean pulled an envelope out of his jacket pocket. He wore a suit today, sans tie, and looked handsome and professional. I rarely saw him in a suit jacket, because he only wore them in court or when interviewing a new client. He extracted two pages from the envelope and unfolded them. "Would you like to read it for yourself?"

Alissa nodded and held out her hand, and Sean got up to hand over the pages. She scanned the words, rather rapidly, I thought, but I remembered she was an experienced reader. Her reading comprehension ought to be good.

She handed the pages back to Sean.

"Any questions?" he asked.

"I think I have the gist of it," Alissa said. "He mentioned Marty and me by name as his heirs. Nothing about my mother. They hated each other." Her matter-of-fact tone didn't faze Sean.

"Yes, that's correct. You and your brother inherited equally. Did your brother leave a will, by any chance?" Sean asked.

Alissa shrugged. "I doubt it. He wouldn't have thought about it, probably. He was always living in the moment, expecting some big thing to happen." She gestured toward the papers Sean held. "Like inheriting a fortune from our grandfather."

"In that case, with your brother deceased, you are the sole heir to everything your grandfather possessed," Sean said. "It's worded carefully, and it means exactly that. What your grandfather possessed or owned. He did not own this house or the farm."

"Yes, I know. Your dad has explained that to me." She paused. "I guess it means, though, that the contents of the house belong to me. Is that right?"

"Yes, it is. You will also inherit any money in his bank or savings accounts. I am already working on discovering the extent of the funds in those accounts."

"He always talked big, like he had a lot of money," Alissa said. "Probably won't be a lot, but anything is better than what I've got now."

"You can also sell all the items in the house," Sean said. "There are several reputable dealers in Athena or Memphis who could handle it for you."

"That's what Charlie said," Alissa replied. "I guess I should go through the house and see what's here. Except . . ." She faltered.

"Don't worry about that now." I gave Sean a warning look. "There are other things to deal with first."

"Speaking of those things," Sean said gently. "I can help you with the arrangements for your brother, if you like."

"That would be good," Alissa said. "Marty handled our grandfather's cremation and everything. I think Marty would want to be cremated, too."

"If you're sure about that, I'll make the arrangements for it. The body should be released soon," Sean said.

A shadow passed over Alissa's face, but she simply

nodded. "How much will it cost? I don't have much in my savings."

"Don't worry about that," I said. "I can cover it for now, or Sean's law firm will. You can reimburse us through the estate."

"That's right," Sean said. "I'll go over it all with you so that you know exactly what the costs will be."

"Thank you. You're both really kind," she said. Diesel meowed loudly, and she smiled. "You too. Especially you." She rubbed his head and down his spine. He arched his back and chirped.

"Would it be okay if we went back to your house now?" Alissa said.

I really wanted to hang around here, hoping for more information on what Dr. Seton had found. I also wanted to have time to explore the house, but I understood why she would like to get away from here.

Sean evidently picked up on my hesitation. "I'll be happy to drop you by there. It's on the way to my office, and I need to get back there anyway."

"Is that okay with you?" I asked.

"Can Diesel come with me?" she said, glancing at the cat.

"If he wants to," I said. "I always let him decide." I patted the cat on the head. "You can go home with Alissa if you want to."

Diesel meowed in response, but I wasn't sure whether he intended to go home with the young woman.

"If you're ready," Sean said, nodding to Alissa.

"Sure." She rose from the settee. "What about you, boy?"

Diesel moved toward me and meowed. "I think that means he wants to stay here."

Alissa looked disappointed. "That's okay. Ramses and Azalea will be there, won't they?"

I nodded. "Azalea will be there until five, at least, and I'll be home with Diesel before then."

"See you later," Alissa said.

Sean escorted her out. She looked so small beside my tall son, who stood even taller than usual in his high-heeled boots.

After I heard the front door close, I turned to the cat. "I'm glad you stayed with me. You've been really nice to Alissa. You've made her feel better."

Diesel gazed up at me and trilled, throwing in a couple of chirps. I wished, not for the first time, that I could interpret his sounds. It really did sound like conversation sometimes.

"Let's explore the house, okay?"

Diesel padded alongside me. I turned in the doorway of the parlor and pulled out my phone. I wanted to take pictures of each room as it was now. There might be a few pieces of furniture or knickknacks that I would want to buy from the Hales for the house. That settee, for one. It needed to be reupholstered and repadded, but it looked and felt sturdy.

I took multiple shots in each room, Diesel following me patiently through the house. I had no idea how long I had spent. I made sure to get several pictures in the small room that had frightened Alissa so badly. A thorough search of its contents didn't reveal anything useful, however.

We ended in the kitchen, where I surveyed the appliances. The refrigerator was a good twenty years old, I thought, an outdated model. I was surprised it was still working. It would have to be replaced. The kitchen should be remodeled anyway. The floor was stained, the tile an ugly yellowish brown, and the walls dingy with grease and smoke. The whole house would have to be cleaned top to bottom whether I sold it or kept it.

I looked at the door that led up to the attic. Did I really feel like tackling the attic today? I doubted I would find any other grisly surprises there. The bones were more than enough for my lifetime.

I checked my watch. I had been here for over three hours, and it was close to nine forty-five when we arrived here. I realized that I was hungry, so I went back to where I had left the cooler. I withdrew the container of snacks from the cooler, along with another bottle of still water. Then I retrieved the bowl I'd used for the cat from the front porch.

As I snacked on cheese and crackers, Diesel lapped up more water. I gave him a couple of small bites of cheese. Cats couldn't tolerate large amounts, but Diesel had never demonstrated any kind of gastric issue with small amounts. He also couldn't have any of the grapes Azalea had included.

I finished my snack and put the remainder of the food away in the cooler. Diesel watched me but didn't beg for more once the lid of the cooler came down. He went back to finish the water in his bowl. We went outside for a few minutes to walk in the yard. He disappeared behind a bush, and I heard scratching sounds a few seconds later. After a short time, he reappeared, and we went back into the house.

There had been no sign of Kanesha and her officers, or of Dr. Seton and Fleur, other than the vehicles in the driveway. I figured they would have to emerge from the woods before much longer. Surely they would be allowed time for lunch. How much could Dr. Seton accomplish without more equipment? I wondered. Or assistants who knew what they were doing. I imagined he had a few graduate students who would normally assist in a situation like this. Or maybe the deputies Kanesha had chosen for this assignment were sufficient.

All this not knowing what was going on was driving me a little nuts. I was spending far too much time obsessing over these points. Perhaps I should go up into the attic after all.

I knew that the contents of the house now belonged to Alissa Hale, not to me, but I didn't think she'd mind my snooping. Especially if I uncovered some valuable object, or multiple objects, for her.

"Come on, boy," I said. "I'm going up to the attic again."

When I had reached the top of the stairs, I could see, even in the dim light, that the dust on the floor had been considerably disturbed by the investigation.

I should have brought a flashlight with me, I realized. The overhead light fixture provided a decent amount of illumination, but that didn't extend into the corners of this large room. Diesel rambled around, sniffing here and there, occasionally poking at a box or an object with his right paw.

I spotted a trunk to examine. I moved slowly through the accumulated boxes and lifted the lid. The groaning of the metal fixtures startled me momentarily, but I pushed the lid back and glanced inside the trunk.

I used the flashlight app on my phone to make it easier to see the contents. *Aha*, I thought when I espied what looked like photograph albums. There had to be four or five in the trunk, and I started pulling them out. I stacked them on top of a nearby box, and there turned out to be six of them. Medium thickness, so I could carry them all at one go.

I was excited. These albums might reveal the mystery woman's identity.

TWENTY-FIVE

|||||||||||||||||||||||||||||||||||||||||||||||||||||||||||||||||||||||||||

I hurried down the stairs as quickly as I could without stumbling over my own feet and falling. Diesel came down behind me. The albums weren't in the best of condition. No telling how long they'd been in that trunk in the attic. They did exude a scent of camphor, and the camphor had a done a good job of keeping bugs out of the trunk. I set them on the kitchen table and opened the top one.

The photographs had yellowed, and the tape that had held them in place had dried out. I didn't recognize anyone in the photographs, but from the clothes I thought the pictures dated from the fifties, if not a bit earlier. I pulled out one of the loose ones and turned it over. Only a date appeared on the back. October 1953. Several years before I was born.

I examined the front again, peering more closely at the faces of the four people in the picture. A man and a woman. Mr. and Mrs. Hale, perhaps? There was another couple who appeared to be older. When I examined their faces more closely, I felt a tingle of recognition. They were my grandparents.

I put the picture back in its place in the album. I wondered if these albums had belonged to my grandparents. Surely Aunt Dottie would have taken any such things when my grandfather died. She wouldn't have left these behind.

I scanned the other photographs on the page and didn't see my grandparents in any of them. I decided they must belong to the Hale family after all. I closed the album and picked up the stack.

"Let's go back to the parlor," I said to Diesel, who had been watching me patiently.

He trotted ahead of me down the hall and into the parlor. He jumped on the settee but left room for me to sit beside him. I pulled the small coffee table closer to me and set the albums down. With the aid of a lamp on the table beside the settee, I was able to see the photographs more clearly.

I went slowly through the first album, checking each photograph carefully. I didn't recognize anyone in the photos other than the man and woman I thought were the Hales. My grandparents didn't appear in any other photos. I didn't recognize the setting for the photos, either, so these must have been made elsewhere. I laid the album aside and picked up the next one in the stack.

This one yielded nothing of interest. I checked the back of one photograph and inscribed there was the date 1957. At least I was moving forward in time. No result from the third or fourth one, either, though by then the pictures had moved into the 1960s. A young boy appeared with the Hales in a number of pictures. He appeared to be five or six by the end of the album.

The fifth one was a jump back in time to the 1940s. After a quick scan I put it aside. I was beginning to feel that my search through these pictures was hopeless, unless there was another cache of albums in the attic. I would go through this sixth one, and then I would head home. My head ached from the strain of examining pages of old photographs, many of which had faded badly. I checked my watch to find out it was nearly three-thirty.

I decided I would take the last album home with me. Alissa might recognize people in them from family photos her mother might have taken with her.

"Come on, boy, let's go home," I said.

My car stood alone in the driveway. I had no idea when the other vehicles had departed. I had been too engrossed in the albums to hear anything. I thought it odd that Kanesha hadn't come back to give me an update. She might have attempted to while we were in the attic, but I hadn't heard her if she had called out for me.

Once the car cooled down a bit, the drive home was actually pleasant. Diesel lay stretched out on the backseat, and I had the album I'd brought on the passenger seat. I hoped Alissa wouldn't see anything in it that would upset her, but I wouldn't force her to examine it.

Azalea might recognize the people, I realized, and now I wished I had brought the rest of the albums with me. I debated turning back to retrieve them, but by now we were back on the highway heading into Athena. I was ready to get home. For one thing, I was hungry, and Diesel must be ready for his dish of dry food by now. I could make myself a sandwich to tide me over until dinner.

On that happy thought, I continued on to the house.

When I turned into the driveway, Diesel sat up as he always did. He appeared to know when we arrived home, and he was ready to exit the car before I parked in the garage. We met Azalea and Ramses in the kitchen. After we greeted them, I inquired after Alissa.

"Upstairs reading or taking a nap," Azalea said. "Been up there ever since she got back. She didn't say much. Was she upset about something?"

I told Azalea about the poor girl's experience with the one room in the house. Azalea frowned. "I wonder who that woman was. Miz Hale was gone by then, and it sure wasn't that child's mother. I don't know about any other woman living there."

"Did Mr. Hale have a sister or a cousin who might have come to live there after his wife ran off?"

"Not that I ever heard," Azalea said. "That don't mean it didn't happen, though. I seem to recollect that he did have a sister, but I think she married a man from Itta Bena and moved over to the delta a long time ago."

"It's definitely a mystery, then." I went to the sink to wash my hands before I made a sandwich. "What's for dinner tonight?"

"Stewart's going to make something for you," Azalea said. "Remember, I told you on Monday I had to leave early tonight?"

"That's right, you did," I said. "You've got a special service at your church. Are you going to be singing?"

"With the choir, yes, I am," Azalea said.

Azalea had a lovely voice. She had sung at Sean and Alex's rather impromptu wedding. Thinking about it still made me smile. She was one of the mainstays of her choir, too. That much she had let slip.

"Is Mrs. Luckney a member of your church?"

Azalea nodded. "She'll be there tonight. She stands right behind me in the choir."

"What about Mr. Luckney?"

"He usually comes with her, but not always. You got something you want me to tell him?" Azalea asked.

"I'd really like to talk to him tomorrow, if it's convenient for him."

"I'll pass that along. Is the afternoon all right? He usually stops work at lunchtime on Saturdays."

"That would be fine," I said. "Thank you. Now, you go and have a wonderful service."

She gave me one of her rare smiles before she went to gather her things. She checked the one bag she carried besides her purse, the bag that Ramses liked to sneak into so she'd take him home with her. Evidently Ramses was still with Diesel, and Azalea nodded.

"He'd best stay here this weekend. I've got a lot to do, and I don't need him following every step I make, acting like he hasn't had a bite in his mouth since he was born."

"I'll make sure he doesn't starve," I said.

Azalea departed, and I checked the refrigerator for a snack. There was some cold chicken, but there was also ham. I loved ham sandwiches, and I extracted the ham, along with mayo and some Vermont cheddar.

The landline phone rang while I was in the middle of making the sandwich. I wiped my hands and picked up the receiver.

"Hi, Charlie, Aleta Boudreaux. How are you?"

"I'm fine, Aleta. How nice of you to call. What's up?"

"I've got some good news for you," she said. "After talking to you, I consulted some of the historical society's board members, one of them being Miss Dickce Ducote, and they agreed with my suggestion."

"What was that?" I said, intrigued.

"You being a librarian and utterly trustworthy according to Miss Dickce, I have permission to give you a key to the building so you can go in and look through the archives."

"That's extremely kind of you, and the board." I hadn't expected this. "I promise I won't disturb anything."

"According to Miss Dickce, you can just about walk on water." Aleta laughed. "I reckon we can trust you with our archive."

"You can," I said eagerly. "I've really been wanting to examine those papers related to my family."

"I've got another surprise for you," Aleta said with a chuckle. "I actually found them for you. I got curious after we talked, and I hunted around in the boxes and there they were. You'll find them at the reception desk."

"Thank you so much. When can I get the key?"

"If you can meet me there in the morning, say at eight-thirty, I can give it to you then. I have to be somewhere at nine, and I'm booked the rest of the day."

"That's perfect. I'll see you then."

Elated by this fortuitous turn of events, I went back to my sandwich and finished making it. I cleaned up before I sat down to eat. Diesel and Ramses had rejoined me, and I parceled out the bits of ham I had cut for them.

The sandwich hit the spot, along with the can of my diet soda, and I felt I could last until dinnertime. I laughed suddenly. My behavior was rather like that of Ramses. I could have waited until dinner, I knew, but I wanted to eat now.

The sandwich finished, I wiped my fingers and pulled the album toward me. I regretted that I hadn't had time to show it to Azalea. I was counting on her to be able to put names to at least some of the faces, but there would still be time on Monday, no doubt.

I had flipped open the album when my cell phone rang. Who was it this time?

"Hi, Sean, what's up?"

"Dad, are you at home now?"

I replied that I was.

"Did you find out anything more from Kanesha? I have a call in to her, but she hasn't called back yet."

"Not a word," I said. "They all left while I was busy in the house. I went through and took pictures of every room, and then I went into the attic and poked around. I found some photo albums and looked through them. I brought one home for Alissa to look at. I'm hoping she might recognize some of the faces."

"Is Alissa there with you now?"

"No. She's been upstairs in her room since you brought her back, according to Azalea. I haven't been home all that long."

"I'm not ready to tell her this, but based on my preliminary findings, I think she's going to inherit several hundred thousand dollars. Even after taxes."

"That's wonderful," I said, pleased for the young woman. Maybe now she could work only one job and even go to school.

"Yes, but I'm concerned about the source of the money," Sean said. "The thing is, I found a small notebook in the papers the grandson brought to me. The notations are cryptic, but there are what look like amounts of money, along with initials, that cover a good twenty pages in it. I'm beginning to suspect that old Mr. Hale was a blackmailer."

TWENTY-SIX

||||||||||||||||||||||||||||||||||||||||||||||||||||||||||||||||||||||||||||

"That's outrageous," I said. "Are you sure?"

"No, not sure, I don't have any real evidence," my son replied. "But I'm having trouble coming up with any other answer at the moment. His income from the farm wouldn't have amounted to this much, because he spent money pretty freely. The one savings account I located hasn't had any withdrawals in twenty years, only deposits."

"What about the initials? Any clues there?"

"G.J.," Sean said.

"Gil Jackson," I replied. "Maybe connected to his alleged bootlegging?"

"That's what I'm thinking," Sean said. "Either Hale was a partner in it, because Jackson was operating the still on the land he leased from Hale . . . or Hale threatened to expose him unless he got paid."

"Depends on how much land Jackson owns outright,"

I said. "He could always move the still onto his own property if Hale threatened to expose him for using the leased land. I think it's more likely they were partners, and those are Hale's profits."

"Then there's a heck of a lot of money in moonshine," Sean said. "Jackson must produce a lot of it."

"I don't know anything about that business," I said. "It must be lucrative, though, or else people wouldn't do it."

"Same with any business," Sean said.

"Are you going to tell Kanesha about this?"

"Not yet," Sean said. "I have to consider my client's interests, and there's no proof that Hale got the money through illegal means."

"I'm not sure how you'd prove it anyway," I said.

"*Aye, there's the rub*," Sean said, with a hint of humor in his tone.

"You're doing it again," I said, mock-severely. "Quoting Shakespeare is a bad habit."

"A little *Hamlet* isn't so terrible." Sean laughed. "I need to get back to the brief I'm working on. Talk to you later, Dad. Just wanted to tell you what I'd found."

"Thanks. Give my love to Alex and Rosie."

I put the phone down and continued perusing the album. I recognized the clothing styles of the late sixties in these colored photographs. They had yellowed like all the others, thanks to their storage in the attic, even though it was ventilated. Heat rose, and Mississippi summers could be brutal.

I finally found a face that was somewhat familiar. A young man of about sixteen, I reckoned, who must be Martin Hale Jr., Alissa's father. He'd been a couple of years behind me in school, I thought. I would have to check with Melba on that. She would remember. I couldn't remember half the people in my high school class, but Melba knew the names of every one of them. My high school yearbooks were packed away somewhere, and I didn't have the energy to dig them out. I was pretty sure I had correctly identified Martin Jr.

He was the only one who looked at all like someone I might have known. I closed the album without examining the last few pages. This hadn't been much help, thanks to my almost nonexistent knowledge of the Hale family.

I debated whether to go upstairs and check on Alissa. I didn't want to disturb her sleep. I figured she could use the rest. Working two jobs meant a grueling schedule, and being away meant she could relax as much as the circumstances warranted.

She obviously loved her brother, but she was by no means blind to his faults. Nor to her grandfather's, or at least how her mother had painted them to her children. I had no idea whether their father had favored his own father, or if he was different in character. Her stepfather must have been, for she seemed genuinely to have admired and cared for him. She never really had the chance to know her own father.

My thoughts turned to the historical society and its archives. I was excited by the thought of actually being able to examine papers related to my family's history. I was sure that Mrs. Carraway had included the most pertinent facts in her book, but there might be things, as she had informed me, that she thought were better left out. Had there been any scandals attached to the Harris clan?

I would be surprised if there were. My parents had been quiet people, and I knew nothing to my grandfather's detriment. He might have sown some wild oats in his youth, but my father had never told me any stories about his own father that would lead me to believe that.

I realized, not for the first time, how very little I knew about so many aspects of my parents' lives, and in turn, even less about my grandparents'. Was it because I had never expressed enough interest to encourage my father to talk to me about such things? Had I been so involved in my own life that I never stopped to think how important that information might be to me later in life?

The answer to that last question was an emphatic *yes*. I had been too wrapped up in school, then starting my own family, to take the time to sit down and talk with my parents about such things. I regretted that more than ever, now that I was a grandfather myself. I had little to pass down to my children and grandchildren about their forebears. I resolved to learn more about the family history so I could share it with Sean and Laura and their families. I thought they would be interested. I wished I hadn't waited so long to become interested myself.

I was still lost in these reflections a few minutes later when Stewart entered the kitchen from the garage. He carried several grocery bags that he put down on the counter before turning to greet me.

"Hi, Charlie, you're looking pretty gloomy," he said while he began to empty the bags. "I'm going to do a quick stir-fry tonight, and there's fresh salad greens, too. How does that sound?"

"Delicious," I said. "I'm not really gloomy, simply thinking about the fact that I know so little about my own family. Not my children, I mean, but my parents and grandparents."

"That's not unusual," Stewart said. "I don't know a lot

about mine, either, other than their being dead for a long time." He grinned. "Don't look at me like that, I was just trying to make you smile. I'm sorry if I offended you."

"No need to apologize. I was feeling a bit maudlin, I suppose. Can I help with that?"

"No, this won't take a minute. I'm going to put everything I don't immediately need away, and the rest can sit here while I go get that pest of a dog and take him for a walk."

I would have offered to take Dante for his walk, but I knew Stewart loved spending time with his pest, as he called him. "All right. I'll sit here and look glum until you come back."

"You do that if you must," Stewart said. "Or you could be thinking about the marvelous dinner I'm going to make for us. Haskell should be here for dinner tonight, unless plans have changed."

"That's good," I said. "Look, did he say anything to you about Alissa? He surely realizes she's his cousin."

"He knows that, but right now he thinks it better that she doesn't know. All because of the mystery of what happened to his aunt." Stewart shook his head. "I wish his mother weren't so bullheaded. Whatever happened to her sister surely couldn't be that bad."

"She obviously thinks it was, or else she wouldn't be holding out on her son," I said.

"She's right out of the Victorian age in some ways," Stewart said. "I'm surprised she hasn't covered the legs of all the furniture in the house so the naked limbs don't offend anyone's sensibilities."

"She must have a hard time in this world the way it is these days," I said.

"She belongs to one of those hellfire and brimstone

churches out in the country. At least they draw the line at handling snakes, or so I'm told. She's the only one in the family who goes. Haskell's dad has more sense." Stewart stowed the empty bags in the recycle bin. "I'll be back soon."

"I'll probably be right here," I said.

If Haskell did make it home for dinner, I thought, he might be willing to share more information about what Dewey Seton and his dog uncovered. He hadn't been with the group at the farm, but I knew Kanesha would have brought him up-to-date. Whether she had instructed him to keep it to himself was the question.

I had been so focused on the identity of the woman whose bones Diesel and I had found, I realized, I hadn't given much thought to the murderer of Marty Hale. Kanesha might have had a break in that investigation that I knew nothing about, and that was often the case. In the past I hadn't heard about forensic evidence until after the fact. I speculated that her team might have found something at the crime scene that could help identify the murderer.

That was the problem with being on the outside. The playing field, if you wanted to call it that, was uneven. Kanesha was sharp, no question about it. By the time I figured out the identity of the killer, she was almost always there, too. Simply by a different path, with clues to which I had no access.

I decided I would probe a bit with Haskell. If nothing else, he might admit they did have evidence to follow up on. If I got that much out of him, at least it would tell me that Kanesha had made progress. More than I had done, certainly.

I tired of sitting at the kitchen table, waiting for others

to appear. I decided to go up to my room and change my shirt. I hadn't realized how much dust I had picked up in the attic. Neither Azalea nor Stewart had said anything to me, but I suddenly felt grubby.

Diesel and Ramses came with me up the stairs, though they both turned the opposite way on the landing. They were going to check on Alissa, and that was fine.

When I came out of my room several minutes later wearing a clean shirt, I didn't see the cats or the young woman. I walked back downstairs and into the kitchen. Alissa was seated at the table, thumbing through the album. Diesel and Ramses, predictably, lay on the floor on either side of her chair.

"Good evening," I said.

Alissa looked up and smiled. "Good evening. I had a nice long nap, and I read awhile." She indicated the album. "Did you find this at the farm?"

"I did, along with five other albums." I sat and examined her expression. She didn't appear upset. "I brought only this one here, though. I hope you don't mind. They're yours now."

Alissa shook her head. "Fine with me. I know some of the people in these photos, but only because I've seen similar ones that my mom has in California." She slid the album toward me and indicated a picture at the top of one page. "See there? That's my grandfather and grandmother, and that's my dad. He was probably fourteen in that photo. Mom has the same one. My dad gave it to her when they were dating, she said."

I was right about Mr. and Mrs. Hale in the photos I had already seen. And Martin Jr., too. His face in this photo was clearer, and he did look familiar after all. I really must remember to ask Melba about him. I recognized the setting. The front porch of my grandfather's house.

"Have you been all the way through yet? See anyone else you recognize?"

"No, I only started a couple of minutes ago," Alissa said. "You know, it's really kind of weird seeing these pictures of my grandmother. That's the only way I know her. She must have died right after this."

"Let's see when this picture was taken." I pulled it loose from the album and turned it over. The date was July 1972. Not long before she disappeared from the family. I replaced the photo, and Alissa turned the page.

Many of the pictures we looked at had been taken either somewhere in my grandfather's house, on the porch, or in the front yard. I didn't recognize other locations. Mrs. Hale dropped out of the record after three more pages, and I checked the date on one of the photos. August 1974.

"When did your grandmother die, Alissa? Do you know?"

She shook her head. "In the early seventies sometime, I think. I don't know the exact date. Dad was about sixteen when she died."

Or disappeared, I added silently. I wondered whether I should tell Alissa that her grandmother was rumored to have run away. I would have to think about that carefully. Sooner or later she would find out, but I didn't know that I wanted to be the one who told her. I should probably leave that to Haskell, her cousin, if he admitted the relationship.

Alissa turned another page, and suddenly she froze.

In a choked whisper, she said, "That's her. That's the woman in the room." Her hand trembled as she tried to indicate the photo.

I pulled it from the album. It came loose easily. I examined it carefully. There were two people in the photograph, a man and a woman. I didn't know who the man was, but the woman . . . the woman had no hands.

TWENTY-SEVEN

"Do you recognize her? Other than as being the woman in the room?" I tried to keep my tone casual, but I was excited. This was a huge breakthrough. There couldn't be two handless women in this case.

Alissa, though still obviously upset, took the photograph back and looked at it. After a moment she shook her head. "I don't know who she is. She has no hands. I think that's what scared me about her. I was a little kid."

"You don't recognize the man, either?" I asked.

Alissa looked again. "No, I don't." She turned the photo over to find the date. The back was blank.

"I need to call the sheriff's department about this picture. Would you mind looking through the rest of the album to see if there are any more pictures of her or this man?" I asked.

Alissa grimaced but said she would. She didn't question me, and I was glad that I didn't have to explain why yet.

Miranda James

I called Kanesha's cell phone rather than the department number. To my surprise, she answered right away.

"What is it?" she said, her tone brusque as ever.

"I believe I've partially identified the woman whose bones I found," I said.

Silence rewarded me. I had rarely made Kanesha speechless.

After a long moment she said, "How? How could you do that? And what did you mean, partially identified?"

"I don't know her name," I said, "but I found a photograph of a woman with no hands in a photo album that belonged to Martin Hale. The elder one, that is. I have it here at my house. We're going through the album to see if there are any more of her or of the man who's with her. I don't know either of them, but somebody will."

"I'm on the way. Haskell should be there soon. Turn the photograph and the album over to him immediately, please." She was gone.

I had to admit to a moment of deep self-satisfaction. I had found a piece of crucial evidence, mostly thanks to Alissa. I regretted that Alissa had been frightened by the picture, but now that she had seen the woman again, and realized that she had no hands, perhaps some of the horror would fade from her memory.

I walked back into the kitchen. "Any luck?"

"No, that's the only picture with either of them," Alissa said. "What did they say when you told them about the photograph?"

"Chief Deputy Berry is on her way here. Haskell should be here any minute. We are to turn the photograph and the album over to him. The sheriff's department will try to find out who that woman was."

228

"Was?" Alissa frowned. "How do you know she's dead?"

"I believe she is the person whose bones Diesel and I found in the attic." I drew my chair near hers. "I didn't tell you this before, because I thought it might bother you. The hands and feet were missing from the skeleton I found. Now that we've found this picture, and you recognized the woman as the one you saw in that little room, we have more information that will help lead us to her identity."

"That's good," Alissa said, rubbing her arm. "The memory is still scary. Not as scary as it was before I realized why she frightened me. She must have suffered pretty bad to end up that way." She paused, frowning. "But there was something else. I'm sure of it."

I thought about that for a moment, then inspiration struck.

"She might have had prosthetic hands, or maybe claws. You know, the pincer type?"

Wide-eyed, Alissa looked at me. "I think you're right. Claws. That must be what scared me. But I can't say for sure. All I really remember is being frightened of her. I was too little to understand."

I squeezed her shoulder. "You can forget about it now, or try to. Once we find out who she was, her ghost will be well and truly laid."

"Maybe." Alissa looked doubtful. "But how did her skeleton end up in the attic? That's super creepy."

"It is. Her bones got dug up at some point and stored in the attic. I have no idea why, though, unless it was meant as a prank of some kind."

Alissa grimaced. "That's the kind of thing Marty would have done. Maybe it was him."

"I think it was done well before your brother came here," I said, and I explained about the undisturbed dust in the attic when Diesel and I made our discovery.

"You don't understand. Marty came to stay with our grandfather for a couple of weeks about three years ago," Alissa said.

"I thought he hadn't come back here since your family moved to California," I said, stunned.

"That was the only time," Alissa said. "Grandfather said he was sick and needed help. He paid for Marty to fly here, and Marty stayed for two weeks. Maybe three. He didn't have anything good to say about our grandfather when he got home. He made Marty work like a dog."

This was a bombshell on top of the photograph. Had Marty somehow found the bones, disinterred them, and hidden them in the attic as a prank?

"You'll have to tell Deputy Berry about this," I said. "They might be able to determine whether your brother did dig up the bones and put them in the attic."

"I don't know how," Alissa said. "Can you leave fingerprints on bones?"

"I have no idea," I said, though I would find out. If nothing else, I might call my newly rediscovered childhood friend, Dewey Seton, and simply ask him.

Alissa brightened. "I know. I'll call my mom. She ought to know who that woman was."

I felt a fool. I should have thought of that myself. "That's a great idea, and anything she knows would be a big help."

Stewart returned from walking Dante while Alissa was on the phone with her mother, and thanks to the barking dog and the chattering cats, I couldn't hear Alissa's side of the conversation. I gave Stewart a quick up-date and told him Haskell should be here any minute.

I'd barely got the words out when Haskell came walk-ing into the kitchen. I tried to tell him what Alissa and I had discovered, but Dante barked even louder at the sight of his adored human. Laughing, Haskell scooped him up and said he'd take him upstairs with him while he changed out of his uniform. Stewart went with them.

Once they'd departed, quiet reigned again, except for Alissa's brief responses to her talk with her mother. From Alissa's expression, I judged that something was amiss. Seconds later Alissa put her phone down and turned to me.

"This is really crazy," she said slowly.

"What's wrong?" I asked.

She gazed up at me. "I told my mom about what hap-pened today, and about the photograph. She says she doesn't remember ever meeting a woman like that while she lived in that house. She can't explain what I saw."

I frowned. Would her mother deliberately lie to Alissa about something like this simply to torment her daughter?

"Let's look at the picture again." I sat beside Alissa and we pored over the photograph. I noticed something right away that hadn't registered before, having been too shocked by the sight of the woman with no hands.

"Their clothes are funny looking," Alissa said. "Like right out of an old movie."

"You're right," I said. The clothes were definitely not contemporary with those of the other pictures in the al-bum. The man and woman looked to be in their thirties, and the clothes dated from the forties. I recognized the styles. Laura had worn a similar dress in a production of a World War II–era play she had done in Los Angeles.

"How could this woman have been in the house, in that room, and your mother not know it?" I asked.

"I don't know," Alissa said. "Unless my mom was lying to me for some reason."

"Has she done that before?" I asked.

"Yes, she has," Alissa said, her expression grave. "Marty was always her favorite. That's one reason I loved my stepdad so much. I was his favorite, and he wouldn't let Marty pick on me or make fun of me when he was around."

I realized that I had conceived a thorough dislike of Marty Hale, and that now extended to his mother. I had only Alissa's word for all this, and I cautioned myself not to believe everything she told me about her family. I had only known her a brief time, after all. Diesel had really taken to her, though, and that was usually a good sign.

"I have read, more than once, that little children are more open to the paranormal," I said. "They don't know that such things as ghosts are not supposed to exist, for example, and when they see things the adults around them don't, it usually gets dismissed as an active imagination."

"You think maybe I saw a ghost in that room?" Alissa looked uncertain.

"If your mother is telling the truth, I'm not sure what else to think," I said. "If it weren't for that photograph, I'd say maybe some stranger had wandered into the house to steal something, and you saw her and frightened her away."

"Even my mom wouldn't have left me alone in the house," Alissa said. "Someone else would have been there, I'm sure. They would have seen her, too."

I looked at the photograph again, to check the woman's feet. She was sitting, and the man stood next to her, a hand on her shoulder. Her handless arms were crossed, wrist against wrist, in her lap. I couldn't see any feet, but I suspected the chair she was in was a wheelchair, one of the old high-backed kind.

"I'm sure you're right," I said. "The problem is, your mother is the only one, besides you, who lived in that house at the time who's still alive. I'm sure Kanesha will want to question her, and if your mother was lying to you for some reason, Kanesha will get the truth out of her."

"I hope so," Alissa said. "I'd rather think Mom is lying than that I saw a ghost." She shivered.

I heard the doorbell. "That must be Kanesha. We'll be right back."

Diesel remained with her, but Ramses followed me to the front door. I scooped him up before I opened it, because he often tried to run outside.

I invited Kanesha in and closed the door firmly behind her before I put Ramses down. Kanesha looked at him and grimaced. "My mother loves that silly cat, the Lord only knows why."

I chose to ignore that comment. Azalea had told me recently, during one of Kanesha's visits with her, she had left the room for something and come back to find Ramses in her daughter's lap. Kanesha was stroking him and smiling. I would keep that to myself for now.

"Let's go in the kitchen. Alissa's there, and you can see the photograph," I said.

Kanesha followed me, Ramses like a small dog at her heels. He was probably confused because she was ignoring him.

Alissa and Kanesha exchanged greetings, and I handed the deputy the photograph. Kanesha took the chair across from Alissa and studied the picture. She looked up. "You don't know these people?"

"No, I don't," Alissa said. "When I was really little, before we moved to California, I think I saw her in that room where my brother was living at the farm. She frightened me. That's all I remember, really."

"Alissa called her mother a few minutes ago," I said. "Asked her about this woman, and her mother claims she never saw her at the farm."

Kanesha frowned. "Are you trying to tell me you saw a ghost?"

"I don't know," Alissa said. "I was only two, I think. I didn't remember any of it until I walked into that room. Then it terrified me again."

"Would your mother lie to you?" Kanesha asked.

Alissa nodded. "Sometimes she does. It was always Marty and her against me."

"Let me have your mother's phone number, and I'll call her." Kanesha pulled out her phone and punched in the number as Alissa recited it.

"Mrs. Willoughby, this is Chief Deputy Kanesha Berry in Athena, Mississippi. How are you?" Kanesha paused to listen. "I hope you have time to talk with me. I have a serious matter to discuss. It's about an old photograph your daughter found in an album from the farm."

Kanesha's expression remained impassive as she listened. Apparently, Mrs. Willoughby had a lot to say, because Kanesha didn't respond for what seemed like several minutes.

"I see," Kanesha finally said. "That's all you know?" Another long pause.

I glanced at Alissa, not surprised at the hurt expression I saw. Her mother had no doubt lied to her deliberately, and I wondered what kind of parent would treat a child so badly. Not a woman I'd ever want to know, that's for sure.

"Thank you, Mrs. Willoughby. I'll be calling you again when I have more questions." Kanesha ended the call and regarded Alissa with what looked like sympathy.

"Your mother asked me to apologize for her. She said she was only playing a joke on you and would have told you the truth," Kanesha said.

"It's okay," Alissa said, her tone flat. "I thought she had to be lying to me. As usual."

Kanesha arched an eyebrow, then relaxed it. "Your mother says the woman stayed in the house for only a couple of nights. Apparently, she was some relative of your grandfather's, but she didn't know the exact relationship. The only name she heard was Maudie."

Alissa shook her head. "I don't think I've ever heard that name before."

"Your mother said the woman was quite elderly," Kanesha replied. "She had prosthetic hands and got around in an old wheelchair. Your grandfather never explained what had happened to her hands and feet."

"An accident of some kind, I suppose," I said.

"Now that we have a name, or part of one, we'll work to uncover her full identity," Kanesha said. "I'd like to know how she ended up in an unmarked grave, and who put her bones in the attic."

"I think I can answer one of those questions," Alissa said.

TWENTY-EIGHT

||||||||||||||||||||||||||||||||||||||||||||||||||||||||||||||||||||||||||||||||||||

Alissa's statement surprised Kanesha, though she hid it quickly. "Tell me what you know," Kanesha said.

First Alissa explained that her brother had visited their grandfather several years ago and spent two or three weeks with him.

Kanesha frowned at that. "I wish you had told us this sooner."

"I'm sorry," Alissa said. "I didn't think about it until today. Anyway, Marty was always pulling tricks that he thought were funny. I never did, but my mother always laughed and egged him on."

I suspected most of those jokes were at Alissa's expense, and I would have wagered that Kanesha thought so, too.

"The way I see it," Alissa went on, "Marty must have been poking around in the woods and come across the grave. He would have thought it was hilarious to dig up the bones and hide them in the house."

"That's as good an explanation as any," Kanesha said. "I'll share this with Dr. Seton, and perhaps he can find some corroboratory evidence."

Alissa nodded. "I hope you find it. I hope you find out who she was, too. It's really sad. I wonder why my grandfather put her in that grave in the woods."

"That's a very good question," Kanesha said. "I'm not sure that's one we'll ever be able to answer. Unless Dr. Seton comes up with something to explain how she died."

Did Kanesha think Mr. Hale had killed this woman? Either deliberately or accidentally? Wouldn't someone have missed her?

Kanesha rose. "If you'll replace the photograph in the album where you found it, I'll take the album now to the office. I want to get to work on identifying this woman."

Alissa complied with the instructions. Kanesha wrote out a receipt and gave it to the young woman. "I appreciate your help," Kanesha said.

"I really haven't done much," Alissa said, "but you're welcome anyway."

I walked with Kanesha to the front door. "I'm glad you called Mrs. Willoughby and got the truth out of her. Can you imagine a mother playing that kind of trick on her child? It's outrageous."

"It is," Kanesha said. "She's going to have to come here at some point, and I look forward to questioning her in person. Good night."

I closed the door behind her and turned to see Stewart coming down the stairs.

"Kanesha's gone?" he said. "I was going to invite her to stay for dinner. There'll be more than enough."

"She was anxious to get back to the office to start work on identifying the mysterious woman in the photograph," I said. "Is Haskell coming down soon?"

"He's taking a shower," Stewart said. "Won't be long. I'm going to start dinner." He headed for the kitchen, and I went with him.

While he worked I brought him up to date on everything. He shot a sympathetic glance at Alissa when I mentioned her mother's cruel trick. His mouth tightened momentarily, and I thought he might say something cutting. He evidently thought better of it and focused on the meal preparation instead.

When Haskell appeared a few minutes later, I began to give him an update. He held up a hand to forestall me.

"It's okay, Charlie. Kanesha called and gave me the details."

"Good." I really didn't want to go over it again, for Alissa's sake.

Alissa greeted Haskell before she turned to me. "If you don't mind, I think I'll go upstairs until dinner. I'm almost through with my book, and I want to see how it ends."

"You go right ahead," I said. "I'll call when the food is ready."

Diesel and Ramses accompanied her.

"Poor kid," Haskell said. "Kanesha told me about her mother. What a piece of work." He took a place at the table. Stewart retrieved a beer from the fridge and gave it to him.

I decided I needed a beverage, too, but not beer. I pulled a can of diet soda from the fridge. A little caffeine would be good about now.

"Looks like you're closing in on at least one part of the case now," I said to Haskell.

He nodded and took a swig of his beer. "And you want to know if we've made any real progress on the murder."

"Yes," I said. "I'm sure y'all know more than I do, and for Alissa's sake, I hope you're close to an arrest."

"Maybe," Haskell said. "We did find a few things that could tie the murderer to the scene. I can't go into what they are, because we're not entirely certain who left these things behind. We have a pretty good idea, though."

"That's good." I was disappointed that he obviously wasn't going to tell me any more than that, but at least it was progress.

The landline phone rang, and I got up to answer it. After I had identified myself, the caller said, "This is Asa Luckney, Mr. Harris. My wife said you wanted to talk to me."

"Yes, I would, Mr. Luckney. About my grandfather."

"I dropped Oralee off at the church, and I can come talk to you now if it's convenient."

"It is. Thank you so much." I gave him the address, and he promised to be here in about ten minutes.

"Asa Luckney, one of the men leasing land from the farm," I said to Stewart and Haskell. "He's coming here to talk to me."

"What is it you're hoping to find out?" Stewart asked. "Things about your grandfather that you don't already know?"

"Yes, that's part of it," I said. "My grandfather supposedly took a great interest in Mr. Luckney, and I've been wondering why he gave Martin Hale a life lease on the property instead of Mr. Luckney. Given what I know of my grandfather, who was a teetotaler, according to my father, I can't see him entrusting his property to an alcoholic."

"Maybe because Luckney is Black and Hale was white," Haskell said blandly.

"Possibly," I said, "but that wasn't the way my parents thought, and I don't believe my grandfather thought that way, either. My dad said my grandfather threatened to whip him if he ever caught my dad being disrespectful to anyone, Black or white."

"That's certainly different from my family." Haskell grimaced. "They're all pretty racist to this day."

"I'm sorry to hear that," I said.

Haskell shrugged. "They're never going to change, and I've pretty much accepted that."

Stewart changed the subject by talking about the meal he was preparing. He and Haskell talked about the merits of the various ingredients. Haskell was apparently partial to water chestnuts, and Stewart assured him there would be plenty of them in the mix.

I let the conversation flow around me. I was impatient for Mr. Luckney to arrive. I hoped he would be amenable to answering my questions about his relationship with my grandfather. And about my grandfather's decision to give Martin Hale that lease.

The doorbell rang, and I went to answer it. Instead of Asa Luckney, however, I found Gil Jackson on the stoop.

"Sorry to barge in like this." Jackson stepped inside before I invited him in. I frowned and shut the door.

"What can I do for you, Mr. Jackson? I'm expecting someone to arrive any minute now."

"I want to talk to you about that land I'm leasing," he said. "No beating about the bush. I need that land. I'd rather buy it outright, but I'll continue to lease it if that's what you want."

"You're supposed to talk to my son about this," I said. "He's handling the estate. I'm not going to agree to anything without his knowledge."

"Yeah, I know," Jackson said. "I don't like dealing with lawyers, though, even if he is your son. I figured we could come to a gentlemen's agreement, just between you and me."

I started to say there was only one gentleman in the room, and it wasn't him. But that wouldn't be productive. No point in insulting the man, even though I thoroughly disliked him now.

"I'm afraid I'm going to have to disappoint you," I said in icy tones. "You will have to deal with my son. Now, if that's all you have to say, I will ask you to leave before the person I *invited* here arrives."

Jackson shot me a hard look. He was not pleased, but I didn't care. If necessary, I would call Haskell out from the kitchen to help me deal with him.

The doorbell rang again, and I went back to the door. This time Asa Luckney stood there. "Good evening," I said. "I really appreciate you taking the time to come by and talk with me."

Luckney nodded and came into the house. I remained by the door. "I'll say good night now, Mr. Jackson."

He didn't take the hint. "What the hell are you doing here?" He scowled at Asa Luckney.

"I came to talk to Mr. Harris. What are you doing here?" Luckney scowled back.

"You're trying to get him to lease all the land to you and that drunken son of yours." Jackson sneered, and for a moment I thought Mr. Luckney might strike him.

"That's enough, Mr. Jackson. I think you should leave now. My business with Mr. Luckney has nothing to do with you."

Jackson moved toward the door, still glowering. Before he stepped onto the stoop, he turned and looked at me. "I'm not going to forget about this. I'll take you to court if I have to. I'm going to keep that land whether you like it or not."

"We'll see about that." I slammed the door in his face and locked it.

Asa Luckney laughed. "He oughta be used to that by now. Nobody wants him in their house."

"He is not welcome in this one," I said. "He just barged in when I opened the door. Why don't you come into the living room, Mr. Luckney? We can talk in there."

Luckney nodded and followed me. I switched on the lights and indicated a comfortable chair. He sat where I indicated, and I parked myself on the sofa across from him.

"I expect you're wanting to know about your grandfather," he said. "You wasn't all that old when he died, as I recall."

"Yes, about six, I think," I replied. "I don't remember much about him."

"The best thing to know about him," Luckney replied, "was that he was a good man. He always treated me right. I respected him, and he respected me. Back then, that wasn't common. There was a lot of crazy stuff going on, but he stuck to what he believed in and treated me like he always did."

"I'm glad to hear that," I said, touched. "My father raised me that way, and he said that about my grandfather. I'm glad to know it's true."

"You can count on that," Luckney said.

"I was told by someone that my grandfather thought a lot of you."

"I believe he did," Luckney replied. "I worked for him from the time I was about thirteen, and he always treated me good. Told me I had a knack for farming."

"I'm really surprised that my grandfather gave Martin Hale that life lease on the farm instead of to you," I said. "I know my grandfather was a teetotaler, and Hale was an alcoholic back then."

Luckney looked uncomfortable. This was obviously a sore point with him.

He eyed me for a moment, and I wondered how he would respond.

"Your granddaddy told me not long before he died he was going to give me the farm for my lifetime," he said. "But Martin Hale conned him into changing his mind somehow."

TWENTY-NINE

"I suspected as much," I said. "Do you have any idea how Hale made him change his mind?"

Luckney shook his head. "No, sir, I sure don't. Hurt me pretty bad, I tell you. I thought for some reason Mr. Robert took against me before he died. I went to see him in the nursing home the day he died, and he acted happy to see me. He couldn't talk much, but he did say, 'I'm sorry, Asa.' Then he went to sleep. I waited to see if he would wake up, but he didn't. Found out later he died that night."

"He must have been apologizing for the nasty shock you were going to have," I said.

"I reckon so," Luckney replied. "I never could figure it out, what Mr. Hale did to change your granddaddy's mind like that. It took me some years, but I finally got a chance to lease some of that land. Though not as much as I wanted. A few years later Mr. Hale leased a big part of the farm to Gil Jackson."

That definitely hadn't set well with Mr. Luckney, I judged by his expression.

Impulsively, I said, "I haven't decided yet what I'm going to do about the farm, Mr. Luckney, but I will assure you now that you won't lose by my decision." I felt that I needed to make up somehow for my grandfather's inexplicable change of heart and mind.

His expression brightened. "Thank you, Mr. Harris. I appreciate that. Is there anything else you want to know?"

"I could probably keep you here for hours talking about my grandparents," I said with a smile, "but I know you need to get back to church. We can talk another time, if you are willing."

"I'll be glad to." He rose and extended a hand to me. I stood and shook it, then I escorted him to the door. He thanked me again before he walked out of the house.

A welcome contrast to Gil Jackson, I decided. Jackson was crude and quarrelsome. If he hadn't acted the way he had, I would have been more inclined to agree to his continuing to lease the land. After his unwelcome visit tonight, I had decided he wasn't going to get his lease renewed. Unless I had no choice in the matter. Sean would know how these things worked.

I returned to the kitchen, tantalized by the scents of the stir-fry. I spotted on the table the salad Stewart must have put together while I talked to Jackson and Mr. Luckney.

"Smells wonderful," I said.

"Not much longer," Stewart said. "Go ahead and call Alissa down, and then you can serve yourself salad."

I did as Stewart asked. I walked about halfway up the stairs and called out to Alissa that dinner was ready. If her door was open, she should be able to hear me. I waited for a response. None came, so I climbed to the second floor.

I knocked on the closed door, and Alissa came to open it.

"Dinner's ready," I said.

She nodded. "I'll be down in a minute." She turned away from the door, and Diesel and Ramses came out to follow me down to the kitchen.

Haskell was eating salad when I walked in. I helped myself and chose a dressing from the several bottles on the table. Diesel immediately came to sit beside me and placed a paw on my thigh. Ramses gave his attention to Haskell.

"This is salad," I said to my cat. "You don't like salad, remember?"

Diesel warbled and withdrew his paw. He sat by my chair and looked sulky.

In between bites of salad, I told Stewart and Haskell about my unexpected visitor. Haskell scowled, but Stewart said, "The man is totally uncouth. I'd like to set Miss Manners on him. She'd whip even him into shape."

I had to laugh at that. Gil Jackson was probably beyond even Miss Manners's abilities. Haskell voiced that same thought.

Stewart shrugged. "Somebody needs to bang him upside the head, then, knock some sense into him."

"The sheriff's department has been trying to do that for years," Haskell said in a mild tone. "Not literally, of course. One of these days he's going to slip up, or his source in the department is going to be exposed. Then we'll get him."

The current sheriff was a good ol' boy. Kanesha had challenged him in the most recent election. It had been close, but he had won by a slender majority. I hoped Kanesha would run again and win. We needed someone like her running the department.

Alissa appeared and took her chair at the table. Haskell moved the salad bowl closer to her, and she thanked him. I wondered if he was ever going to tell her about their family connection. Surely he would, once the murder had been solved and the killer arrested. Unless, for some reason, he had no wish to acknowledge her as family.

Stewart's stir-fry was as delicious as expected. The cats were not able to have any because of the garlic in the sauce, but Stewart had set aside some bits of boiled chicken for them so they didn't feel left out. He doled the bits out to all of us, and Alissa giggled when she received hers.

"These cats are spoiled, aren't they?" she said.

"They sure are." Haskell grinned as he gave Ramses a small bit of the chicken.

Conversation around the table for the rest of meal had nothing to do with the murder or the bones in the attic. By tacit agreement we avoided those topics. Alissa told us about living in central California. Haskell talked about growing up on a farm here in Athena County, and Stewart shared a few anecdotes about his eccentric uncle. He did not mention that his uncle had been murdered, however. I chipped in a few anecdotes about Houston, and we all enjoyed ourselves.

I praised Stewart for the excellent meal, and Alissa chimed in. Stewart and Haskell shooed us out, saying they would clean up. I knew they liked doing domestic things together, so I didn't demur. Alissa tried to insist on helping, but they wouldn't hear of it.

"I finished my book," Alissa said when we'd reached the foot of the stairs. "Would you mind if I picked out another one?"

"Of course not. Help yourself. I'm going upstairs to read myself. Let me know if you need anything."

"I will." She hurried past me with a smile, and I waited to see her enter the den before I went upstairs. Ramses had stayed with Stewart and Haskell, ever hopeful for more chicken, I felt sure. Diesel came up with me and settled himself on the bed in his regular spot.

After removing my shoes, I padded over to the desk, where I had several books I hadn't yet read. I chose a nonfiction book, a popular history of medieval England, and brought it back to the bed with me.

Helen Louise was late in calling that night, and she apologized profusely. "We didn't get back to the hotel until a little after midnight," she said, giggling. "I knew you'd be mad if I didn't call, though."

I laughed, though her phone call had awakened me from a sound sleep. "I'm glad you called, honey. Sounds like y'all had more fun than usual tonight."

She giggled again. "Too many hurricanes at Pat O'Brien's." She hiccuped suddenly, then apologized.

"I see. Well, you go on to bed and get some rest. Don't try to talk tonight," I said.

"Okay, sweetie. Love you," she said.

"Love you, too."

I put down the phone, smiling in the dark. Helen Louise rarely drank to excess, and I feared she would be regretting this episode when she woke up in the morning. Hurricanes had two or three kinds of rum in them, along with fruit juices. I recalled the one I'd had the last time I visited Pat O'Brien's as being on the strong side.

The call had roused me enough that it took me a while to go back to sleep. I thought about the mysterious "Maudie," and what had happened to her. Had Marty Hale really dug up her bones and hidden them in the house? That was a bizarre thing to do, but Alissa seemed to think he would have done it.

Then I thought about Asa Luckney. I wondered if I would find out somehow *why* my grandfather changed his mind right before he died. Perhaps there would be something in the papers at the historical society. I was eagerly anticipating going through them in the morning.

Finally, I drifted off to sleep, and when my alarm went off later that morning, I awoke a bit groggy. I sat up on the side of the bed, and Diesel came to sit beside me, leaning against me. I rubbed his head and yawned. Ramses wasn't with us. He might have spent the night with Alissa, I supposed.

I was the first one downstairs, and that surprised me. Usually Haskell was up early, even on weekends, and I often found him drinking coffee when I appeared. Given that the case hadn't been resolved, I thought he might have been out the door earlier. In an ongoing homicide investigation, the hours he worked were long and tiring. I hoped he'd had a good rest.

Sure enough, I found his favorite mug in the sink. I filled my own mug and set it on the table. There was no paper today, so I contented myself with my phone after I finished adding cream and sugar to my coffee.

No earth-shattering headlines in the world this morning, thankfully. I put my phone down. I fried a couple of eggs and browned two slices of toast for my breakfast. I allowed Diesel a couple of bites of toast, but he had to content himself with the wet food I gave him before I went back upstairs.

Aleta Boudreaux was waiting for me when Diesel and I arrived at the historical society building near downtown.

"Good morning," she said brightly. I would have recognized her for her abundant curly hair as a library patron if I hadn't been expecting to see her.

I returned her greeting. "Thank you so much for arranging this for me. I can't tell you how excited I am to find out more about my family."

"You're welcome." She bent to coo at Diesel. "You're such a handsome boy. I wish I could take you home with me, but I don't think that will be allowed."

He meowed in response, and she laughed. "You'd swear he knows exactly what you say to him."

"I wouldn't be surprised," I said.

"Here's the key." Aleta produced it from a pocket in her slacks. "Let me show you how it works. The lock can be a bit stubborn sometimes."

We approached the door, and she instructed me on the proper way to get it unlocked. I watched carefully and felt sure I'd have no problem with it.

She walked in with me and showed me the light switches. She then pointed to the reception desk. "Your papers are there. I'll get out of the way now. You just lock up after you're finished, and you can drop the key off on Monday. One of the board members should be here until noon."

I locked the door behind her. Diesel had been wandering around investigating the room. I closed the doors leading out of the space, because I didn't want him wandering loose in the museum. He wouldn't deliberately damage anything, or at least I hoped he wouldn't, but there was no point in setting him up for failure.

I found a thick folder in the center of the desk. I pulled a notepad and pen from my briefcase and set the latter aside. I had allowed myself three hours for this, and I had left notes for Stewart and Alissa of my whereabouts, along with my cell number for Alissa.

Eagerly, but with care, I opened the folder and began to examine the papers. The first items I encountered were copies of land documents, deeds, to some of the property in Athena belonging to my family in the early nineteenth century.

I pressed on, scanning and putting aside certain documents for a lengthier perusal. I found several letters that I was tempted to read immediately, but I steeled myself to carry on, laying them aside.

The first time I thought to check the time, it was already ten-thirty. I had been too engrossed in my task to realize I'd been here that long. I put down the document in my hands and stood up. Diesel had been asleep near my feet. He stirred and looked up at me, yawning.

"I'm going to walk around the room a couple of times," I said. "My back is stiff."

Diesel chirped and stretched while I suited deed to words. After a few minutes of moving around, my back loosened up, and I resumed my seat.

The next document I picked up turned out to be a family tree that began in the early 1700s, I was thrilled to see. I started to jot down the names, dates, and relationships, focusing on my line of descent. I would add the others in later. The tree came down all the way to my father in my line and ended there.

I noticed something unexpected with my grandfather and great-aunt. In between their names was another name, Allan Wilfred Harris, and his dates. Allan had married a woman named Jincy Harrell. They had a son, Horace. No wife was listed for Horace, but there was a dotted line down from his name. He'd had a son named Martin.

Mr. Hale was my cousin.

THIRTY

||||||||||||||||||||||||||||||||||||||||||

Esther Carraway had left this out of her book. There had been no mention of a connection to anyone named Hale. I speculated that Martin Hale's father might not have married his mother. If so, Esther Carraway had let me find this out for myself.

At this late date, I wasn't scandalized by the discovery. I looked again at the tree, and I saw that my great-uncle Allan had died not long after Martin Hale was born. Why hadn't my grandfather ever mentioned the relationship? Why hadn't my aunt or my father done so? Surely they had to know about my great-uncle's son and his grandson.

But he was Martin Hale, not Martin Harris. That argued for his being illegitimate.

I looked more closely at the family tree. I put it under a brighter light, and I noticed that the ink adding Martin to the tree looked different from the ink on the rest of the paper. The handwriting was slightly different as well. I wondered who had added Martin to the tree, and why.

Had this been done maliciously? Was it even true?

How would I find out?

I decided that I needed to copy the papers containing the diagram of the family tree. I looked around, and sure enough, there was a copier in the room. I turned it on and waited for it to warm up. I made a couple of copies of the original. I put one of them back in the file and took the original and the second copy with me.

"Come on, boy," I said to Diesel. He followed me out and waited while I locked the door and pocketed the key.

I drove straight to Esther Carraway's house, hoping that she would be at home.

My luck was in. She answered the door. She opened it wide and motioned me in, along with Diesel.

"I apologize for showing up unannounced like this," I said, "but I really need to talk to you about something." I handed her the copy of the family tree. I had left the original in the car.

"I wondered how long it would take you to find it," she said as she accepted the pages. "Come in and sit down."

Diesel sat by her legs, and Mrs. Carraway, already dressed for the day, patted his head. "I'll always be glad to see you, handsome boy." She looked over at me. "I told you that I didn't wash anyone's dirty laundry in public. It was there for you to find and do whatever you thought proper about the information."

"I presume you added Martin Hale to this," I said.

"I did."

"What proof do you have that he was my great-uncle's son? Illegitimate, I presume."

She nodded. "Yes, he was born out of wedlock. I heard it from his mother herself, not long before she died."

"Who was she?"

"A woman from Alabama, named Maudie Magee," she replied. "Really a tragic story."

The name Maudie stunned me. Surely there was no coincidence in the name. Had Martin Hale buried his own mother in an unmarked grave?

"Why wasn't he Martin Magee, then?" I asked.

"He was adopted by a family named Hale who farmed near your grandfather. I don't know if your grandfather ever knew, though I suspected he found out when I heard about the terms of his will."

That would answer the question of the life lease, I thought. My grandfather had done it for his illegitimate nephew, family being family after all.

"Shocked a lot of people, I can tell you," Mrs. Carraway said. "Martin Hale and I were probably the only two people who knew the reason. He didn't tell anyone, and neither did I. He didn't want people to know he was a bastard. At least, that he was born that way." She gave me a grim smile.

"Tell me more about his mother," I said. "When and how did you meet her? And what happened to her?"

Mrs. Carraway sighed. "Wasn't long before she passed away. She married a man in Alabama, name of Magee. Her husband had died, and she wasn't well herself. She'd been in a bad accident and lost both her hands and her feet."

"That's awful," I said. "I've seen a picture of her."

"I'd like to see that sometime, if I might."

I promised to show it to her.

She went on with the story. "She'd somehow found out who had adopted her baby. Someone I knew in Alabama, where she still lived, put her in touch with me. She asked me what I knew about Martin Hale, and I told her the plain facts. Not about his character, mind you."

"That was kind of you," I said.

She shrugged. "A friend of hers took her to your grandfather's farm to meet her son. That was about twenty-five years ago, and she was old by then. I never heard from her again. I presumed she went back to Alabama and died there. I didn't ask Martin Hale about her. It wasn't my business."

I wondered whether I should tell her I was pretty sure where Maudie Magee had died. The story of the bones in the attic had run briefly in the paper. The sheriff's department had hoped someone would come forward about them. Mrs. Carraway had obviously not made the connection between Mrs. Magee and those bones.

I decided that she deserved to know. I explained it to her gently.

She didn't appear all that shocked. I figured she had run across many scandalous things in her research into the past of so many local families.

"I forgot one thing," Mrs. Carraway said suddenly. "Mrs. Magee told me she had letters from Allan Harris, Martin's father, that proved he knew about the baby. He was planning to marry her, or so the letters said, but he was killed in the South Pacific during the war."

"World War Two," I said.

"Yes, I believe he was a marine."

"How sad for her," I said. "I wonder if my great-grandparents knew about the relationship."

"Mrs. Magee told me they did, and they didn't approve. She didn't come from a family like the Harrises. They were poor sharecroppers."

I didn't like to think of my ancestors as being snobs, but it wasn't an unusual attitude at that time.

"I really don't understand why Mr. Hale buried his birth mother in an unmarked grave," I said.

"There's a family cemetery somewhere in those woods behind the house. Was that where she was buried?"

"I don't think so. I've never seen the cemetery."

"It's probably completely overgrown now. No one to take care of it for decades," Mrs. Carraway said. "I expect she must have died in the house, and Martin Hale didn't want anyone to know who she was. So he probably buried her himself."

His own mother, left in an anonymous grave, until her own great-grandson dug her up to play a prank on his grandfather. Sad and macabre all at once.

"I wonder what happened to those letters," I said, struck by a sudden thought.

"Martin Hale might have burned them," Mrs. Carraway said. "Or they could still be somewhere in that house. Have you looked through everything yet?"

"No, ma'am, I haven't, but I'm going to now. Mr. Hale's granddaughter, Alissa, is here from California, and she's staying with me. Once I tell her the story, I know she'll be as eager to find those letters as I am."

"I wish you good luck," Mrs. Carraway said. "Maudie Magee deserves that someone in the Hale family knows her story."

"I'll make sure they know," I said. "You can count on it."

"Good," Mrs. Carraway replied. "Now, is there anything else?"

I rose, realizing this was a polite hint to go. "No. I

can't thank you enough for your help with this, Mrs. Carraway."

She smiled briefly and took my hand. "You're welcome." When she released my hand, she stroked Diesel's head a couple of times. "Bring Diesel back to see me sometime."

I promised to do that, and she showed us to the door. I drove straight home, because I couldn't wait to share this information with Alissa. I would give Sean a call before we left for the farm and give him a rundown on everything. I would leave it to him to relay the relevant information to Kanesha.

After the murder case was solved, I wanted to search the property for that family cemetery Mrs. Carraway mentioned. I couldn't imagine that my aunt would have neglected it completely, or my father, either. But since the property was leased to Martin Hale, they might not have felt they could insist. I couldn't imagine that Martin Hale would have wanted them on the property.

Wait a minute, I thought. My grandfather died before Hale's birth mother came to visit. Unless Hale already knew about his true parentage, he couldn't have blackmailed my grandfather into leasing the land to him.

Perhaps my grandfather had known all along. Maybe he knew that Martin Hale was his nephew. He put up with him, despite his drinking habits, because of the blood relationship. I could see my grandfather doing that, even though he might not want to acknowledge Hale publicly. My grandfather, with his teetotal stance, would not have wanted people knowing that his own nephew, an illegitimate one at that, was a drunk. Hale must have threatened to tell everyone the truth of his parentage if my grandfather didn't leave the land to him.

My grandfather took great pride in his family; that much my father had told me. To his generation, acknowledging a bastard member would have been anathema.

I decided that was the more likely scenario. Unless we found information to the contrary somewhere in the house. That was always a possibility.

As soon as I got home, I called Sean and filled him in on what I had discovered. I could imagine he was dumbstruck for once, because he didn't say a word until I'd finished.

"Holy moly, Dad, that's some story." He sounded dazed. "So Alissa Hale is your cousin. Mine too. That's wild."

"I know it's a lot to take in. I'm going to find Alissa and tell her all this, either before we leave, or on the way to the farm. I'd really like to find those letters if Hale kept them."

"I'll call Kanesha," Sean said. "I have a couple things to do here, and then I'll join you at the farmhouse."

"Thanks," I said. "I appreciate the offer. The more of us looking, the more likely we'll find them."

There was no sign of anyone in the house, at least downstairs. Diesel came up the stairs with me and followed me down the hall to Alissa's room. The door stood slightly ajar. I knocked, and Alissa called for me to enter.

I found her in the armchair in the corner, book in hand, and Ramses draped across her lap.

Ramses. I had forgotten about him. I didn't think taking him to the farm was a good idea. It would be far too easy for him to hide himself somewhere, and it could take hours to find him. He was a devious little rascal, darn him. I despaired of his ever being as trustworthy as Diesel.

I'd figure it out in a moment. First, I told Alissa I had interesting information to share with her and that I wanted to go back to the farmhouse to search for more papers, primarily in the attic.

"That's fine," she said, laying her book aside and pushing Ramses gently out of her lap. "As long as I can avoid that one room. I'm curious to see the attic."

"Good. Diesel is going with us, but I think Ramses needs a babysitter."

"Really?" Alissa frowned. "Can you leave him by himself here?"

"I don't think that's a good idea. There's no telling what he might get into left on his own, and I don't like crating him. I've never done that." At least since he was a small kitten, I added silently. I would tell Alissa before long how Ramses came to be part of the family. Her extended family, as it turned out.

"I'm going to call Azalea and see if we can take him to her house. He's stayed with her quite often on weekends, and maybe she'll be able to keep him for a few hours."

Alissa grabbed her phone and small handbag, and she and Ramses followed Diesel and me downstairs. I was already on the phone to Azalea. She answered right away, and I explained my dilemma. She agreed to keep Ramses the rest of the weekend, and I promised we would be there soon to drop him off.

During the drive out to the farmhouse, I shared with Alissa what I had learned. She listened in silence until I'd finished. The first thing she said was, "This means you're my cousin, doesn't it?"

"Yes, my grandfather and your great-grandfather were brothers, so that makes us second cousins once removed."

"What does that mean? Once removed, that is."

"Your father was my second cousin, and because you're a different generation, and younger, you're once removed."

"Okay, I guess I understand." She smiled. "I'm just glad I have more family besides my mother. You're a nice cousin to have."

"Thank you," I said, touched by her pleasure. "I'm glad to have you in the family."

By now we had turned off the highway and were nearing the farm. Before I realized it, two sheriff's patrol cars sped by me in the left lane, lights flashing. No sirens, though. I wondered what they were doing. Something urgent, obviously.

I turned into the farmhouse driveway. Alissa, Diesel, and I climbed the steps to the porch, and I unlocked the door. I went inside first, and as I did, I glanced into the parlor. I stopped suddenly, and Alissa bumped into me. I held a finger to my lips and pointed.

Someone had moved the settee aside from its usual spot and pushed the rug and the coffee table on it aside. A trapdoor lay revealed, the door open.

THIRTY-ONE

||||||||||||||||||||||||||||||||||||||||||||||||||||||||||||||||

I motioned for Alissa to step back onto the porch, and she complied without hesitation. Diesel went with her. I closed the door softly behind them. I debated whether I should follow them, but I thought it would be a good idea to close that trapdoor. If anyone was down there, he would be stuck inside until I could call for help. I began to have an inkling of what, and who, was down there.

I moved forward cautiously, but despite my care, a floorboard squeaked. I paused, ready to dart for the door. Nothing happened.

I took a few more steps forward and halted.

Then a few steps more until I was only about four feet from the trapdoor. I held my breath. The door opened away from me, so I had to move around to the other side of it to close it. I hoped there was some kind of latch on this side. I couldn't see one. I might have to push furniture on top of it to keep it shut.

The settee was fairly substantial, but was it enough? There was nothing else within a couple of feet, however. At least pushing the settee on top of it would give me enough time to get out of the house and into the car. I should have told Alissa to get in the car with Diesel, I realized.

I bolted to the other side of the door. It was heavier than I'd expected but I managed to lift it and let it drop into place. There was no latch on this side. I uttered a rare curse word and immediately began dragging the settee on top of it. Panting, I headed for the front door as soon as I got the settee in place.

"Where the hell you think you're going?"

I skidded to a stop to see Gil Jackson, rifle in hand, coming down the hall from the back of the house.

"I'm going out to my car," I said as coolly as I could manage. "I'm going home."

Jackson laughed and came to within two feet of me. "Yeah, right. You're not going anywhere, buddy, unless it's down there." He gestured toward the trapdoor.

"I don't care what's down there," I said, taking a step backward.

Jackson turned the shotgun on me. "Unh-uh," he said. "Move." He gestured with the shotgun.

I walked into the parlor, praying that he had no idea Alissa and Diesel had come with me.

"Move that thing off the door," he said, keeping the shotgun leveled at me.

"What if I don't?" I said.

"I'll kill you right here," Jackson said matter-of-factly. "I got nothing to lose now. One more dead guy won't matter to me if they find me."

"You killed Marty Hale," I said. "I thought you had."

"Snoopy little bastard," Jackson replied. "Caught him down there. Didn't know anyone was in the house."

"He found your still," I said.

Jackson nodded. "Wanted the same cut of the profits his grandfather was getting. I told him no, and he threatened me." He chuckled. "Smartass like his grandfather. I marched him out in the woods that morning and took care of him."

"Why didn't you cut him in on the operation?" I said, curious. "He might have been of use to you."

"He was stupid. He let slip that this house didn't belong to his grandfather, but he told me he was going to sue and get it back."

"So you decided to get rid of him, because you'd lose your secret hideaway."

Jackson shrugged. "Seemed like the best option. I didn't know who owned the property until I heard about you. I've been working on clearing out that cellar, and I was just about finished until you turned up just now."

I caught a flash of motion in the hallway behind him, and I hoped he hadn't seen me noticing. He was too certain that he had the situation under control, however. I wasn't sure, but I thought I had seen Alissa briefly. If so, she must have come in through the back door. I hoped she had called the sheriff's department and reported the situation. She could have seen Jackson through the window in the hall from her vantage point on the porch.

What was she doing in the house? She could get herself killed if Jackson found her.

After he dealt with me. I had to keep him distracted.

"How long have you had your still down there?" I indicated the secret cellar.

"Ever since ol' Martin told me about that secret cellar. He had no idea it was there until he started moving furniture around about twelve years ago."

I could see Alissa now, half her body against the cased opening into the room.

"No more stalling," Jackson said. "Open the door."

I pushed the settee off the door. I paused to get my breath back, buying a few seconds to see what Alissa was going to do. Jackson gestured at me with the shotgun.

"Open it." He stepped right up to within a foot of the opening across from me.

I reached down and pulled up the door.

Alissa rushed forward and kicked Jackson hard in the rear. Jackson dropped the gun to try to save himself, and the gun landed several feet away. He couldn't help himself and fell through the opening.

I slammed the door shut, and Alissa helped me put the settee over it. Then we pulled a small chest onto it as well.

"That should hold him," Alissa said, grinning.

"Where did you learn to do that?" I said, still amazed by what she had done.

"Self-defense classes," she said. "When you're my size, you have to learn to take care of yourself."

I went to her and hugged her close to me. She hugged back, her arms tight around me.

"Thank you," I said. "You saved my life." I released her, and she gazed up at me with a tearstained face.

"I had to," she said. "That's what cousins do."

Sean arrived right on the heels of Kanesha and her deputies, Haskell among them.

"Where is he?" Kanesha asked straightaway.

I pointed to the settee and the chest. "Under there." I felt slightly giddy with relief when Kanesha looked at me like I had lost my mind.

"There's a trapdoor under all that," I said.

Kanesha gestured for two of her deputies to clear the furniture away.

"His shotgun is over there." Alissa pointed, and another deputy went to retrieve it.

"He might be badly injured," I said. "Alissa kicked him hard in the rear, and he fell in. We slammed the door immediately."

"Good for you." Kanesha directed one of her deputies to call for an ambulance.

"She saved my life," I said.

Sean went immediately to Alissa. "Thank you. I hear we're cousins. You had one heck of a welcome to the family."

She grinned. "It was exciting. I just wish I could do it again." She sobered. "That man killed my brother. I hope he broke his neck."

Sean and I exchanged looks. I hoped Jackson hadn't, because I wanted him to go to jail for the rest of his life.

"The still is down there, too," I said. "That's why you never found it."

Kanesha muttered something that I didn't catch. I hoped it wasn't directed at me, because I had managed, without intending to, to solve two problems at once for her. I'd found the murderer and the bootlegging operation. The latter she might never have found out, but she might have evidence that linked Gil Jackson to the murder.

I asked her about that, and she nodded.

"Fibers left at the scene. We were on the way to serve

a search warrant to find the source of the fibers when Alissa called. We drove straight here to prevent him from killing anyone else."

"Thank you, but luckily Alissa saved me. I think he would have killed me once he got me down in the cellar. He had no idea Alissa was in the house. I'm sure he would have buried me down there, and no one would know what had happened to me."

"I'd have torn this house apart, Dad." Sean looked angry, and I hoped it wasn't at me. I had stumbled into this innocently. I hadn't sought Jackson out.

"I'd like for y'all to leave the room," Kanesha said, her tone brooking no argument.

Sean motioned for Alissa and me to follow him into the room across the hall.

"Where is Diesel?" I had momentarily forgotten him.

"In the car," Alissa said. "I'll go get him."

"No, let me," I said, anxious to see him and reassure him that I was unhurt.

All four windows of the car were slightly cracked, so he had air flowing. It was warm in the car, but not dangerously so. I had parked in the shade of the large oak, and Diesel appeared fine. He yawned and came out of the car, chirping happily. I sank to the ground and drew him into my lap.

That's when it hit me, how close I had come to losing my life. I put my arms around Diesel and tried to steady my nerves. I hoped Laura and Helen Louise wouldn't join Sean in reading me the riot act. I had no way of knowing of the existence of the still in the house, nor that I would find Gil Jackson there with a shotgun. If I hadn't been so eager to find my great-uncle's letters to Maudie Magee, I could have waited until later to return to the farmhouse. By then, Jackson would have removed his still, and I would never have been the wiser. At least until I discovered the secret cellar, though that was far from certain.

Sean called to me from the porch, sounding alarmed. "Are you okay, Dad? Is something wrong with Diesel?" He hurried across the porch and down the steps.

I released Diesel and got slowly to my feet as Sean approached. "He's fine, and I'm okay."

Sean grabbed me and pulled me into a fierce hug.

"Damn you, Dad, I swear I'm going to get a microchip implanted in you so we can keep track of you."

I started laughing, and Sean released me. He smiled. "I was terrified when I walked into that room," he said.

"Thanks to Alissa, I'm fine, fully intact," I said. "Did they get Jackson out of that cellar?"

"Not yet. They're waiting for the ambulance. He's alert and cussing to beat the band. They think both his legs are broken, a few ribs, and one of his arms."

"Can't say I feel sorry for him," I said.

"I don't, either, the bastard," Sean said. He normally didn't use words like that or curse in front of me, but I understood how high his emotions were running right now. I felt like uttering a few bad words myself.

Diesel butted his head against Sean's leg and meowed loudly. I thought Sean might have frightened him a little, but then I realized Diesel simply wanted to reassure him.

Sean squatted on his heels, nose to nose with the cat. "Okay, buddy. I'm okay. I'm glad you weren't hurt. It's a good thing you missed the action."

I didn't want to contemplate what might have happened if Diesel had been with me. Jackson would have probably taken delight in killing him in front of me. I had more to be thankful for. I owed not only my life to Alissa, but Diesel's, too.

Alissa joined us in the yard. "Deputy Berry said it was okay for us to go home." She grinned. "In fact, she told me she insisted on it."

Sean and I laughed.

"I insist on it, too," I said, and Diesel meowed.

THIRTY-TWO

When the whole family gathered the next day for dinner, our usual custom on Sundays, Sean pulled me aside to give me an update on Gil Jackson.

"Mostly just broken bones," Sean said. "They had to remove his spleen, but he'll make a full recovery. As soon as he can leave the hospital, he'll be arraigned and indicted. You'll have to appear at the trial, but that's a ways off yet."

"I'll be happy to testify," I said. "Does he know how he ended up in the cellar?"

Sean chuckled. "The deputies made sure he did. He was apparently pissed as hell that a little woman had done that to him."

"Serves him right." I laughed, too.

I had instructed Sean to inform Marv Watkins, the smarmy real estate agent, that I would under no circumstances be selling my land to him and his development group. He would have to look elsewhere for the site of his grandiose houses.

Helen Louise had arrived home around five o'clock last night, and she asked me to her house for dinner. For once, I left Diesel at home. I knew Alissa would take good care of him. I wanted some time alone with my fiancée.

I waited until she had shared the high points of her vacation with me, and over dessert—one of my favorite chocolate cakes from her bistro—I told her about all that had happened while she was gone. I kept details to the minimum without making the story hard to understand. I knew that, with her quick mind, she would grasp all the necessary implications.

I also discussed with her my plans for some of the land. I had decided that I would follow through on my grandfather's original promise to Asa Luckney. Instead of leasing the land to him, however, I was going to sell it to him for a dollar an acre. He could buy the land he had been working for so many years, plus the land that Gil Jackson had leased. As much as he wanted. I planned to keep the house and about a hundred acres around it, including the woods, where I suspected the family cemetery must be. Helen Louise heartily approved of my decision.

When I finally finished telling her everything, she sat back, wineglass in hand, and regarded me solemnly.

"All right, Charlie Harris," she said, her tone stern. "This is the last time I leave town without you. You're not fit to be left without supervision. I want to get you to the altar in one piece, you understand?" Then she grinned.

"I'd like to get there in one piece myself," I said, picking up my wineglass. We toasted each other and drank.

We celebrated our reunion upstairs, sans cat for once.

Today she and Stewart busied themselves in the kitchen. They had shooed the rest of us out. We waited for the summons to dine in the living room. Sean and Alex were present with my granddaughter, Rosie, who would soon be one year old. Frank and Laura had Charlie with them, keeping a close eye on him as he meandered around the room. Diesel divided his time between Rosie and Charlie. He loved them both, but I believed Charlie was his favorite because he was the first. He was fourteen months old now, and he chattered to Diesel incessantly when they were together.

Alissa and Haskell formed part of the group as well. Haskell had told her last night about their relationship. She had hugged him impulsively.

"Another cousin," she said. "This is wonderful. Finding my family is an amazing gift. I don't want to go back to California."

I didn't blame her, given what little I knew of her mother. I was thinking about what to do to help her stay here, and I had a couple of ideas. She had an associate's degree in literature from a community college in California, and that might help her get a job at the college library here. I knew of two current openings that she might be a good match for.

Haskell had shared with me privately that he had confronted his mother about his aunt this morning, and she had finally revealed the truth. His aunt had severe mental problems and had been admitted to the state mental institution at Whitfield. His mother found this so shameful that she didn't allow anyone except her husband to know. She had driven her sister there herself, and Mrs. Hale, wife of the old man, had voluntarily committed herself.

Mrs. Bates was deeply ashamed by all this, not an un-common attitude in those days. Haskell asked me not to tell anyone. He had already told Stewart. Mrs. Hale had died some years ago at Whitfield.

Sean had already talked to Alex, Frank, and Laura about Alissa, so they were aware that there was a rela-tionship. Sean hadn't gone into detail with them, how-ever. He promised that I would make everything clear to them today. I could tell Laura was bubbling with curios-ity. She had tried to get me to start explaining, but I in-tended to wait until the dessert course to satisfy everyone's demands for information.

The conversation remained desultory until Helen Louise summoned us to the dining room. One topic was foremost in everyone's mind. I held firm, however. We left Charlie and Rose sound asleep in their separate cribs with Diesel on guard duty while we ate.

Our family meal today consisted of pot roast, pota-toes and carrots, steamed broccoli, creamed corn, and freshly made yeast rolls. For dessert, there would be hot apple pie and vanilla ice cream. After I said the blessing, we all tucked in, chatting about nothing in particular while we ate.

When the time came to clear the table for dessert, I was not allowed to help. I had been told I was the patri-arch, and my help was not required. I sat and sipped my iced sweet tea and watched everyone else, except Alissa, work. Despite her new status as a family member, she was not yet familiar with the clearing-away routine.

We talked about books until dessert arrived. Once everyone was around the table again and attacking the apple pie, I began to talk.

"I hope you will let me tell this my way," I said, "and

save questions for later." I glanced around the table and saw the nods of affirmation.

"Thank you. First I want to say that, out of these tragedies, past and present, we have a blessing. We have discovered Alissa, and I am delighted by that."

"Hear, hear," said everyone around the table, and Alissa blushed.

"Thank you," she said, then motioned for me to continue.

"Most of this story is about family," I began. "I owe the story I'm about to tell you to Jordan Thompson, actually, because she recommended a local history book to me. Esther Carraway is a native of Athena with a deep interest in the town and the county and all their families. In the book Jordan handed me, I discovered information about the Harris family. Information that, frankly, surprised me, because I was entirely unaware of it."

I paused for a sip of my tea. "I discovered that the Harrises were once a wealthy family in Athena, thanks to my ancestor's mercantile business. He prospered and eventually bought property out in the county, where he built a house for his wife. She apparently didn't care for life in town and preferred the quiet of the country. With the Civil War, my ancestor lost the business in town and became a farmer. He managed to accrue more land in time.

"His wife came from an antislavery family, and he employed only free men, both white and Black, I surmise, on the farm."

"My grandfather died when I was a small boy, and my father, for whatever reason, never told me this about his family. Aunt Dottie never did, either. I don't know if they were unaware of these facts, or if they simply didn't think they were important or interesting. While I was growing up, I wasn't that interested in American history, because I became fascinated by English history instead.

"Inheriting my grandfather's house was a complete surprise. My father had never mentioned this, either, though surely he must have known the terms of his father's will. He had no interest in farming, and he could see that I had none, either. Perhaps that's why he never told me. Had he and my mother not been killed relatively young, he might have told me at some point."

Time for more tea. I wasn't used to talking at this length.

"That's what really sparked my interest in the family's history, inheriting the house and the farm. I never knew Martin Hale, the tenant for life, and I doubted that he knew, or cared, who I was. He led his grandson, also named Martin, to believe that the land belonged to him. It wasn't until after he died that the younger Martin found out his grandfather had lied to him about that. Apparently, it wasn't unusual for the elder Martin to indulge in self-aggrandizement, but it had unfortunate effects. I'll come back to that.

"Back to the family tree. I met with Mrs. Carraway to find out more about the family. Her sources for the information in her book came from papers in the county historical archive. I wasn't able to consult those papers until yesterday." I withdrew the copy of the family tree from my shirt pocket, unfolded the pages, and passed them to Laura, sitting on my right.

"This tree takes the family further back to the Revolutionary War era. I want to investigate that in more depth, but I discovered something intriguing that I had to find out about right away. Mrs. Carraway had told me when I talked with her that she had no interest in publicizing scandalous bits of family history in her books. If people wanted to find out about them, they could look for it themselves. As it turned out, that's exactly what I did.

"I first discovered that my grandfather and my aunt had a brother I'd never heard about, Allan. He died, unmarried, in the South Pacific during the Second World War. I don't know why they didn't talk about him, but families are funny like that. My dad never mentioned him, either, but he surely must have known his uncle. He was nearly an adult when his uncle was killed." I shrugged. "One generation's scandal is no big deal to another, I think you'll find. The scandal in this case is that Allan fathered an illegitimate child with a woman named Maudie Magee. He died not long before his son was born, leaving Maudie a single, unmarried mother in the mid-1940s. She gave him up for adoption, and a couple in this county named Hale adopted him."

I heard several gasps. "Yes, Martin Hale was my father's first cousin and Aunt Dottie's nephew. I doubt they knew who he was, but I think they might have known that the child existed somewhere. I do believe my grandfather possibly knew Hale was his nephew, though."

I told the story of Asa Luckney, my grandfather's protégé, and how he expected to have the life lease once my grandfather died. "I'm pretty sure Martin Hale had found out about his biological father's family, and he confronted my grandfather not long before he died. My grandfather had kept Hale as a worker despite the fact that Hale was an unreliable drunk. My grandfather was a teetotaler. I think he had to know who Hale was or he wouldn't have tolerated his behavior.

"Grandfather changed his will shortly before he died, leaving Martin Hale life tenancy to the farmland and the house. I suspect Hale had threatened to expose the family scandal if he didn't. Later on, Mr. Luckney and Gil Jackson sublet land from Hale, who was probably content to live off the lease money. We discovered that he also was sharing in the profits from Gil Jackson's bootlegging operation."

I paused for dramatic effect. "That operation had been taking place for the last dozen or so years in a secret cellar beneath the parlor in the farmhouse."

That really got reactions. Helen Louise shook her head and said, "Shades of Nancy Drew and the Hardy Boys. Secret cellars. I want to see it."

"You all can as soon the sheriff's department is finished with it. Back to Martin Hale and the bones in the attic. We're pretty sure they belonged to his natural mother, Maudie Magee. She came to visit her son about twenty-five years ago. Tragically, Mrs. Magee had lost both her hands and her feet in an accident, as yet undetermined, and she frightened poor Alissa, who was about two years old at the time."

Alissa nodded self-consciously but didn't speak.

"Mrs. Magee was in poor health and evidently died there in Hale's home. She had no family left in Alabama, where she came from. I suspect he didn't want anyone to know who she was, because he didn't want people to know he was illegitimate. He dug a grave in the woods and put her there."

"How did her bones end up in the attic?" Laura asked.

"According to Alissa, her brother, Marty, came to

visit their grandfather for a few weeks three years ago. She thinks Marty stumbled across the grave, excavated the bones, and hid them in the attic as a prank." I shrugged. "I don't have any idea whether Mr. Hale ever found them. If he did, he left them where they were."

"Creepy," Laura said.

"Mr. Hale went to California recently to visit his grandchildren. His only son was killed in an accident when Alissa was a baby. While there, he suffered a massive stroke and died. Not before, however, giving his grandson a false picture of his financial position. Marty came to Athena thinking he had inherited a house and a farm, only to find out that his grandfather was only a tenant for life.

"In the meantime, Marty was busy nosing around. He discovered the still in the cellar, and he found Gil Jackson in the house. Jackson had no idea Marty was there. This was the day of that storm. Sometime that morning, before the storm hit, Jackson took Marty out into the woods and killed him. He left the body where it dropped, and a tree uprooted in the storm fell on the body. The sheriff's department found some fibers Jackson left behind, so they had forensic evidence to tie someone to the scene. They were also aware of Jackson's bootlegging, but they had never been able to find the still."

"They couldn't because it was in that secret cellar all along," Haskell said. "Clever. If you hadn't stumbled into him in the house, we might never have found it."

"True, but frankly I wish you could have found it another way. Jackson planned to kill me, but he had no idea I had a secret weapon." I smiled at Alissa. "She saved my life, and Diesel's, too. She kicked Jackson in the behind and knocked him into the cellar."

"Three cheers for Alissa." Frank lifted his glass, and everyone else except the honoree lifted theirs, too. Alissa blushed and stammered her thanks.

When we'd finished, I raised my glass again. "To family."

ACKNOWLEDGMENTS

The usual suspects played their usual important role in getting this book to publication stage, although I imagine most of them thought it might never happen. Bountiful thanks to my editor, Michelle Vega, and to the entire Berkley team, including Jennifer Snyder, Elisha Katz, and Brittanie Black, for being unfailingly helpful and professional.

The other set of suspects hang out at Nancy Yost Literary: Nancy herself, my agent for more years than either of us would care to count, a staunch advocate for her writers, and her team: Sarah E. Younger, Natanya Wheeler, and the helpful interns who take care of the business end of things.

Two good friends, Don Herrington and Stan Porter, sustain me in the day-to-day, putting up with my idiosyncrasies (while sharing their own), and helping me make it to a new day intact. My two long-distance cheerleaders and beta readers Patricia Orr and Terry Farmer, who always know just how to encourage me with the right words of criticism.

Finally, as always, I have to thank the readers who continue to hold Charlie and Diesel close to their hearts. Without you, none of this would be possible.

Keep reading for a sneak peek of the next
Cat in the Stacks Mystery
by *New York Times* bestselling
author Miranda James

HISS ME DEADLY

I frowned at Melba Gilley, my coworker and longtime friend. "Sorry, I just don't remember anybody called Wil Threadgill."

Melba returned my frown with a scowl. "Honestly, Charlie, I wonder about your memory sometimes. Maybe you ought to be taking one of those supplements they're always talking about on television."

Diesel, my Maine Coon cat, chirped loudly and moved against my leg. He apparently didn't like Melba's tone.

"I don't have your encyclopedic memory for everyone who has lived and died in Athena, Mississippi, over the past fifty-odd years," I replied, trying to keep my tone even. "Remember, I was gone for twenty-five years or so." I rubbed Diesel's head to reassure him that I was fine.

"True," Melba said. The scowl receded, to be replaced by a thoughtful expression. "Do you remember *Fred* Threadgill?"

I thought for a moment. That name did ring a bell. "Yes, I think so," I said, drawing out the words. "Wasn't he in high school with us? But a little older?"

Melba nodded. "That's Wil."

"So Fred is Wil?" I asked, still puzzled.

I ignored the eye roll.

"His name was Wilfred," Melba said. "He never liked

anyone to call him Wilfred, so he went by Fred back in high school."

"When did he become Wil?" I had vague memories of a tall, skinny, redheaded guy who never had much to say to anyone. He'd always seemed to be lost in his own little world.

"When he went to California and became a famous musician," Melba said, a note of triumph in her voice.

"Okay, but why am I supposed to have heard of Wil Threadgill?"

I could see that Melba was trying to hold on to her temper. I wasn't deliberately trying to aggravate her. My knowledge of the California music scene was fairly limited, despite the fact that my daughter, Laura, had spent several years there trying to establish her acting career. I knew the famous actor names, of course, like Meryl Streep, Robert De Niro, and Diane Keaton, as well as the greats from the Golden Age, like Katharine Hepburn, Cary Grant, Bette Davis, and Jimmy Stewart. But musicians? Not so much, unless they were from the sixties and seventies, like the Supremes, the Beatles, ABBA, and the Carpenters.

"He's been nominated for an Oscar and a Golden Globe for film scores," Melba said.

"That's impressive," I replied. "But I never watch those awards shows. I guess that's why I didn't recognize his name." I hadn't been to the movies in I didn't know how long. My late wife, Jackie, and I used to go occasionally, but neither of us was a big movie buff. We both preferred Golden Age Hollywood in all its glamour. I reminded Melba of this.

She sniffed. She was an avid moviegoer and knew who all the current stars were, as well as who wrote the movies' scores and probably even who the best boys were, among other trivia. "I'll let it pass this time," she said, her tone mock-severe. She pulled out her phone, tapped on it several times, then thrust it at me. "This is Wil."

I took the phone, and Diesel warbled. Surely he didn't want to look at the phone? I patted his head as I examined the photograph of Wil Threadgill.

The long red hair, streaked liberally with gray, hung well past his shoulders. His thin face and shy smile recalled the high school loner to my memory. "His hairstyle has changed, but I remember the face." I gave the phone back to Melba. "I really didn't know him. He always seemed like he wasn't really in the present."

Melba sighed as she gazed at the picture and then put her phone away suddenly. "Wil has always been a dreamer. A misfit, too, I guess. He never felt like he really belonged here."

"A conservative, small Southern town," I suggested. "When he wanted to rock and roll." Diesel warbled again.

"Something like that," Melba said. "I had such a crush on him. He was really a sweet guy, and we were friends, sort of. I think I was as close to him as any other girl was, but all he was really interested in was music."

"Did he have a band?" I asked. "In high school, that is."

Melba nodded. "There were four of them. They got together in the eleventh grade. Called themselves Southern Drawl."

I laughed, and Melba grimaced.

"Yeah, not a great name," Melba said. "It wasn't Wil's choice. The other three outvoted him. They played some gigs around here, but then Wil just up and disappeared one day. It was right after school let out for the year. He never came back for his senior year."

"He went straight to California?" I asked. "What about his family here?"

"There was only his daddy, and they didn't get along," Melba said. "His daddy died about twenty years ago. I thought Wil might come home for the funeral, but he didn't."

"That's sad," I said. "So he really had no other ties here."

"No strong ones, anyway," Melba said. "He actually wrote to me that fall he went to California and told me where he was. A short note, that was all, but he included his address." She shrugged. "I wrote him every once in a while, and sometimes he'd answer. He moved a lot, and then finally I stopped getting letters from him."

Having known Melba since we were kids, I knew she had been hurt by this. She was the most loyal person I knew, and I figured she had really been in love with the guy. I heard a trace of pain in her tone as she talked about him. I reached out and patted her arm. "I'm sorry," I said.

Melba shrugged again. "It was a long time ago, and I got over him. I haven't thought much about him for over twenty years, except hearing him on the radio or seeing his name pop up in the credits at the movies." Diesel moved close to her and rubbed against her legs. She smiled and stroked his head.

"What brought him to your mind again, then?"

My question earned me a trademarked Melba snort of exasperation. "Charlie, don't you *ever* read the campus newsletter? The announcements from the president's office?"

"Sometimes, but since I'm not full-time, I don't pay a lot of attention to anything other than library news or the theater department." My son-in-law, Frank Salisbury, served as head of the department, and my daughter, Laura, his wife, was a faculty member.

"Wil's getting an honorary degree," Melba said, "and he's going to be here a couple of weeks conducting clinics with students in the music department."

"Not bad for a guy who never finished high school," I said, and I meant it.

Melba narrowed her eyes at me, but evidently satisfied that I wasn't attempting sarcasm, she nodded. "He's done really well. With talent like that, he had to succeed."

"Did he ever get married?"

"Not that I know of," Melba said.

"Is he gay?" I asked.

"No, I don't think so. I just don't reckon he's the settling-down type. I could be wrong. He might arrive with a couple of women in tow. You never know about these Hollywood types," Melba said.

I wondered if Melba were still carrying a torch for Wil Threadgill after all these years. She had never had much luck with men, and that always surprised me. She was a good, loving, smart woman, but maybe *too* smart and *too* good for the men she encountered in Athena, Mississippi.

Melba was like a sister to me in many ways, and yet I hesitated to ask her right out, "Are you in love with him still?"

She solved my dilemma by suddenly telling me, "I think I'm still in love with him, Charlie. Otherwise the thought of seeing him again wouldn't have me all discombobulated like a teenager. Isn't that the stupidest thing you ever heard?"

I shook my head. "First loves are always special. I don't know that you ever truly get over them."

Melba shot me a sympathetic glance. She knew my first love was my late wife, Jackie, who had died of pancreatic cancer several years ago. We had been devoted to each other, and I still missed her, though I had made my peace with her death. I had even found another woman whom I loved, my dear Helen Louise Brady. We were engaged to be married, if we could ever agree on where to live after the ceremony.

"I kept hoping he'd come back," Melba said, and her wistful tone made my heart ache for her. "But he never did. He would always sign his letters *Love, Fred*, and then later, *Love, Wil*, but I learned not to take that literally."

"I'm sure he did love you, as far as he was capable," I said. Almost as if on cue, Diesel trilled loudly. "Artists who are that driven to succeed can suppress a lot. They also sacrifice a lot. He is the poorer for not ever coming back to you, or inviting you to come to California."

Melba turned away, and I knew she had teared up. She couldn't stand to let anyone see her in what she considered a moment of weakness. I pulled some tissues out of the box on my desk, got up, and took them to her, pushing them into her hand. She didn't look at me, and I returned to my chair. When I faced her again, she had regained her composure.

"Thank you. He wrote me a couple weeks ago." She stopped abruptly.

I waited a moment, but she remained silent.

"What did he have to say?" I asked. Diesel remained by her side, his head on her lap. She stroked him absent-mindedly.

Melba frowned. "It was an odd letter. He acted like we hadn't lost touch all those years. Maybe in his mind, we hadn't. He sounded like the same old Wil, for the most part."

"But?" I prompted her when she fell quiet again.

Melba's gaze met mine and held it. "The last bit of the letter has been worrying me. Wil said he thought coming back might be a bad mistake. Stirring up old feelings and causing unhappiness. He said things could get ugly."

"What things?" I asked, rather disturbed by this.

"He didn't say," Melba replied. "He might be talking about the guys in the band. He did leave them in the lurch right as they were getting some decent gigs."

"That's nearly forty years ago," I said. "Surely they're not still angry with him after all this time."

Melba shrugged. "Sounds ridiculous, I know, but some people hold grudges a long time."

"He might have to face them and apologize," I said, "and that wouldn't be pleasant. Surely he's man enough to do that."

"I sure hope so," Melba said. "But I know one of the guys from the band, and he's the one I'm afraid of."

"Why? What do you think he might do?" I asked.

"Kill Wil," Melba said, and her obvious sincerity shook me.

Miranda James is the *New York Times* bestselling author of the Cat in the Stacks Mysteries and the Southern Ladies Mysteries. James lives in Mississippi.

CONNECT ONLINE

CatInTheStacks.com
MirandaJamesAuthor

Ready to find
your next great read?

Let us help.

Visit prh.com/nextread

Penguin
Random
House